# FOREVER

# What Reviewers Say About Kris Bryant's Work

### Home

"Home is a very sweet second-chance romance that will make you smile. It is an angst-less joy, perfect for a bad day."
—*Hsinju's Lit Log*

### Scent

"Oh. Kris Bryant. Once again you've given us a beautiful comfort read to help us escape all that 2020 has thrown at us. This series featuring the senses has been a pleasure to read. ...I think what makes Bryant's books so readable is the way she builds the reader's interest in her mains before allowing them to interact. This is a sweet and happy sigh kind of read. Perfect for these chilly winter nights when you want to escape the world and step into a caramel infused world where HEAs really do come true."—*Late Night Lesbian Reads*

### Lucky

"The characters—both main and secondary, including the furry ones—are wonderful (I loved coming across Piper and Shaylie from Falling), there's just the right amount of angst and the sexy scenes are really hot. It's Kris Bryant, you guys, no surprise there."
—*Jude in the Stars*

"This book has everything you need for a sweet romance. The main characters are beautiful and easy to fall in love with, even with their little quirks and flaws. The settings (Vail and Denver, Colorado) are perfect for the story, and the romance itself is satisfying, with just enough angst to make the book interesting. ...This is the perfect novel to read on a warm, lazy summer day, and I recommend it to all romance lovers."—*Rainbow Reflections*

**Tinsel**

"This story was the perfect length for this cute romance. What made this especially endearing were the relationships Jess has with her best friend, Mo, and her mother. You cannot go wrong by purchasing this cute little nugget. A really sweet romance with a cat playing cupid."—*Bookvark*

**Against All Odds**
*(co-authored with Maggie Cummings and M. Ullrich)*

"This story tugged at my heartstrings and it hit all the right notes for me because these wonderful authors allowed me to peep into the hearts and minds of the characters. The vivid descriptions of Peyton, Tory and the perpetrator's personalities allowed me to have a deeper understanding of what makes them tick and I was able to form a clear picture of them in my mind."—*Lesbian Review*

"*Against All Odds* is equal parts thriller and romance, the balance between action and love, fast and slow pace makes this novel a very entertaining read."—*Lez Review Books*

"I started reading the book trying to dissect the writing and ended up forgetting all about the fact that three people were involved in writing it because the story just grabbed me by the ears and dragged me along for the ride. …[A] really great romantic suspense that manages both parts of the equation perfectly. This is a book you won't be able to put down."—*C-Spot Reviews*

**Temptation**

"This book is an emotional roller coaster that you're going to get swept away in. Let it happen…just bring the tissues and the vino and enjoy the ride."—*Les Rêveur*

"This book is a bag of kettle corn—sweet, savory and you won't stop until you finish it in one binge-worthy sitting. *Temptation* is a fun, fluffy and ultimately satisfying lesbian romance that hits all the right notes."—*To Be Read Book Reviews*

## Falling

"This is a story you don't want to pass on. A fabulous read that you will have a hard time putting down. Maybe don't read it as you board your plane though. This is an easy 5 stars!"—*Romantic Reader Blog*

"Bryant delivers a story that is equal parts touching, compassionate, and uplifting."—*Lesbian Review*

"This was a nice, romantic read. There is enough romantic tension to keep the plot moving, and I enjoyed the supporting characters' and their romance as much as the main plot."—*Kissing Backwards*

## Listen

"[A] sweet romance with a touch of angst and lots of music."—*C-Spot Reviews*

"If you suffer from anxiety, know someone who suffers from anxiety, or want an insight to how it may impact on someone's daily life, I urge you to pick this book up. In fact, I urge all readers who enjoy a good lesbian romance to grab a copy."—*Love Bytes Reviews*

"If you're looking for a little bit of fluffy(ish), light romance in your life, give this one a listen. The characters' passion for music (and each other) is heartwarming, and I was rooting for them the entire book."—*Kissing Backwards*

## Forget Me Not

"Told in the first person, from Grace's point of view, we are privy to Grace's inner musings and her vulnerabilities. ...Bryant crafts clever wording to infuse Grace with a sharp-witted personality, which clearly covers her insecurities. …This story is filled with loving familial interactions, caring friends, romantic interludes and tantalizing sex scenes. The dialogue, both among the characters and within Grace's head, is refreshing, original, and sometimes comical. *Forget Me Not* is a fresh perspective on a romantic theme, and an entertaining read."—*Lambda Literary Review*

"[I]t just hits the right note all the way. …[A] very good read if you are looking for a sweet romance."—*Lez Review Books*

### Shameless—*Writing as Brit Ryder*

"[Kris Bryant] has a way of giving insight into the other main protagonist by using a few clever techniques and involving the secondary characters to add back-stories and extra pieces of important information. The pace of the book was excellent, it was never rushed but I was never bored or waiting for a chapter to finish…this epilogue made my heart swell to the point I almost lunged off the sofa to do a happy dance."—*Les Rêveur*

### Whirlwind Romance

"Ms. Bryant's descriptions were written with such passion and colorful detail that you could feel the tension and the excitement along with the characters…"—*Inked Rainbow Reviews*

### Taste

"*Taste* is a student/teacher romance set in a culinary school. If the premise makes you wonder whether this book will make you want to eat something tasty, the answer is: yes."—*Lesbian Review*

### Jolt—*Lambda Literary Award Finalist*

"[*Jolt*] is a magnificent love story. Two women hurt by their previous lovers and each in their own way trying to make sense

out of life and times. When they meet at a gay and lesbian friendly summer camp, they both feel as if lightening has struck. This is so beautifully involving, I have already reread it twice. Amazing!"
—*Rainbow Book Reviews*

## Touch

"The sexual chemistry in this book is off the hook. Kris Bryant writes my favorite sex scenes in lesbian romantic fiction."
—*Les Rêveur*

## Breakthrough

"Looking for a fun and funny light read with hella cute animal antics, and a smoking hot butch ranger? Look no further. ...In this well written, first-person narrative, Kris Bryant's characters are well developed, and their push/pull romance hits all the right beats, making it a delightful read just in time for beach reading."
—*Writing While Distracted*

"[A]n exceptional book that has a few twists and turns that catch you out and make you wish the book would never end. I was captivated from the beginning and can't wait to see how Bryant will top this."—*Les Rêveur*

# By the Author

Jolt

Whirlwind Romance

Just Say Yes

Taste

Forget Me Not

Shameless (writing as Brit Ryder)

Touch

Breakthrough

Against All Odds
(written with M. Ullrich and Maggie Cummings)

Listen

Falling

Tinsel

Temptation

Lucky

Home

Scent

Not Guilty (writing as Brit Ryder)

Always

Forever

# FOREVER

*by*

## Kris Bryant

2022

# FOREVER

ISBN 13: 978-1-63679-029-9

This Trade Paperback Original Is Published By
Bold Strokes Books, Inc.
P.O. Box 249
Valley Falls, NY 12185

First Edition: May 2022

## Credits

Editors: Ashley Tillman and Shelley Thrasher
Production Design: Susan Ramundo
Cover Design By Kris Bryant

# Acknowledgments

I'm a romantic at heart. I believe in true love and the power of it. How people meet and fall in love fascinates me. The internet, dating apps, reality shows, and even bumping into somebody at the grocery store or the local coffee shop. We're searching for love the minute we're born. We date, we break up, we find somebody else who makes our heart flutter, we nurse another broken heart. It's a cycle, but we are bound and determined to find our soul mate. It all has to do with hope. When I decided to write a book about a dating reality show for lesbians, I wanted to kind of poke fun at reality shows, but at the same time, show that there are people who still believe in finding love and do in such an unorthodox way. We don't know what to believe. Are the shows real or are people just in it for fame? There are couples who have met on television dating shows and are still together. I thought it would be fun to write that story. The coldness of reality TV vs the warmth of true love.

Here we are, two years into a pandemic and I'm finally finding my stride again. It's because I have an amazing support group. My family, my friends, my readers, and even my co-workers. I need people to keep me on track. Writing dates with besties Fiona and KB Draper help keep me accountable. Seeing my writer friends again after a zillion years really helped with my mental health. Melissa, GFB, Carsen, Paula, Rey, Morgan, Friz and so many others—thank you for including me in your lives and checking in when mine is upside down. A giant shout-out to my patrons. We are growing and doing amazing things as a group around the world, one shelter at a time. Deb has made 2022 the year of Kris Bryant's amazing book covers! I'm in love with all of them. Her talent astounds me. Thank you for seeing what's in my head.

Ashley slashed, and I mean with the sharpest knife, or, you know, a red pen, the last 12,000 words of *Forever* and told me to try again. I did and I love how this book ends. She's a genius and I look forward to her edits because she makes me a better storyteller and Shelley makes me a better writer. Without the behind-the-book-scenes help from editors, proofers, typesetters, and designers, our polished books wouldn't make it into our readers' hands and hearts. Thank you, Sandy, for working with me on plot points and dreaded blurbs, and thanks to Radclyffe for publishing our books and giving us the platform to share our stories.

My readers are wonderful. Your support has been phenomenal over the years and I want you to know that I see and appreciate every tweet, post, and shout-out on social media. Thank you for your sweet emails and messages. I can't tell you how important those are to me. You are the best!

# Dedication

To my sister
because I will love you forever

## Chapter One

"Flickering Wicks, organic candles. This is Jane. How may I help you?" Jane, my best friend and part-time helper, nodded as she listened to whoever had called. "Sure. Just a moment." She tried to hand the phone receiver to me.

"Tell them I'm not interested."

"They specifically asked for you. I don't think it's a telemarketer." Jane waved the phone at me as though I didn't already know I had a call.

"Can you find out who it is?" I was putting together a small bouquet of flowers with a candle order that had to go out today, and it was already almost two in the afternoon.

"Cole Campbell," she said.

I froze right as I was sticking baby's breath between a cluster of pink and purple roses that I'd picked up from Wholesale Petals, the flower store next door. The thin stem broke as I squeezed. "No."

"No, it's not Cole, or no, you don't want to take the call? I can't keep him on hold forever." She shrugged.

I took a deep breath and waited until the blood flowed back through my icy veins. "No. I won't take the call."

"I'm sorry, but Savannah's busy right now. Can I take a message?"

I didn't even want her to take a message. I stabbed baby's breath into the small arrangement until it looked more like a bridal bouquet than an I'm-thinking-of-you-fondly gift. Then I pulled strands out until I found balance. A sharp poke on the back of my arm made me pull back, thinking a bee had stung me. It'd happened before working around flowers. "Ow." Jane was jabbing me repeatedly with the point of a folded pink note.

"I think you're going to want to see this," she said.

"Just throw it on the counter. I have to get this arrangement ready before Andrew leaves for the day." I wasn't lying. I liked to get all orders out by two, so if one was delivered to someone's work, they still had a few hours to show it off. She stared at me until I was done with the floral part of the arrangement. "Can you hand me two rose and chamomile canning-jar candles?" The arrangement, *Summertime Romance,* included a small wicker basket with roses, two of our small organic candles, customer's choice, and handfuls of heather and baby's breath as filler to make it worth the eighty-nine-dollar price tag. Andrew made more money delivering it than I did creating it. Delivery charges were sky-high in the Scottsdale area, but nobody seemed to mind.

"Is it ready?" Andrew threaded his fingers through his sandy-colored hair and pushed it away from his face, then rested his gangly elbows on the counter. The warehouse flower shop next door and I had a pretty good thing going. Andrew, whose parents owned it, delivered for me during the summers and pocketed all delivery charges, and I got all flowers at cost. "It sure is. Here's the address. And slow down." He was a good kid, but he liked to speed, and sometimes customers complained.

"Will do, boss. Text me if something else comes in." He zipped off and guiltily looked back at me when the side of the arrangement hit the entrance door. A quick check, thumbs up, and he disappeared, leaving the tiny bell on the door swinging furiously.

Jane and I watched him peel out of the parking lot. "It's not that I don't appreciate his need to get people their arrangements," I said. "It's just I don't want him to die or kill anybody in the process."

"Can we talk about the call now?" Jane followed me back to the sales counter and pointed to the pink slip of paper with more writing than I wanted to see. I dreaded it but was also extremely curious why someone from *When Sparks Fly* would be calling me. Jane, like everybody else in this town, knew that years ago I was on a dating show, and the outcome was horrific. I took a deep breath and picked up the message.

> *Cole Campbell*
> *Meador Entertainment*
> *(786) 555-3555*
> *Wants to talk to you about being the flame on an anniversary show. He says you'll be perfect since you're a fan favorite and everyone wants to see you get a happily-ever-after.*
> *Call him.*

My emotions played tug-of-war with me. The embarrassment of getting dumped on a television show had been awful, but the chance at redemption intrigued me. Ten years ago, Cole was a recruiter for the show and found me poolside and hungover during spring break in Florida. I blamed youth and ignorance for saying yes. Who didn't want to be on television? I had been twenty-two and not looking for love, but it was exciting to have all eyes on me.

At the time, *When Sparks Fly* was a new dating show for lesbians, and I was out and proud. I spent the summer after graduation in a posh apartment in the Florida Keys with other lesbians partying, having fun, and dating the same beautiful woman: Katie Parson. At first, it was a competition. We all just wanted to win for the glory and to drink free alcohol as long as possible. When it got down to four of us, something happened. I fell for her. One day I realized the words I rehearsed every day before stepping in front of the cameras were real. I was in love. The handful of faithful viewers thought so, too. I was a favorite to win even though I was young and naive.

Sadly, Katie didn't feel the same. Not only did she send me packing, but she humiliated me in the process. She said I was too young and she didn't need a puppy following her around. I was heartbroken and angry for allowing the show to let her shred me on national television. I'd signed up for a dating show, but Katie was cruel. Cole chased me down and apologized, but I was done. Thankfully, since I wasn't in the top two, I wasn't obliged to return for follow-up shows.

"Are you going to call him?"

"Hell, no."

Jane held her hands up and walked away slowly. "Okay, okay. I get it."

But Jane didn't get it. She was lucky and found love after college, had two kids, and started working with me once the kids went to school and camps. She was never a meme of a girl with an ugly cry. Nobody hounded her for interviews or laughed at her when she ventured out into public. But everything died down after a few years, and I was able to expand my college project and open a small organic candle shop in the heart of Scottsdale.

"I'm sorry for snapping at you. I just like my life. It took me a while, but I've put the show and the humiliation behind me."

"I know you have, but the rest of the world hasn't. People still love you and hate Katie." Jane tapped the note on the counter. "Wouldn't you like a little redemption?"

"Fine. I'll call him, but after work. And after a glass or two of wine."

"They pay their bachelorettes or whatever," she said.

"Really? Huh." If that was true, I didn't want it to sway me either way. I hadn't been paid to be a contestant. At least not with money. I had a free place to stay, stocked refrigerator, all the alcohol I could drink, and a wardrobe of bikinis.

"That's what I read somewhere," she said.

I casually reached for my cell phone and posted the latest arrangement on Flickering Wicks's Instagram account. I showed Jane only because I didn't want her to think I was googling how much the flame was paid on *Sparks*, even though that was exactly what I did next. "Holy shit! The last one made a quarter million without any endorsements. That was just her salary for being on the show."

"Ha! I knew you couldn't resist looking." Jane raised her hands in the air in a touchdown move.

I scowled at her and then sighed. "The money would save this place."

"And you aren't dating anyone," she said.

"Isn't on-air dating just a ruse to get in front of cameras? The contestants are in it for either a career boost in television, modeling, or music." The irony of my words didn't escape either one of us, but Jane was gracious enough to blow past it.

"Maybe you can show the world that someone can find love on a show. You did it before, and a lot of people were pulling for you. You're thirty-two, and it's time to open yourself to something other than swipe-right-app bullshit or whatever single people do now," Jane said.

I wanted to defend my dismal dating, but she was right. I worked, and that was it. I never hung out anywhere I could meet people the old-fashioned way—in person and, most times, by chance. "Oh, it's not that bad." But it was. It was hard to work six days a week and then expect to be refreshed for a night out. Most of my free time I spent with Jane and her family in comfortable clothing and very little makeup.

"At least listen to him. I'm always telling you to put yourself out there. You're gorgeous, own your own business, and have a great heart. You'd be the perfect sparklorette. Isn't that what they call them?" Jane always knew the right words to say to make me either push myself or laugh.

I laughed. "Social media dubbed the contestants sparkettes, and the name stuck." I rolled my eyes at how ridiculous that sounded. "And the bachelorette is called the flame. I wish they had a better name for her."

"Then they should call her the sparklorette. Oh, and use sparklers instead of candles."

"And burn us all on the first night? I like my smooth skin. Plus, sparklers are loud and obnoxious."

"Like the show isn't?" Jane raised her eyebrows at me.

"Wait. I can't tell if you want me to go or not. The way you're making fun of it, I'm guessing I should just throw away this message." I held up the pink slip and waved it in front of her.

"You know I'm kidding. Just call Cole and hear him out."

I slipped the note into my back pocket and tried to forget about it. Jane and I talked about our new summer exclusive scents that would be released next week, including Water Lilies, Huckleberry Sugar, and a new candle called Campfire, which smelled like roasted marshmallows and burning wood. I even used a wooden wick to mimic the sound of a crackling fire. We needed a boost, and I knew this candle would bump sales. "I'm going to work on the display tonight. Want to come over and help? Or do the kids have things on the schedule?"

"Tyler has baseball practice and Tamryn has dance, but they're at the same time, so I could probably swing by for about forty-five minutes. What did you have in mind?"

"Fire pit, roasting marshmallows, and maybe a small tent. If we set up the shot just right, the tent should cover the fence. It'll look like we're camping in the great outdoors and not in Scottsdale." I used social media platforms to sell our products instead of paying for advertising. My videos were a hit. I offered different discounts on different apps so I knew where I was getting the most business. It didn't hurt that I had a semi-celebrity past. Several of my followers had been with me since my stint on *Sparks*. But running a business cost a lot of money, especially in downtown Scottsdale. I had three employees—Jane, Andrew, and Dawn. Dawn was my only full-time employee. If I agreed to do the show, Jane would have to put in more hours, and that wasn't fair to her since her kids were out of school for the summer.

"Sounds great. Maybe a few glasses of wine?" Jane asked.

"For the video shoot or for us?" Either way sounded fine.

"Why not both?" Jane was always the logical one.

"You're on."

"Hello, Cole. It's Savannah Edwards." I was home, and even though I was planning to wait until after Jane left, curiosity and anxiety won, so I made the call. I tried to keep my voice calm even though my hands were shaking.

"Savannah. Thanks for returning my call."

I immediately regretted it. Anger hidden under layers of denial quickly surfaced, and I squeezed my fingers into a tight fist at their fast appearance. "What can I do for you?"

"We're shooting a shortened ten-year-anniversary show. If you're interested, we would love for you to be the flame this time. You were always a fan favorite, and you're still popular after all these years. Any chance you're single?"

I had a feeling Cole had a dossier of my life since I left the show and already knew everything about me, including my lack of a love life. "I'm not in a relationship. I don't really have a lot of time since I opened my own business."

"A candle business, right?"

He probably knew my net worth and that I was barely scraping by. I hated that anything could be found online. "Yes. It would be hard to leave the business for any length of time."

"Do you think you can get away for a day? We'll fly you out here, talk about the show and the perks, and get you home the same night. Savannah, the show has made great progress since its debut. We've grown by leaps and bounds, and our new hostess is amazing. *When Sparks Fly* is a successful prime-time show, and several of our flames and sparkettes have found love."

According to the internet, three out of the ten flames from the show were still with their partner from the show. Katie Parson's relationship had failed after a few months. When I googled her name earlier, it said she was still single. "Lauren Lucas is hosting now." I'd seen the show, but only bits and pieces. It still stung.

"She's added so much class and legitimacy to the show," he said. "I think you'll be really impressed with what it has become."

My curiosity won. My only day off was three days from now. "How about Sunday? It's the only day the shop is closed, and I can get away then."

"Sounds perfect. What's your email address? I'll send you the details."

I gave him my email and disconnected the call. Then I rolled my shoulders to alleviate the tension that had settled there during the past five minutes.

"Where are you?" Jane peeked her head into my kitchen, entered when she saw me, and handed me a six-pack of White Claw.

"Why are you so pale? Are you okay?" she asked.

"I just got off the phone with Cole." I was still processing. "He wants me to visit on Sunday and talk more about it. They're going to fly me out there."

Jane squeezed my arms. "That's great. Right? I mean, it doesn't hurt to listen to them and make them treat you like a queen."

"That gives me three days to get a mani-pedi and find something decent to wear," I said. I hadn't had a decent wardrobe in years. Most of the money I made went right back into the shop.

"We can skip the video shoot and go shopping instead." Jane looked at her watch. "We have plenty of time."

I thought about it, but I needed to stay level-headed. "It's okay. The video is important. I have a hundred summer dresses. I'm sure one will work." I would panic-shop during my lunch break tomorrow. Tonight was about Flickering Wicks and keeping the doors open.

After several takes, we ended up with a video I liked that included a plate of s'mores, a fire in the background, and marshmallows roasting on a thin stick. I moved my phone so the video ended with a shot of the new candle with the snazzy label and crackling wick. After Jane left, I added information about the business and my voiceover. I texted the final product to her.

*Looks great! I'm excited for release day and your meeting with WSF.* She ended the text with a happy-face emoji.

*Thanks. Let's see how sweet they can make the deal.*

I put my phone down and cracked open one of the White Claws. Cole's call was an awakening. I had been alone too long. Maybe the show could help me find my soul mate. It had made me fall in love before, but maybe this time, somebody would fall in love with me, too.

## CHAPTER TWO

A private jet. Nice touch, Cole." The four-and-a-half-hour flight to Florida was manageable with my very own flight attendant. I watched two movies and ate a hearty breakfast.

"Savannah, you look more beautiful today than you did ten years ago." Cole air-kissed my cheek. He looked polished and refined. Very different from the cute frat boy who approached me a decade ago during spring break.

"Executive producer, huh? Congratulations."

The old Cole would have shrugged and smiled. Instead, he gave a curt nod. "Hashtag career goals. Shall we?" He held the door open to the building and nodded to the security guard sitting at the desk.

I was surprised he was taking me to their office building. I thought maybe we'd do a light lunch somewhere chic, and he would woo me over trendy salads and chardonnay. He hit the fifth-floor button.

"We have the fourth and fifth floors, and the studio, of course."

"Of course." When the doors opened, I almost gasped. The decor was sophisticated. Meador Entertainment and its subsidiaries were listed on the wall behind the reception desk. A receptionist smiled brightly at us. "Welcome, Ms. Edwards."

"You all work on Sundays?" I whispered to Cole.

"Only on special occasions," he said.

He nodded at her, and she buzzed the door to let us in. "Take a left." He pointed down the hallway and waited for the door to latch behind us.

"Do you need all this protection?" I remembered only Lou the security guard stationed outside the rented penthouse, but I didn't recall anyone bothering us.

"*When Sparks Fly* is a big show. Plus, Lauren is a celebrity. Since she left CNN to lead *Sparks,* she pretty much calls the shots," Cole said.

He opened the door to the conference room, and I froze in the doorway. Six people sat at a large oval table staring at me.

"Ms. Edwards. Thank you for coming. Please, have a seat." An attractive older man with gorgeous hair shook my hand and introduced himself as Peter Meyers, Meador Entertainment's chief financial officer. I was introduced to everyone, certain I wouldn't remember a single name by the end of the meeting. I sat and waited for somebody to start talking.

"I'm sorry I'm late." Lauren Lucas breezed into the room and smiled at me. Her cream-colored suit with a sapphire shell stood out in the room full of dark suits and conservative ties. Honey-brown hair tumbled in curls down her back. She stared at me with sparkling blue eyes that matched her blouse. "It's so nice to meet you. I'm Lauren Lucas." She shook my hand, and when she smiled, a dimple formed high up on her cheek.

She was a proverbial breath of fresh air and more beautiful in person than on-screen, which was rare because most people looked better on television. I was both excited and completely self-conscious around her. I didn't care about the show executives and producers in the room. "Hi. I'm Savannah Edwards." I didn't recognize my own voice. It sounded husky and a bit too sexy. I cleared my throat and took a sip from the ice water in front of me. She sat four seats down and across from me.

"Since we're all here, let's get started," Peter said. He handed me a leather portfolio with a contract and a ton of other papers.

I closed it and folded my hands so they rested on the soft leather. "First of all, I want to know why you picked me. Out of all the other seasons and the hundreds of contestants, why me?" I glanced at Lauren, who quickly masked her smile as she bit her bottom lip and wrote something in her notebook.

"Ten years ago, we didn't know the direction of *When Sparks Fly*. We wanted to have a dating show that focused solely on women. In the beginning, it was about partying and everyone making out. It wasn't serious like *The Bachelorette*," Peter said. Everyone at the table knew most of the show's budget during season one had gone to the Tipsy Rooster liquor store in the Florida Keys. "We started off that way, but we've since changed the direction of the show. There's a real need for a serious reality show about women loving women." He nodded in Lauren's direction. "With Lauren's help, we were able to add a level of sincerity to the show, and the switch has been amazing. Amazing," he repeated.

As I looked around at the posh digs, I agreed that the switch was a good call. "Okay, so again, why me?"

"You're exactly what we are looking for. People believed you then, and they're going to believe that you want a relationship now. That *is* what you want, right?" Peter sat back in his chair and looked around the room as though he had just revealed a secret that everyone already knew.

A heated flush settled on my neck and cheeks. I was embarrassed to have every single person in that room judge me. I had gotten my answer, but it was hard to hear. I was thirty-two, single, and preparing to sign up for a dating show that had once destroyed me.

"You're familiar with the show, you've always been a fan favorite, you're attractive, and you're genuine. Everybody loves the girl next door," Lauren said. "You have your own business, you know what you want, and you haven't settled for anything but what's best for you."

I got lost in Lauren's brilliantly blue, trusting eyes for a moment. "Um, yeah, thank you. Honestly, I feel a little exposed right now."

"Can we have the room?" Lauren asked. The seven men immediately pushed up from their chairs and left. Each one nodded and smiled at me on his way out. Lauren moved closer and sat in the now-vacant chair across from me.

"Why me, though? I'm nobody. I'm somebody who signed up for a show years ago and got dumped on television."

She pointed at me and smiled. "That's exactly why. People need to see you happy and moving forward with your life. They are invested in you. The show still gets emails about you. And about Katie Parson, whom they all dislike very much."

I smiled at her. "Yeah. I'm not really a fan either."

The lilt in her laugh made my stomach quiver. "I know you have reservations, and I would, too, but I promise that we will do everything possible to make it an amazing experience. The new board and policies focus on taking care of the flames, contestants, and crew. And we have only ten contestants this time around. Once you tell us what you're looking for, we will make sure the contestants check all your boxes."

I wanted to believe her. She made me excited about dating again. Her words boosted my confidence. When was my last date? Three months ago? Theoretically, everyone on the show would be people I would be interested in, so it was better than a dating app. "Tell me the plan. Is there an apartment somewhere like before?"

She patted the closed leather portfolio in front of me. "We plan to start at two mansions in Key West. The contestants will be at one, and you'll be at another." She opened the binder and showed me photos of the places. Not surprisingly, both were high-end. "We'll have a quick trip to Mexico when it gets down to four contestants, and, of course, the final two you'll take home to meet your family and/or friends."

I sat back in the chair. "This is a lot to take in."

"I know you have a business to run and that this will take you away for a good three months. You'll receive a ten-thousand-dollar signing bonus that will hopefully allow you to hire somebody while you're away. And then there's the salary for playing the flame. Since it's a shortened season, it's only a hundred and fifty thousand dollars, but you won't have to worry about food or lodging. Everything is provided. And you'll have your own makeup and hair stylist."

The proposal sounded too good to be true, but I had no reason to doubt Lauren. "Is there a catch?"

"What do you mean?"

"You're not going to blindside me with an ex or ask me to hand over my firstborn if I find the perfect woman?" I was only kind of joking.

"We're not looking to manufacture drama. It's really a straight-forward contract."

"Would you do it?"

"Um, well. Interesting. No one's ever asked me that question," she said.

I didn't know a single thing about Lauren. I didn't know if she was married, straight, single, bi, pan. She was incredibly femme, but that could just be her persona for the show. My gaydar didn't ping at all.

"I would do the show. They vet each contestant and do a background check and a deep dive on their social media accounts. The contestants will be people who want a long-term relationship and aren't necessarily in it for fame, but no promises."

Even though Lauren was aware of my dating history, I knew I couldn't ask if she was married or dating. It wasn't my business. We were here for me, and I needed to decide. "If you say it's legit and something you would do, then where do I sign?"

She smiled, and the tiny dimple that popped up high on her cheek made my knees weak. Regardless of the outcome of the show, it was going to be a nice treat to see her every day for the next three months.

## CHAPTER THREE

"They said I have the shoulders of a football player."

Jane snorted over the phone. "First of all, that's funny, but not at all true. I'm only laughing because you described Buzzy perfectly. I just found their Insta, and I'd say I'm sorry, but they do amazing work. They are one of the hottest wardrobe stylists now."

I wasn't allowed on social media now that the show was technically underway, but I was allowed to check in with Jane with a flip phone the show provided since she was running my business. Once they started recording the first episode, they were cutting me off from her and the rest of the world for at least two months.

"Well, maybe they didn't come right out and say it, but apparently I have bad posture and walk like a Neanderthal."

"Stop it. You're graceful. They're just used to dealing with red-carpet affairs and people who have been dressing for galas their entire lives," Jane said.

I looked at myself in the mirror and straightened my shoulders, which forced me to push my average-sized boobs out. The strapless, sexy black dress I was wearing made me feel naked and vulnerable, which was par for the course, given that I was going to expose my heart on national television. Again. "I've been waxed in places I never imagined could be waxed." I never thought the small hairs on my arms were noticeable, but Buzzy sent me to the waxer, who removed hair from my arms, legs, bikini area, and even the thin tiny ones above my navel. As offended as I was at the time, I had to admit that I looked fresh.

"I never noticed you were hairy except on your head."

I leaned closer to the mirror. "They did compliment me on my eyebrows, but the waxer still found a few strays." The facial this morning had felt wonderful. "And my face looks ten years younger. Remind me to spoil us at a spa once this is all over."

"I'm going to hold you to that."

"You deserve it for running my business for three months." I'd given Jane my signing bonus to work more hours and find part-time help. We had enough inventory for at least a month with steady business. Jane knew how to make candles. She just didn't have the experience or time.

"Don't worry about the store. If things get crazy, I'll sign on Lee from next door to help." She'd already hired Andrew's older sister, Annabeth, to work the afternoons until school started. Lee, their mother, popped over enough to know our business. She could slip in and help if things got too wild.

"Sounds like you've got this. Okay. They're waving at me for hair and makeup. Talk to you later."

"Right this way, Ms. Edwards." Mandee, my hair and makeup artist, was the polite, very quiet break I needed after an endless round of tongue clicks, head shakes, and judgment-filled combination of English and German from Buzzy, my wardrobe magician. Their words, not mine.

"You have such thick, gorgeous, dark hair," Mandee said.

"That's probably the nicest thing anybody has said to me today," I replied.

She shrugged. "Don't worry about Buzzy. They are like that with everyone. Deep down, they're harmless and a true pussy cat. Just wait until they flip the switch. You'll notice when that happens."

Mandee pulled up my hair on both sides in a half updo and let several waves of curls roll down my back. An hour later, it looked as though I were in a wedding. It was a spectacular effect. After spraying more product on my hair to keep it from moving at all, she started on my makeup. I couldn't help but smile when she finished. I looked great and felt beautiful.

"Let's get you over to your photo shoot." We had several promotional teaser videos to make, but I was afraid to move or blink. Thankfully, everything happened at my mansion.

Denise Lawry, the director, explained we were taking a ton of photos and filming two promotional videos. One would show my back as I looked out at the ocean. The other one featured the inside of the house and ended on a blurry shot of me, focusing on a candle in my hands. Nobody knew who the next flame would be, and they were building up the reveal. They would start promoting the show next week.

Tonight, I was scheduled to sit down with Lauren and Denise and discuss the contestants—what to expect when meeting them and how to respond to the initial meeting if something didn't feel right. Filming would start Wednesday so that the first episode would drop in a month. With a shortened season, they predicted the final ceremony in ten weeks. Seemed like a short time, but unlike *The Bachelorette*, this show didn't necessarily end with a proposal.

"Put your hands on the railing and place one foot behind the other, like you're toeing the ground behind you. Breathe normally and just enjoy the view," Denise said.

The film crew would come in from the front door, glide through the living space, and pan in on me on the balcony. The drone would fly straight up but not show my face. I thought the technique was ridiculous, but they knew what worked in film and television. When I heard Denise yell "Action," I took a few deep breaths and relaxed. I heard them move closer and closer until Denise yelled something else. We filmed three times before she was satisfied. I was instructed to turn around slowly and smile at the camera when she gave the command. I did that five times.

My first scripted word was "Surprised?" Then I was to act coy or smirk. That remark required more takes than I cared to count. I wasn't as smooth as I thought I was.

"That's a wrap for now. Mandee, take her over to the photographer, and we'll get several snaps of her in this dress. Then let's put her in something more comfortable."

Three hours flew by, and after my stomach rumbled loudly for the third time, Mandee insisted on a quick lunch break. A part of me wanted to gobble everything in front of me, but the clothes Buzzy had picked fit perfectly, so I limited my intake to fruit, veggies, and a yogurt. I eyed the plate of carb-filled bagels like a starved eagle would a field full of unsuspecting mice but avoided it because my willpower sucked.

"We're going to have you change into these yoga pants and this sweatshirt. I'll fix your hair once you've changed."

"Is this Buzzy-approved?"

Mandee hid her smile by turning to face the rack of clothing. I was sure she knew what a pain it was to work with Buzzy.

"Yes. They're good with the look. I'm going to reapply your makeup so it appears more natural, like you're just hanging out on a Sunday afternoon scrolling on your phone or watching romantic comedies."

I snorted. On the rare occasions when I had downtime, I never wore a bra or makeup. Maybe I made it out of bed that day, but most of the time I stayed under the covers and got caught up on social media and different TV shows piling up in my queue. "Sounds good." After removing my makeup and reapplying a fraction of what she just took off, she styled my hair in a bun and left a few tendrils down. "I might have to take you home with me after this." I could never get this look on my own. I saw her blush and realized she took my words wrong. "I mean as a stylist. Your makeup skills are magical." Her embarrassment gave way to my own, and I tried hard to stop the flush from blossoming on my cheeks. She skillfully worked around it.

"There. You look wonderful. Let's get you over to Norman."

I hissed out a deep sigh of relief and followed her to the other side of the house, where the show's photographer had a small studio set up in the large library. Nobody was allowed in the room unless photos were scheduled. I sat and followed Norman's directions to move my arms here, cross my legs this way, tilt my head up, smile, not smile. The lights were so blinding I didn't even see Lauren slip into the room.

"Are we almost done here, Norman? We have a dinner meeting with Denise in a little bit." She leaned over the laptop and scrolled through the photos that automatically downloaded to it. "By the way, your photos are incredible."

Her voice made my skin tingle. I realized another reason they'd picked her besides her class and beauty was her soothing voice. And she was charming.

Norman fell under her spell immediately. "Okay, Ms. Edwards. We're done for today," he said.

Lauren winked at me over his shoulder. I relaxed my shoulders and rolled my neck. A break sounded wonderful. I couldn't believe we'd been doing this for almost eight hours. Lauren pulled me up from my sitting position on the set's floor. Her hand was firm and warm, and I instinctively took a step back because I was in her personal space. She was slightly more casual today, with her hair pulled back in a long ponytail and minimal makeup. Her outfit was still professional, and I wondered if she knew what yoga pants were or had ever walked on grass without heels.

"Do you have a preference for dinner?" Lauren asked. "Unfortunately, we can't be seen out in public, or we'd blow our secret of you as the new flame wide open."

"Right now, I could eat anything," I said.

She waved me off when I grabbed the hem of the oversized sweatshirt to pull it over my head. "Just leave that outfit on. You look cozy. Plus, after being under the lights for so long, you're probably slightly chilly."

She wasn't wrong. I sank back into the Supima-cotton softness and smiled. I hoped I was allowed to take some of the wardrobe home because I could live in this sweatshirt. "Seriously, anything with protein and carbs sounds delicious." I was thinking cheeseburger, fries, and a milkshake but didn't think that choice would be an option.

"Perfect. Josef with an ef, our chef, makes a fantastic citrus shrimp. It's delicious."

I should have checked my reaction before sharing it.

"Or whatever your nutritionist suggests," Lauren said.

I sighed. "I know I have to watch my weight now, so sure, we can have that." I was dying for a cheeseburger with fat, greasy steak fries, but I had a wardrobe to fit into, and Buzzy clicked their tongue enough at me when they had to adjust my dress every time I moved.

Lauren cocked her head as though she felt sorry for me. "I won't tell Buzzy. Plus, it's the first day of filming promos."

Was she really this nice? I figured they paid her a lot of money to make sure the flames were comfortable, but was it a twenty-four-hour, seven-day-a-week job? "Honestly, I'd love a cheeseburger. I'm sure there's something healthy about it, right?" I winced as I waited for her answer.

She crinkled her nose in the most adorable way before breaking my heart. "I promise Josef will cook something so delicious you won't even miss the calories."

I almost harrumphed, but at least she was trying. I already knew it would have to be sparkling water, so I didn't even push for a milkshake. She'd probably suggest a sugar-free, almond-milk froth, if such a thing existed. "Sounds great. Lead me to the kitchen." Surely, Josef with an 'ef' could throw something at me to nibble on while he hacked up some house plants for us to eat.

Denise was sitting at the kitchen island drinking a beer and writing notes on her tablet with a stylus. She was in her late fifties, with short, curly hair that had a dusting of gray close to the scalp. Her glasses were tight against her face, and she pulled them off when we approached. "What do you think of the place, Savannah?"

"This mansion is beautiful. Too bad it's not really mine. I would love to live in Key West forever. Having a beach right outside is a dream come true."

She handed me a longneck without asking, and I took it out of respect and, quite frankly, fear. She was intense.

"How was the photo shoot?" She looked at Lauren when she asked, and I wasn't sure if I should answer or not.

"Savannah is very photogenic. Norman got some great shots."

"I haven't been this excited about the show since you came on board," Denise told Lauren.

"This is going to be a wonderful season," Lauren said.

It seemed impossible that somebody this sweet and nice was in the television business. I felt like a third wheel while they were having their moment.

Denise slid Lauren a beer when she sat in the high-back chair across from us. That put her two feet from me. She was truly a stunning woman. Her natural tan made her light blue eyes pop. A brush of mascara that lengthened her lashes appeared to be the only bit of makeup she had on. Her hair had natural blond streaks. She looked like a poster advertising the All-American woman. She was probably around my age, maybe older, given her resumé.

"How did Meador Entertainment convince you to join the show?" I asked. It seemed like a good starting point for any conversation.

Denise sat back in her chair with a sigh, as though she'd heard this story too many times, and Lauren gave a shaky laugh.

"Well, I was looking for something light after reporting overseas for CNN. One can handle only so much death and destruction." She took a sip of beer and grimaced. "Also, I've given up on beer. I'm going to grab a glass of wine instead."

She seemed nervous sitting with us. I watched as she expertly extracted the cork of a red and poured a glass.

"Anybody else want one?"

Since I wasn't fond of the beer either, I nodded and slid my longneck away from me. Denise couldn't be mad at both of us.

"It's not the greatest, but it was cold." Denise shrugged and finished her bottle with a final pull.

"Here, drink this." Lauren handed her a cold water from the refrigerator. "Stay hydrated. New season, full steam ahead." She gracefully poured a second glass that she put in front of me. Her nails were perfectly shaped and polished. She was camera-ready, too.

"You worked for CNN. That's quite the accomplishment at such a young age," I said.

"I was able to travel the world and got clout for covering stories nobody else wanted."

"Why did you stop?" I asked. After a slight pause, her full lips touched the thin rim of the wineglass for a delicate sip. Was she always elegant?

"It was time to settle down."

"I get that. I really do." I clinked my glass against hers and couldn't help myself from asking the obvious question. "Did you? You know, find somebody to settle down with?" Both women gaped at me. I held my hands up and leaned back. "Really? That's offensive? I'm here so you can film me dating ten people for national television, but my questions are too much?" I held back a laugh. I didn't want to offend them, but their reluctance to answer was pretty funny, considering how exposed I already was. "Isn't this dinner the opportunity to get to know one another so we can feel more comfortable on set? You know everything about my love life during the last ten years. I've taken drug tests, STI tests, signed a thousand waivers, and that question is too much?"

Lauren squeezed my hand. "You're completely right. This *is* a chance for us to get to know one another better. I'm so used to being private that I've forgotten what it's like to just have a chat with a normal person who isn't trying to interview me or pry," she said.

Her hand was warm and soft. I wanted to smile at her comforting gesture, but it was hard because I couldn't remember the last time somebody touched me other than during a handshake. I ended up biting my lip to keep a frown from settling in. But just then a man arrived armed with two grocery bags and a knife roll.

"What's for dinner?" Denise asked.

I'd forgotten she was in the room with us. Lauren stood to peek inside the bags he dumped on the counter. "What are you making us?"

He turned. "Hello, Ms. Edwards. I'm Josef with an 'ef.'" I almost laughed, but he was dead serious. That detail was obviously important to him.

I nodded and ignored the sarcastic barb teetering on my tongue. "Nice to meet you, Josef." I might have placed more emphasis on the "ef" than I should have, but he appeared not to notice.

"I have steak, asparagus, and a salad, but I can make you whatever you would like," he said.

I quickly forgot the cheeseburger I'd so desperately wanted. "That sounds wonderful." Also healthier.

In fifteen minutes, he blended a butternut squash and roasted red-pepper hummus and placed a healthy serving of it with pita bread in front of us. "This is while you wait for the grill to heat. How would you like your steak prepared?"

We gave him our order and moved into the sitting room for privacy. I wanted to hear more about Lauren, but Denise had blown past that conversation and started discussing the contestants.

"Whoever started calling them sparkettes on social media should be shot. It's bad enough we have a candle ceremony, but trying to erase that name has been a nightmare." She turned to me. "I'm very passionate about this show and have done everything in my power to change it from a fuck-party house to a solid, entertaining show."

That remark ruffled my feathers. "Hold up. Don't forget I was in the original fuck-party-house season. The idea was there, the execution was not. Also, we didn't fuck, just for the record."

Denise shook her head. "I'm sorry. I didn't mean to offend you. The first season was a trial, and you're right. It wasn't like that. But the second and definitely the third and fourth seasons were."

"I didn't watch them," I said. As a matter of fact, I didn't watch any seasons, not even my own. I caught a few bits and pieces, but seeing it still stung.

"Those seasons were pretty bad. They were like *Temptation Island*, only sleazier, if that's even possible," Denise said.

"Worse than anything on MTV?" I asked. They both nodded. "Good thing I did only one season."

"And that's why you're so popular. You were the sweet one, and it was obvious you fell in love with her-who-should-not-be-named," Lauren said.

That remark made me smile. "A lot has happened since then." Not really. At least not with my love life. But I had my own business, and while it wasn't thriving, it was mine.

"Tell us about your company," Lauren said.

I appreciated the subject change. "I make organic candles. Strange, huh? It started in college, for one of my entrepreneurial classes. Everybody loves candles, but most of them burn chemicals that aren't healthy."

"So, your project started before the show?" Denise looked at me with surprise.

I frowned. "Did you think I created the store because of the show? No. Truly one of life's coincidences. And let me tell you, the candles for the show are horrible."

"They have to last long and look good on camera." Denise shrugged.

"I kind of have the perfect candle for you." I fired off a text message to Jane, which took forever since it was a flip phone. "We'll have them by Friday. And if we don't use them, that's okay, but if you like them, then it's a win-win for all of us." I was so proud of myself for pimping my own line to the show and not backing down, even when Denise rolled her eyes.

"It can't hurt," Lauren said.

Lauren sat back and stretched her long legs out. I couldn't stop myself from glancing at them. They were perfect.

"Shall we talk about the sparkettes?" she asked. Her smile was borderline devious, and for a moment, I regretted my decision, but then she gave me a genuine smile. "Seriously. I think you're going to like the contestants we picked."

## CHAPTER FOUR

My anxiety made an appearance just as we started filming. I was fine up until Lauren asked me, on camera, if I was ready to meet my dates. I froze. I couldn't speak. She turned to Denise.

"Let's take a quick break."

She grabbed my hand and pulled me into a private room, then made me sit. I dabbed at the sweat beads along my upper lip with a tissue she handed me.

"Don't worry about ruining your makeup. We have people to fix it." She sat in front of me and took my hands. "I know this isn't easy for you, but just remember that you're in control this time. Katie isn't here, and I know you won't be mean or cruel to anyone. And you might just find the perfect person." Her beautiful smile made me feel a smidge better.

"I don't know what's wrong with me. My heart started racing. Is this what a panic attack feels like?"

"I'd ask you to put your head between your knees, but the dress prohibits that possibility. Do you want me to loosen it? Will that help you breathe better?"

I waved her off but dropped my head. "No. I just need cool air and space to breathe."

She cranked the thermostat until the cold air made me shiver. I smiled gratefully at her when she handed me a cold water that magically showed up at the door. "I'm so embarrassed."

"Don't be. This is not the first time this has happened. Trust me."

Lauren sat next to me and rubbed small circles on my back. She was entirely too close, but I found myself leaning into her personal space. She smelled lovely.

"How are you not a sweaty mess right now?" I looked at her perfectly made-up face and unwrinkled suit. The lights were making me sweat, and she was poised, without a drop of perspiration anywhere.

"I'm comfortable in front of the camera and have been for twelve years. It's been a few years for you. You'll get used to it again."

Her smile reassured me, and her touch on my back comforted me. "Thank you." I took a deep breath and stood. "I'm ready. Let's do this." I chalked up the tingles I felt when she squeezed my hand to excitement for this new chapter to start.

No one entered in a horse-drawn carriage or via water slide or any other over-the-top way. The meet-and-greet took place inside the grand hall of the sparkettes' mansion. Denise had planned for the patio, but she quickly adapted to the rain. The sparkettes were to enter, introduce themselves, and then grab a drink or seat so I could meet the next one. High-top tables and alcoves of comfortable loveseats accommodated more private time once introductions had been made.

It was hard not to openly gawk at the first contestant. She was stunning. I mentally repeated "you're on camera" several times as she approached. Her evening gown was black and sexy and showed a generous amount of cleavage, but tastefully so. Her hair was a dark brown, almost black, and her eyes were so green I thought they were fake. The green popped beautifully against her tanned, smooth skin.

"Hi, Savannah. I'm Ophelia. I'm a life coach out of Ft. Lauderdale right here in sunny Florida, and I'm very excited to get to know you better. I didn't like the way things ended for you on the show ten years ago, and when I heard you were the new flame, I knew I had to meet you."

I was holding her hand longer than I should have. "It's nice to meet you, too, Ophelia. I'm excited to chat later." I was. She seemed genuinely interested in me. Every part of me soared. I was expecting attractive women tonight, but she was on a whole different level. It was hard not to watch her walk away, but I faced the door for the next contestant. Every single person smiled and took my breath away. I was never going to remember names. We took a break after meeting the first four women. Mandee needed to freshen my makeup, and I really needed to get out of these shoes. I followed her to my dressing room and kicked off the heels.

"I love dressing up as much as the next girl, but these are some killer stilettos."

"Do you want me to call wardrobe and get a shorter heel?" Mandee asked.

"No, thank you. That's sweet, but just having them off is heaven." I rubbed my feet for a few moments as Mandee prepped her brushes. I raised my eyebrows in surprise when we heard a soft knock.

"Come in," Mandee and I said in unison. She shrugged at me.

Lauren peeked her head in. "Just checking on our star. How are you holding up?" She was extremely attractive in her dark gray belted skirt suit with black shell. Her hair was pulled back in a bun, and even though she was styled to not outshine me, she looked incredible. I tried to swallow my silly grin whenever she was near. Lauren was a friend, or at least she had the potential to be one.

I waved her in. "Wow is all I can say. It's a lot different being on this side of things."

Mandee tapped the back of the chair, so I leaned back at attention for her to powder my nose and tighten my updo.

Lauren squeezed my hand. "You're doing great. You're charming and very responsive to the women. Your attitude comes across nicely on-screen." She moved to the side when Mandee hovered above me with a mascara wand.

"How are we doing on time?" It had been almost an hour, and I'd met only four people.

"We're doing well. It'll go smoother now that you know what to expect. The rest of the night should be easy."

"So far, I've been very impressed."

"How much of this are you remembering? It can be overwhelming," Lauren said.

"I remember Ophelia the life coach, Lyanna the pharmaceutical sales rep, Madison the lawyer, and I can't remember the nurse practitioner's name. She had blond hair and dark brown eyes and was very outgoing."

"Ava. She's from New Hampshire."

"Ava. That's right. So, you already know everyone?" I asked.

Lauren's smile was stunning. I was self-conscious of my crooked bottom tooth while staring at her perfectly straight and dazzling white ones.

"I've had the intel for weeks. I have to chat with them when you aren't around, so it's in my best interest to be aware of everything."

"You know, you should give me the intel, too. Then we can talk about them." I flashed her my cheesy grin and crinkled my nose in hopes she would cave. She shook her head at my obvious attempt to gather information on the sparkettes. I playfully groaned.

"Watching you get to know these contestants is the fun part, and so far, your reaction has been exactly what people want to see."

"What do you mean?" My cheeks flushed with embarrassment.

"The excitement in your eyes. We all see the hope of something good and, of course, the sparks," she said.

I rolled my eyes and laughed. "You had to go there, huh?"

She shrugged. "Eh, it's my job. I have to come up with the sappy—"

"Corny."

She nodded. "You're right. Corny lines, but some people out there like those kinds of lines. I mean, when you're in love, you don't mind hearing sap—I mean corny lines or getting predicable flowers on special occasions. People think money is what everyone wants. But let me tell you, it's love."

The smile on her face didn't quite match what I saw in her eyes—a flash of pain behind the brightness—and her hand shook ever so slightly as she smoothed back the side of her hair. Nothing was out of place. It was just a way to occupy her hands. I recognized the signs of nervousness. Had I blinked I would have missed it all. I took a deep breath. "If I'm not out of line, I just want you to know that whatever happened to you in the past, I hope that you have found the right person or are on your way to finding them."

The muscle in her jaw tensed a few times before she spoke. "I'll get there."

Her words were soft, but I heard the conviction in them. We were both determined to find somebody. I wanted to gently press since we were kind of having a moment, but one of Denise's gofers burst in without knocking and startled us.

"You're both wanted on set. Boss wants to finish shooting tonight."

"Knock first, troll," Mandee said as she finished putting up her makeup brushes.

Wide-eyed, he quickly shut the door. Both Lauren and I stared at her.

Mandee shrugged. "That's my kid brother. He wants to make it in showbiz. This was the only gig I could get him."

Lauren and I laughed in relief. It was good to get the nervous energy out. I didn't think Mandee was mean-spirited, but then I'd learned never to assume things in show business.

"You look gorgeous." Lauren turned to Mandee. "Is she ready? Are you done doing all the necessary things?"

Mandee stood back and looked at me, her gaze darting from the top of my head down to my neckline. One quick tug on the left side of my dress and then she nodded. After days of trying on clothes in front of Mandee, I wasn't alarmed by her fingers on my breasts. "She's perfect and all yours again."

I blushed because Lauren was watching us. It happened so fast that neither one of us had time to react.

"Ready?" Lauren asked.

"Yes."

For the first time in the show's history, one of the contestants was nonbinary. It clicked that Lauren said "people" a lot instead of "women." I'd known it was possible because the producers had asked a lot of questions about my dating preferences. When the fifth contestant introduced themself, I was really glad they'd made the cut. Their brown hair stood tall in a pompadour, and their blue eyes twinkled under the lights in the greeting room.

"Hi. I'm Alix. My pronouns are they/them. I'm a tattoo artist from Portland, Oregon. I hope tattoos aren't a turnoff, as I have several of them."

Their suit fit them to perfection. Black pants tapered down to black wingtip shoes. Their white shirt was unbuttoned just enough to see ink along their collarbone and in the middle of their chest. To say I was intrigued was an understatement. "Alix, you look incredible. I love tattoos. I don't have any, but I'm open to suggestions, and I'm looking forward to seeing more of yours." I shook my head at my own flirtatiousness. "Hi. I'm Savannah." More ink peeked out from the cuffs of their jacket when they held my hand in both of theirs. They winked at me.

"I'll be sure to find you inside."

Alix was the first person I watched walk away. I raised my eyebrows with interest and slowly turned to focus on the door for the next contestant.

Another brunette with blue eyes entered, but her hair was long and wavy. I met her sweet smile with one of my own.

"Hi. I'm Emma from Louisville, Kentucky, where I'm a preschool teacher." Her accent melted me.

"Hi, Emma. It's nice to meet you. I'm Savannah."

She surprised me by giving me a hug. I wasn't keen on people being immediately in my personal space without my permission, but she didn't threaten me. As a matter of fact, she felt nice and soft against me. "Can I just say that I didn't like what happened the last time you were on the show, and I'm happy that you're giving it one more try? I'll see you inside."

The final four were a blur. A teacher, a professional soccer coach, a speech pathologist who definitely caught my eye, and a mother of a four-year-old who blogged for a living about how to be a great parent. Lauren joined me after Charlotte, the blogger, slipped behind the velvet curtains.

"Well, you've officially met all the contestants. What are your initial thoughts?" she asked.

I knew the question was coming. Denise had prepared me so I could minimize the ums and ahs in my answer. "I'm very impressed. Some really wonderful people are in the other room. I'm excited to find out more about them and see if we have a spark." I loathed that line, but Lauren smiled like I'd said exactly what she wanted.

"Let's not keep you." She motioned for me to go ahead of her and followed me.

"Cut," Denise said.

I didn't realize how stressed I was until Denise ended the scene. I cupped the back of my neck and rolled my head. My neck cracked, and I immediately felt the tension leave my body.

Lauren winced. "Better? Because that sounded painful."

I shook my fingers out in front of me. "Sometimes I get so tense I forget to move. It sounds ridiculous."

"No. I get it. This isn't easy. Let's take a short break and head to the secret info room."

"Ooh. The secret info room?" I exaggerated the word secret and then frowned. "Wait. Why is there a secret info room?"

"It's not really a secret. It's just a room with the contestants' head shots and a little bit of information about each of them. You can just hang out there without any cameras. Study faces, facts, anything you want."

I didn't want to admit that I could remember only three names and couldn't recall who had children and who didn't. Ophelia and Alix stood out the most. I followed Lauren to a small room off the entryway that housed a baby grand piano. The walls were lined with bookshelves devoid of books. Instead, the shelves held framed headshots of the ten people I'd just met. Each photo had an info card with full name and where they were from. It wasn't a lot, but I could spend a few minutes studying faces and remembering names. I stopped concentrating when I felt Lauren's fingers on my arm.

"Take as much time as you need. Denise's assistant is letting the group know what to expect this evening and what's acceptable behavior and what isn't. I like to sit in so the contestants see us as a united front." She took a step closer and tucked a loose strand of my hair back under the partial updo. "I'll retrieve you later."

I held my breath and tried not to notice the sweet smell of her perfume or how her eyes were brighter than any of the sparkettes'. Her bracelet brushed my ear until I shuddered. She pulled back.

"Are you okay?"

My cheeks immediately warmed. "You were tickling me." She looked at me in confusion, so I pointed to her small golden bracelet and rubbed my ear, careful to not smear my makeup.

"I'm sorry. I just wanted to fix your hair. You were beautiful before, but now you're simply perfect."

I didn't know anything about Lauren. I didn't even do a deep dive on her when I was asked to return to the show. I always assumed she was straight. Jane always teased me that my gaydar was broken, and even though she was right, something was quietly pinging inside of me. A hunger stirred low in my belly whenever she was near. I knew better than to fall for a straight woman, but for a moment, I felt a tiny spark when she looked into my eyes.

## CHAPTER FIVE

You own a candle store?"
I loathed Madison, the snooty-lawyer contestant, but kept smiling. I tensed my jaw once but stopped when I realized my reaction would come across as bitchy on television.

As soon as I walked into the room, she'd zoomed in and asked if we could go talk somewhere privately. A booth with velvet curtains was set up for that very purpose, as were cameras, and only one camera person would share our space. Thankfully, they were far enough away so their presence wasn't as invasive as I expected. "I started an organic candle business in college for my senior project. I had already graduated when I joined the show during its first season."

"Isn't that strange? Maybe they based the show on you." Her nasally laugh grated on my nerves.

I needed out of this booth. We'd been alone only five minutes, but time felt like a wet blanket weighing me down. It was hard to maintain my enthusiasm. "I think it was just a coincidence."

She smirked as though she knew something I didn't. Obviously we didn't connect. In the first three minutes she talked about her law firm, how she scored a one sixty-two on her LSAT, and that she owned a Porsche and a Range Rover. I almost snorted as I thought about my ten-year-old Toyota Prius with peeling paint and a dented bumper that sat in my driveway getting bleached out by the sun because my garage was full of candle-making supplies. I'd never even sat in a Porsche. Madison would be the one everyone disliked but wanted me to put up with for the drama. I could almost hear Denise telling me to keep her for rating purposes.

How was I going to get out of here? I couldn't fake a headache because I still had to talk to nine other sparkettes. "I should probably go spend some time getting to know everyone."

Madison put her hand on my wrist. "I'm excited to become better acquainted, Savannah."

I raised my eyebrows and smiled. "Thank you for the private chat. I'll see you later." She should have been the one to leave the booth, but I didn't know how to say "get the fuck out" without sounding rude. Besides, if I pushed her out, the audience would hate me after one episode. I left her sitting in the booth.

Alix swooped up beside me with a charming grin and clinked their glass against mine. "I didn't think I was going to get you this soon."

I couldn't stop my smile. "I can't tell you how happy I am to find you," I said.

They leaned in and whispered, "I saw your slight frown when she whisked you away. I was actually on my way to rescue you."

"Thank you. Should we go somewhere a little quieter?" I was peeved that Madison was still in the private booth.

"Do you want to get some fresh air? I know it's raining, but there's a nice, covered deck out back." They pointed to a door behind four hopeful sparkettes, who stood huddled in a group doing everything possible to gain my attention. I politely smiled as I walked by and told them I would find them later. Alix opened the door, and butterflies exploded in my stomach when I felt their fingertips brush my lower back. The humidity was awful, and I knew after my chat with Alix that Mandee would have to freshen me up, but it felt so good to be out of the house that smelled like perfume, flowers, and competition.

"Please have a seat." Alix pointed to a small love seat.

I watched as they unbuttoned their suit jacket and waited for me to get settled comfortably before sitting. "Tell me more about the smooth tattoo artist from Portland."

"I'm impressed that you remembered. Let's see, my brother and I opened our shop three years ago."

"Are you both tattoo artists?"

They nodded proudly.

"That's impressive. You don't hear about two artists in the same family very often," I said. At least I hadn't.

"He's done most of my tats. Anyway, enough about me. Tell me more about you. What do you do? Do you have any pets? What are your hobbies? Do you have a favorite sparkette here yet?"

"Ah, look at you, sneaking that last question in." I was rewarded with a wink. "I own a small organic candle company in Scottsdale, Arizona. I don't have any pets because I work six days a week. Sleep is a hobby I wish I had more time for, and a few people have caught my eye, yourself included."

Alix put their hand over their heart. "I'm flattered."

"So am I."

Our cute banter was going to make for some great television. I could almost hear Denise rave about how charming it was. I nearly groaned when I saw someone approaching.

"Hi. Do you mind if I steal Savannah away?" Thea, the English professor from Boston, quietly crept into our space.

I almost pouted. I had spent only a few minutes with Alix, but I understood we were on a time limit, and people wanted their fair share of time with me. Alix squeezed my hand first and stood.

"I'll excuse myself so you can have this place. It's quieter than inside. Savannah, I hope to spend time with you again soon." Alix nodded at us, rebuttoned their jacket, and strode away. It was hard not to watch the lithe figure disappear into the house.

"Thea, right?"

"Yes. Good memory. I'm sure it's hard to keep us all straight. Well, not straight, but you know what I mean."

"I do. Tell me about yourself." I leaned slightly forward to study her. She looked more professional than classy and reminded me of somebody running for political office. She had a short, layered pixie cut with highlights and hazel eyes that were mostly blue, with intense brown flecks.

"I teach nineteenth-century British literature at a college in Boston."

"That must be rewarding."

"I'm also on the LGBTQ Alliance committee on campus. It is very rewarding to work with young queer people." She leaned closer. "Tell me about you."

By the time I had spent at least ten minutes with each contestant, I was desperate for a break. As if on cue, Lauren appeared by my side.

"Has everyone had a moment or two with Savannah?"

"Not enough," Madison said.

Most sparkettes nodded. Lauren ignored Madison.

"I'm going to steal Savannah for a moment. Keep enjoying yourselves. Good news. No elimination tonight. Only fun," Lauren said.

Celebratory whoops followed by glasses clinking echoed in the vast space. I followed Lauren into the room with the head shots and sat in a chair that hadn't been there before. Two cameramen crammed into the room with us, one focused on Lauren's face and the other on mine. Mandee squeezed in to quickly touch up my makeup and slipped out within a minute. Lauren smoothed back her hair, even though not a single strand was out of place. How was she so cool right now?

"Okay, so I'm going to ask you some general questions. Just be honest, but remember the cameras are rolling." She ducked her head and whispered, "You and I can talk about the nitty-gritty later at your place." Lauren was wonderful at making me feel comfortable in this chaotic world. It was completely different on this side, and I felt a tiny bit of sympathy for Katie Parson.

"Great. I'm ready."

She nodded at me and to the cameramen. "Savannah, it's been quite an evening. What are your thoughts so far?"

I clamped down and refrained from saying "uh" and "um" at the beginning of each sentence. "I've met some really wonderful people here, and I'm excited to have longer, more meaningful conversations with them in the days and weeks to come." Her beautiful smile told me I had nailed the answer.

"It's different being the flame than a sparkette. Has one particular person caught your interest tonight? Have you found anyone you would like to spend some one-on-one time with?"

I had to pick the first contestant for a date tomorrow. It included a swanky picnic on the beach with a giant umbrella, comfy beach chairs, fans, and a whole bunch of food we would barely touch. We would eat before shooting our date, so we didn't have to worry about sand coating the food or the camera catching strips of lettuce in our teeth. "I know who I'm inviting on the first date."

"Why did you pick this particular person?"

It was a toss-up between Alix the tattoo artist and Ophelia the life coach. Both were extremely kind and respectful. If I picked Ophelia for the picnic, Alix and I could have dinner together alone for my next one-on-one, which would be more intimate and romantic. "I picked this particular person because she was not only kind when we met but made me feel good about my decision to be here."

"Should we go back so you can invite whoever it is?"

I nodded. "That sounds great." I was already tired of being under the lights, having cameras shoved in my face, and Mandee buzzing around me ready to erase any shine on my skin. We'd been at this for five hours now. It was almost midnight, and I still had to pick a date and share a final drink with the contestants. I followed Lauren back into the large meeting room, which was now empty of all its thick, weighted privacy curtains. The sparkettes were sitting on a large sectional couch, a chaise unit, and three chairs. All eyes were on me, and a small trickle of sweat started to bead up on my lower back. This was a lot of attention.

"Thank you all so much for taking time out of your lives and careers, and time away from your families to meet me and see if we have a spark. I have a wonderful group of people who are here for the right reasons. Having been in your shoes, I know this situation isn't easy, and I appreciate your sacrifices." I turned to Lauren to signal that I was done.

"Okay, everyone. It's the time of the night when Savannah makes her first date choice. Don't be discouraged if you aren't picked. We have several exciting dates planned this week, with several opportunities to have some alone time with Savannah. Are you ready?"

I nodded and turned to the group. "Ophelia, would you like to take a walk with me?" It was hard to see nine sets of shoulders sag when she jumped up.

"I would love to." Her smile was so genuine that my sudden guilt at the remaining disappointed contestants evaporated.

When we rounded the corner to head outside, I reached for her hand. "Tomorrow we're having a picnic on the beach, but it's going to be a pretty posh setup, so we don't have to worry about getting too much sun." Our date was private because we didn't want the paparazzi to find out ahead of time who was on the show. The reveals were made on a very strict schedule. My commercials were about to drop though. Jane was the only one in my life who knew where I really was. The rest of the employees thought I was visiting my sick mother. She was on a cruise somewhere in the Caribbean and wouldn't stop by for an impromptu visit out of the blue, thus exposing my secret. Eventually, my small circle would find out, but we had to keep everything a secret until it was revealed nationwide. I had cowardly left my mom a voice mail the day before I left, even though I knew I should have had a conversation with her. Honestly, we weren't that close.

"I'm so excited and honored to get the first date," Ophelia said.

Her green eyes were stunning, and I believed every word she said. Maybe I was naive, but I felt she was a part of this show for all the right reasons. I'd forgotten about the cameras around us. We didn't have a lot of time because I still had nine other people in the other room wanting to say good night, but I took a moment and allowed the rush of excitement to flood my veins.

"How was your first day?"

I opened the door to find Lauren balancing two coffees and a box of doughnuts. She looked adorable in yoga pants, a tasteful workout shirt, and flip-flops. It took me a few seconds to close my mouth and find my voice. I was wrong about her. She knew how to be casual.

"Uh, hi. I was just unwinding." Ten minutes ago, I was about to fall face-first on my mattress but decided to shower and scrub my skin of what felt like a pound of professional makeup. I certainly didn't need clogged pores on national television. I stood in front of her wearing an oversized robe and a tight smile, my curly hair still wet. I was vulnerable, exhausted, and raw. Doughnuts and a kind face seemed like the perfect solution.

"Since it's almost four in the morning, I decided this was a better option than wine or more alcohol. I wanted to find out, off camera, how you were doing."

I cleared my throat and stepped back so she could enter. "If Buzzy sees us, we'll both be in trouble. Hurry up and get inside." I ignored the cameras staged around the mansion. She walked past me and went straight upstairs to my bedroom. I followed without question because she obviously had a reason.

"The master suite and the bathrooms are the only places where they don't have cameras. They can't record without your consent. I wanted to get a feel for where you stand on the whole experience from this side without them hearing us. Do you have a few minutes?"

My picnic was at two in the afternoon. I had to meet Mandee at one for makeup and hair. Buzzy had an outfit, including a bikini, ready for me in wardrobe, so technically I didn't have to get up until noon. That was eight hours from now. "Sure. It's nice to have somebody to talk to."

"Two creams, two sugars." She handed me a coffee. "You're my third season. I've seen other flames struggle with isolation."

I sat on the edge of my bed, trying not to worry about how I looked. After two weeks of photo and video shoots, one would think I would be more comfortable in a robe in front of strangers, but something was different about Lauren. I plucked a glazed doughnut from the box and, after I took a bite, moaned at its warmth and freshness. "Oh, my God. This is the best doughnut I've ever had."

"Freddie's. They make the best doughnuts here in town."

I stopped chewing when her tongue peeked out from between her full lips to catch a crumb in the corner of her mouth. How had I never noticed how red and smooth her lips were? I looked away before she caught me staring. "These are so yummy. My stomach wasn't happy with all the champagne. I need to remember to eat before shooting."

"You've definitely earned the right to at least one. We can't have you shriveling away on this show."

I snorted, then covered my face in alarm. "I'm so sorry. I never do that."

Lauren threw back her head and laughed. "That was hilarious."

"That was embarrassing." I was mortified.

She patted my knee. "You're fine. It was actually cute." She took another bite and started the inquisition. "So, you liked Ophelia and who else?"

Even though the cameras weren't on us, I chose my words carefully. I thought her kindness was real, but I'd also thought Katie Parson liked me. Trust didn't come easy. "It's still early. I spent minimal time with each contestant." I shrugged.

"Oh, come on. I saw your face light up a few times. I promise this information stays between us. It's important to have a confidante, especially since you're cut off from the outside world. I want to be your friend, Savannah, and I'm not just saying that. I like you. I find you interesting, and we have a lot in common."

What could a previous CNN overseas reporter and I have in common? "I definitely could use a friend." I decided not to ask her what our commonalities were. Some things were better off unsaid, because what if she was wrong? "Okay, so far Ophelia and Alix are my favorites."

"Alix is so flirty and fun. You'll have a good time with them."

"I'm surprised *When Sparks Fly* approved a nonbinary contestant," I said.

She took a sip of coffee. "They relied on your questionnaire. Somewhere in those thirty pages, you must have circled nonbinary as a dating option."

"Oh, for sure. I'm just surprised the show went with it. Alix is sexy as hell with their perfectly coiffed hair and stunning blue eyes. I mean, they aren't as pretty as yours." Oh, hell. Did I really just say that? "I can tell that Alix is trouble, but the fun kind."

This was the second time she blushed around me. "Thank you."

I skipped ahead so her discomfort at my attention would be forgotten. "I also like Kaisley, the speech pathologist. She's very nice and wasn't aggressive. She told me she has a son. But don't ask me his name. I'm still learning things."

"Kaden. His name is Kaden," Lauren said. "And his name has already been added to her info sheet."

"So, they will add everything I've learned to the info sheets in the side room?"

Lauren nodded. "Less stress on you."

"I love it. Did they always do that?"

She shook her head. "That was part of the struggle early on when I joined the show. I watched a few seasons and jotted down some ideas before I presented to them."

"Wait. You approached them to be on the show?" I was shocked. I thought for sure they had pursued her with stacks of cash. Lauren was an award-winning journalist from a reputable network. *When Sparks Fly* was a show that most people thought was fake. Respect was hard to find on reality television.

"Are you surprised?" she asked.

"Yes, very much so."

She carefully wiped her hands on a napkin, then curled her legs under her. She was as comfortable in casual clothes as she was dolled up. After sipping her coffee, she rested her head against the high wingback chair and took a deep breath. "I wanted something that wouldn't destroy my faith in humanity. I knew the show wasn't a big hit but that, with the right contestants and proper background work, we could have a show that rivaled *The Bachelorette*. Reality television hasn't been kind to the LGBTQ community. All they depict are adults behaving like horny teenagers with bikini malfunctions instead of people deserving of love and romance." She air-quoted "malfunctions" for effect. "Don't get me wrong. You were in the first season, but nobody knew what direction it would take. It's grown so much, and I just wanted the opportunity to shape it into something special. Mold it into something real."

"Was it your idea to contact me?"

She stared at me with unguarded blue eyes, and my knees felt weak. "It was. I watched the first season and thought you were exactly the person who could help change the direction of the show later. You were real. Genuine. You fell in love with Katie, and we were all crushed when she dismissed you. I honestly can't wait until people find out you're our next flame."

I pursed my lips. "But you didn't contact me until just now. It's your third season."

Lauren smiled and stood, indicating she was leaving. "I wanted to get the show right before I invited you. Plus, it was the perfect time. Ten years later, a better show, more perks, and your return will cause a stir. Ratings will climb because the *Sparks* loyalists will tune in, and so will the original fans. Everyone will want to be on your journey with you."

So many questions popped into my head. Was Lauren queer? Why else would she want to be on this show? Was she in a relationship? I couldn't imagine why she was interested in *Sparks*, and I definitely couldn't imagine why she thought I was such a good fit. I was a nobody from Arizona. My looks were slightly above average, even though Mandee somehow managed to make me look hot with her magical makeup brushes. And Buzzy knew exactly how to show off my body without making me look wanton. But none of these questions came out of my mouth. Lauren's story was hers to tell when she was comfortable around me.

"Thanks again for the doughnuts and coffee and the chat. It's nice to have an ally."

"Keep the doughnuts, but don't tell Buzzy." Her long ponytail swayed ever so slightly as she made her way to the door. "Get some sleep. Big date coming up," she said before closing the door behind her.

"I'll be asleep in two minutes," I said.

After she left, I lowered the room-darkening blinds and crawled under the sheets. Would the show be successful? My heartbeat kicked up a notch as I reflected on my evening. Not only did I meet some nice people, but most of them seemed genuine and here for the same reason I was—to find love and prove that it could be done on television.

## CHAPTER SIX

"This is amazing."

Ophelia dropped onto one of the chaise lounges and accepted a piña colada from the server who took our orders before the cameras started rolling. I hated the word amazing. Reality shows overused it, so I told myself not to say it around the cameras. I smiled. "You don't get tired of this climate even though you live here?"

"I do a lot of my life-coaching sessions on the beach. Nothing says peace and harmony like hearing the soft waves of the ocean or feeling the sun on your body." Ophelia closed her eyes and took a deep breath. "You live in Arizona, right? Do you ever get around water?"

"We have several lakes, and my best friend has a boat. Sometimes I go out with her and her family," I said. I'd been out only twice, but having a business was a lot of work, and I couldn't afford to hire many employees. Until now.

"Your skin is so fair. I bet you burn, don't you?"

"I love the sun, but it doesn't love me." Our conversation wasn't going anywhere. "Tell me what you do as a life coach. Is it rewarding?" I honestly didn't know a lot about her job.

"It's extremely empowering to help people achieve personal and professional goals. I have a dozen long-term clients," she said.

"It was probably hard to get away from your job to come here."

"I want to focus more on me right now. I'm financially set, but I don't have a girlfriend. Haven't had one in a few years."

I raised my eyebrows before I realized what I was doing. "A few years?"

"Well, I've dated over the last two years, but nothing serious. My last relationship ended because my career isn't nine-to-five, and my ex-girlfriend didn't like my phone ringing at all hours. She thought I was having an affair." I must've given her a look because she waved her hands in front of me. "Which I wasn't. One of my clients needed personal advice a lot, and I picked my career over my girlfriend. I need somebody who's understanding and knows what it's like to work hard. Having your own business, I'm sure you know exactly what I mean."

"Definitely. It's not easy to be away from my business, but I also know I have to do this in order to take care of myself and my heart. I'm hopeful, even though I just started this process." I held my drink up and waited until she did the same. "Here's to new beginnings and possibilities." I clinked her glass, and we both took a drink. Ophelia's eyes sparkled when she smiled. Only two percent of the population has green eyes, and Ophelia was definitely in that category.

"You have beautiful eyes," I said.

"So do you."

She was being nice. My brown eyes weren't anything special, but since the camera was trained on me, I smiled. "Thank you."

"I thought you were cute ten years ago with your short hair, but the longer hair suits you now."

I wasn't sure what to say. Mandee deserved all the credit. Most days I threw it in a ponytail. Makeup was a luxury. "Thank you." I was uncomfortable and didn't know what to say. It was hard to have a normal conversation with cameras everywhere. They didn't seem to bother her though.

"Do you want to go for a swim?"

Ugh. That meant a bikini reveal. I was a little soft in the middle, but my morning jogs helped keep me toned. I didn't have time for the gym, but nothing beat the high of a three-mile run every day.

I had Neanderthal shoulders because I played box Tetris in the inventory room at the shop that was so tiny Jane and I couldn't be in it at the same time.

"Sure. Let's go." We weren't planning to swim, but more like splash in the water. At least the cameramen would be shooting from a distance so we could have a normal conversation without a camera two feet from our faces. Ophelia dropped her wrap into the sand before reaching for my hand. I slipped out of my shorts, shrugged out of my shirt, and locked my fingers with hers.

We walked into the ocean hand in hand, and I prayed we didn't look terribly awkward. I was already self-conscious and desperately wanted to straighten my bikini bottom, but cameras were on me, and Ophelia was holding one hand. I could feel a tiny bit of my ass cheek hanging out as we waded in. Once the water was at our torsos, we broke apart. I fixed my bottom and treaded water.

"The water feels so good," she said.

"Yes. Lovely."

"I have to be on the beach every day. It's so soothing."

"Do you do any water sports? Surfing? Sailing?"

"I don't go in the water much, but I do yoga and Pilates in the sand," she said. "Watching and listening to the ocean is very therapeutic."

Ophelia had a lovely body, toned and tight. Her dark hair was piled high on her head so she didn't get it wet. I had mine in a long French braid, knowing full well that Mandee would have her hands full getting the salt out of it. I still tried to keep it dry by pulling it over one shoulder. "I'm not around water a lot, so my only form of exercise is jogging. I try to run every morning before it gets unbearably hot."

"Well, you look great. I can tell you keep in shape."

She was going to have to stop with the compliments. I needed a meatier conversation, so I smiled my thanks and changed the subject. "What do you like to do for fun? What does a night out or a free weekend look like to you?"

"I like to dance. My friends and I hit the clubs sometimes. I'm also close with my family, so we get together on the weekends."

"Do you have a big family?" I was an only child. It was just me and my mom. She was going to be pissed that I took three months off work but couldn't spare her a weekend because I was too busy. Plus, she hated that I'd gone on the show the first season. Convincing her this was the right thing to do was going to be tricky.

"I have two older brothers and one younger sister, who all live around Miami."

"Big families are nice. Do you spend a lot of time together?" I moved closer to hear her better, but when our hands accidentally touched under the surface, she evidently took that as some kind of sign.

"We do. I'm sad that I won't get to see them for a bit, but I'm glad that I'm here and getting to know you better."

She pulled me closer until it became clear to me and probably five million viewers that she was about to kiss me. I licked my lips out of habit and accepted her gentle kiss as gracefully as I could while treading water, kicking her a few times by accident.

"That was nice," she said as she ended the kiss. "Let's go back under the umbrella. You're starting to turn pink."

I felt warm, but it could have been from the kiss. I hadn't kissed a woman in months, and Ophelia's lips were full and soft against mine. It wasn't the best first kiss, but it was nice and exactly what I expected. "I could use some more sunscreen and maybe a water." I was used to the heat in Arizona but always wore a hat and huge sunglasses. They didn't want us to wear sunglasses in the water because they wanted to see our expressions, but it was virtually impossible not to squint with the sun reflecting off it.

"Here's a towel." Ophelia handed me a large, fluffy one but not before giving me a full up-and-down, slow gaze. She seemed unapologetic and lifted one eyebrow when I caught her staring. She carefully poked my shoulder. "Yes. Let's get back under the umbrella. You're going to need more sunscreen."

We spent the final hour of our date talking about life goals, college experiences, coming out to our families, our first relationship, and the last one. When our allocated time was up, she had to leave since we were on my mansion's private beach. I slipped into a wrap conveniently there and walked her up to the driveway. Mandee intercepted us before the big walk to fix my makeup and tame my braid that had gone full rogue from the elastic tie. Editing would have fun with that drastic change. The car was waiting for Ophelia in the driveway, and we were at the obligatory end-of-date, awkward-good-bye moment.

"I had a great time getting to know you better," she said and looked around at the front of the mansion. "And you have a beautiful place."

"Too bad it's not really mine," I joked. I knew that remark would be edited out because it was awkward. She didn't look amused, so I recovered quickly. "I mean, thank you. And I had a nice time, too." I went in for a hug, and she quickly kissed my cheek.

"I'll see you later at the house," Ophelia said.

She squeezed my hand, and I waited until she slipped into the car to go back inside. Lauren, who hadn't been around at all today, was sitting on the sofa in the living room when I returned. Even though camera people were everywhere, her appearance startled me.

"Hi."

"Hi."

"You want to talk about the date, don't you?" I asked.

Like clockwork, Mandee swooped in and put something in my hair and fixed the thin collar of my cover-up.

"Should I change? This swimsuit feels very revealing."

Lauren leaned forward. "You can put on your shorts and shirt from earlier if you feel more comfortable."

"See? Even the host thinks I should wear more," I said as Mandee shook her head.

"Let's get her clothes from the beach," Lauren said.

Mandee spoke into her headset, and within a minute, her brother skidded to a stop in front of her and handed her my outfit, still sandy and wrinkled from lying in a pile at the foot of the lounge chair. "Evelyn? I need you," Mandee said.

I didn't know Evelyn, but she, too, came out of nowhere, took the outfit, and promised to return in five minutes.

"Have a seat. We can chat until Evelyn returns," Lauren said.

Nobody was filming. The camera people were standing around quietly chatting among themselves. "Sure. When did you get here?"

"While you were out on your date. I was watching from the video village." Lauren had already shown me the master suite on the bottom floor that housed a lot of monitors and sound equipment, as well as live video feeds. During waking hours, as many as thirty crew members could be in the mansion at once.

"What do you do when you're not chatting with me or the group?" I asked. I didn't know if Lauren lived in Florida or the show put her up somewhere swanky during filming. "Do you live in Florida?"

"The show owns an apartment not far away. I get it when *Sparks* is filming, so roughly half my life is here. My permanent address is in California."

"Do you live on the beach in California?"

"Yes. I have a condo that I Airbnb while I'm filming. Doesn't make sense to let it go empty."

"That's smart." My garage was full of candle supplies, so doing that with my house was impossible. Not that I'd even thought about it.

"When Evelyn comes back with your clothes, we'll discuss the date in detail, including the first kiss."

I wanted to ask her if it looked as awkward as I thought it did or if the world saw my ass hanging out of my bikini, but she was being so professional that I just ignored my concerns and nodded. "Are we headed over to the contestants' place tonight?"

"Yes. Josef will make dinner, and then you'll have drinks with the sparkettes so they can vie for alone time with you. At the end of the night, you pick one person for your dinner date and four for your group date. Start thinking ahead of time about who you want on that one. It should be easy to do."

"Are you and I having dinner again?" I asked. My stomach dropped at her surprised expression. She masked it quickly, but I saw it and didn't want her to get the wrong idea. "We don't have to. I just meant if you didn't have plans, we could do what we did the other night. We can invite Denise." Before I could get an answer, Evelyn showed up with my pressed clothes.

"Follow me, and I'll fix your hair and makeup," Mandee said.

My answer would have to wait until after the interview. A part of me wanted to take the invitation back, but then I was confused, because what was the difference between doughnuts at four in the morning and a light dinner at seven? Did our friendship embarrass her?

"Don't worry," Mandee said. "I'm going to make sure you still look like you were at the beach, but you won't be as shiny and pink."

She helped me into the shirt I swore was brand new and fixed my braid, keeping a few strands out to make it look like I'd spent the afternoon at the beach. She bent over and scrutinized my makeup and my clothes but barely noticed me.

"Okay. You're all set."

Lauren was exactly where I left her. I decided to play it cool and pretend my super-awkward invitation didn't really happen. "Hey. I'm ready."

"Great." She stood and signaled Denise that we were ready.

"Comms check, everyone," Denise said.

The boom operators had already mounted large microphones above us and out of sight of the shot.

"Lauren, give me a check." Scott Raymond, sound engineer, pointed at Lauren for her to talk.

"The future belongs to those who believe in the beauty of their dreams," she said.

I snorted. "Eleanor Roosevelt?"

"Savannah, we're going to need you to not talk during Lauren's sound check," he said.

I winced and mouthed the word sorry to everyone. Lauren smiled at me, said a few more lines, and waited.

"Savannah, it's your turn," he said.

I recited the chorus of "Rump Shaker" by Wreckx-N-Effect. It seemed appropriate for a mic check. I considered it timeless, but Jane hated when I blasted it while we were boxing up shipments.

Nobody moved a muscle. I cleared my throat at my embarrassment. "This is a test. Can everyone hear me clearly?" I stared down Scott until he gave me the thumbs-up.

"Well, that wasn't fun at all," I said to Lauren.

"They're not listening to anything we're saying. All Scott cares about is the sound quality. They have a different set of problems than we do."

"I get that." I really didn't, but I didn't want to be an attention hog. Everyone had a role. Mine just happened to be looking good in front of the cameras.

"Are you ready?" Lauren wore a cream-colored blouse and light gray skirt that hit above her knee when she crossed her legs. Her legs were tanned, toned, and stunning. Her gray peep-toe heels showed bright red toenail polish. For the first time during filming, Lauren wore her hair down. It was hard not to smile at her because she was so attractive.

"I'm ready."

"Savannah, you picked Ophelia for your first one-on-one date. How did it go?"

"It was a very nice first date."

"It looked like you were having fun and sad to see the date come to an end."

I wasn't sad, but I played along. "I need every minute to count because I'm trying to find my perfect match, and time is so valuable. Even though Ophelia and I got to know each other better, I needed longer."

"Did I see a kiss out there in the ocean?"

I lowered my head in embarrassment. The kiss had made it onto the show, which meant it wasn't as bad as I thought. "We had a brief one. I'm not going to lie. It's hard to tread water and kiss at the same time." Lauren's small laugh was captivating and genuine. I loved that tiny dimple.

"We were all excited to see it happen. I think you have a lot of fans who are cheering you on during this process. Did you feel a connection with Ophelia, or is it too early to tell?"

"Ophelia is very smart, sophisticated, and career-oriented. I like those traits. We had a good time together. I'm happy I chose her first." She was impressive, but I hadn't really formed an opinion. She had nice qualities, but some things worried me, too. Ophelia was thirty-three and still went clubbing. Her active lifestyle sounded exhausting. I was a Netflix-and-chill kind of girl. Ophelia liked attention and enjoyed going out. I hoped my actions from ten years ago didn't attract partiers, because I wasn't that person now.

"Tonight's cocktail party will be fun. You have to decide who you want to invite on your one-on-one dinner date and also pick four sparkettes to join you at The Dolphin Research Center, where you will swim and learn how to communicate with dolphins."

"That sounds enjoyable, because I live in Arizona and have never seen a dolphin in the wild there."

Lauren smiled. "It'll be a great group date, then."

"I'm also excited about the dinner date."

"Do you have a contestant already in mind?"

I smiled and lifted an eyebrow. Lauren laughed. Our back-and-forth banter probably made for good television. We chatted for a total of twenty minutes, even though only about five would be used for the show.

"Okay," Denise said. "Let's all break. Grab some dinner. We have a long night ahead."

The camera people scattered, and I made my way quickly to the kitchen to avoid an awkward conversation with Lauren. I had two hours to kill before Mandee returned to prepare me for the cocktail party.

"Hi, Josef. What's on the menu for tonight?" I would forever, in my mind, say "with an ef" every time I said his name.

"Lemon-garlic-butter chicken and green beans. I also have a side salad."

"Please tell me we have dessert, too." I sat at the kitchen island to watch him. Life was boring when I wasn't in front of the cameras. I was never idle at home so didn't know what to do. I couldn't scroll on my phone or turn on the television. I could go rest or watch Josef work.

"Fruit salad."

My shoulders slumped.

"I heard doughnuts were consumed last night, so low-calorie tonight." He shrugged, seeming apologetic.

"Guilty, but worth it," I said.

"I don't blame you. I can't imagine what you do to entertain yourself around here."

"They've kept me pretty busy most days. How much time do I have before dinner is ready?"

"However long you'd like," he said.

"I think I'll go upstairs and rest. Long night ahead." I left off the "of drinking" part because it was implied. Always implied. I made my way up to my room and set the alarm clock to wake me up in an hour. Between the sun and the alcohol, I was exhausted. I barely remembered slipping under the covers. This schedule was grueling.

# CHAPTER SEVEN

I'm not going to lie. I was hurt that you didn't pick me for the first date." Alix held their hand over their heart in mock pain.

I put my hand on theirs and lowered my voice, even though I knew the cameras and microphones would pick up every single word I whispered. "I thought the dinner date would be better for us."

Their eyebrows rose in surprise. "So, I'm not going on the dolphin tour?"

"Unless you want to."

They held my hands and squeezed. "No. The dinner date sounds fantastic." They playfully zipped their lips just before another contestant swooped in for some alone time. I got a kiss on the cheek before they left, which made me smile.

Frankie, a professional soccer coach from Kansas City, handed me a flute of champagne. I thanked her and took a sip. I had at least five glasses of it in the backyard that someone had handed me that I sipped and never touched again. I didn't want to get drunk and wasn't a fan of champagne.

"How are you tonight?" Frankie asked.

Even though it was a cocktail party, a lot of participants dressed down. I wasn't the only one suffering from too much sun today. Judging by the tired, disheveled looks from a few of the contestants, getting dressed up with sunburnt skin and a hangover was too much. Frankie was one. Her body heat made me sit back on the love seat.

She looked miserable and smelled like vodka. "I feel like I'm doing better than you are."

She dropped her face into her hands and groaned. "I'm probably the oldest one here, and I know better. I'm around young twenty-somethings every day. I don't know why I let them get to me."

It was easy to forgive Frankie because she was so open and real. She didn't try to feed me a lie or exaggerate today's events. She was also strong, in shape, and had a crooked smile I knew made women everywhere melt. "What's your job like? Is the Midwest really into soccer?"

"Kansas City just acquired the team two years ago. We aren't filling the stands yet, but we're hopeful."

"Did you play professionally?" I didn't know a lot about women's soccer other than it boomed after the US Women's team won the World Cup years ago.

"I did, but now I coach."

It was going to take a lot to pull info out of Frankie. "What do you do for fun when you aren't coaching?"

"Hang out with my friends. We have bonfires or play games. Sometimes we hang out at the lake."

"Sounds nice. I do that with my friends, too. My best friend has a boat."

"How have you enjoyed being on this side of the show?"

Apparently, we were done learning about one another's likes and dislikes. I took a deep breath and blew it out audibly. "It's so different. I can't believe everything that goes into a production." I reminded myself not to give too much away. I'd signed a nondisclosure agreement, so the information I shared about the show had to be vague. "Everyone has been so supportive and amazing to work with." Fuck. I'd just said amazing again. The one word I vowed I wouldn't say on television.

"It has to be hard, too."

"The hours are different, but I'm not afraid of hard work," I said.

"You own your own business, right?"

Frankie relaxed in the love seat and rested her head on the cushion. Her eyelids started to droop, and rather than go through the embarrassment of having her fall asleep on me, I excused myself. "I'm being summoned, so we can pick this conversation up tomorrow. Do you think you'd be up for a swim with the dolphins?"

Her eyelids rose for a moment, and a small smile slipped into place. "That sounds like so much fun, but I've already had too much sun. I'll pass."

I wasn't sure if she fell asleep right when I turned around, or before. Either way, I wasn't happy. I pasted on a smile and walked inside, where most of the sparkettes were drinking and having a good time in the ginormous kitchen. "What's going on in here?"

"Savannah, hi. Come on over here. Alix was just showing us how to make the perfect Manhattan," Lyanna said.

Alix winked. "Mixology is my true gift to the world. Would you like one?"

I didn't need more carbs from alcohol. I needed them from bread or pastries, and a tray of cheese and crackers sat on the table. "No, thank you. Keep doing your magic. Pretend I'm not here."

"Impossible. You're the prettiest woman in the room."

All the women agreed, but I felt a current of ruffled feathers at Alix's assertion. I blushed, but my faint sunburn hopefully hid my color. Nibbling on a cracker, I watched as Alix explained why the brand of vermouth was essential to the perfect drink.

Kaisley sidled up to me. "Looks like you got some sun today." I knew the least about her. She didn't race up and drag me away the moment I walked into a room, but I remembered her after our initial meeting. I appreciated her standoffishness, even though the show really pushed for the contestants to fight for time with me or just to be in front of the camera. I wasn't sure where everyone stood yet except for Madison. She was clearly here for fame, a relationship a distant second. I refocused on Kaisley.

"I did. I'm used to the heat but didn't use enough sunscreen. Does it look bad?"

She crinkled her nose. "Not bad, but like maybe it hurts. If you need aloe, let me know. I have a tube of it."

"That's so sweet. Thank you so much. I'm sure the show has it for everyone."

Alix interrupted our moment. "In spite of what she said, the first drink goes to Savannah."

I waved them off. This was too much alcohol. I was too old for this shit.

"Come on. Just a sip. I want to know what you think," they said.

Peer pressure and cameras all around the room made me succumb. I took the lowball glass and sipped. My reaction was genuine. It was delicious. "It's excellent. You should make enough for the room."

Applause erupted, and Alix took a bow.

"Want to get out of here?" I asked Kaisley.

She nodded, and we slipped out onto the patio, away from the loud chatter of the kitchen.

"It's quieter out here, even if it's still hot," she said.

"Remind me where you're from?" I couldn't pull up Kaisley's information sheet in my head.

"Aspen, Colorado."

"Nice place. So you aren't familiar with this humidity either. Welcome to a different kind of hell," I said.

"Dry heat and lots of snow where I live," she said.

"Does that mean you ski? I like to, even though I haven't been in years." I went to Vail one Christmas with my mother and turned out to be a natural. I was a full-grown adult but almost threw a childlike tantrum when it was time to leave.

"Oh, you should come this winter, and I'll show you the best places to ski. I love it so much."

"What else do you like to do? You're fit, so you probably hike every weekend," I said. She covered her mouth with her hand as she giggled at my compliment.

"Thank you. I love anything outdoors. I like to camp, fish, ski, snowboard. Now that I have a son, I'm limited on what I can do, but he's actually been on skis already, and he just turned three."

"Oh, my gosh. That's so adorable. Is he any good?"

"I mean, he still trips just walking because he's a toddler, but he's fearless."

"What's his name?" I had it memorized, but too many distractions made my mind blank out. She smiled so hard when she was talking about him, her love for him evident.

"Kaden. He's my everything. It was hard to leave him to do this show, but I felt like you and I had a lot in common, including relationship goals." Tears gathered in the corners of her eyes.

The urge to kiss her and dry her tears was strong. She seemed like she was more what I was looking for than the others drinking in the kitchen. We talked for twenty more minutes before Lauren interrupted and told us to head inside. The next date was going to be announced.

"Hi, everyone. How's the night going?" Lauren asked the contestants.

"Alix made us delicious Manhattans. And we got to spend time with Savannah as a small group," Kaisley said.

"But did everyone get some one-on-one time?"

Some people nodded, including people I hadn't seen until just now. Madison, the obnoxious lawyer from the first night, and Thea, the English professor from Boston, had only just appeared. I didn't give it any thought. I'd had a nice time being part of something that didn't hang on my every word or action.

At everyone's nods, Lauren continued. "I'm going to have a chat with Savannah, and then we'll come back and announce the contestants for the first group date and the lucky one who gets the dinner date. Please excuse us."

We slipped into the secret info room with headshots and more information on each contestant.

"Do you have an idea of who you want on the dinner date and who you want on the group date?" she asked.

I guess I shouldn't have told Alix I was picking them for the single date. Oops. I looked at the ten photos on the wall and mentally selected my four. "Yes."

"Good. I think whoever you choose will have a lot of fun on the group date."

"You should come with us. Maybe when we're done, you can sneak into the water and play with them. I'm assuming *Sparks* has rented the place for the day, right?"

She waved me off. "This isn't about me. This is about you."

I shrugged. It was her loss. I imagined every single crew member would love to swim with the dolphins if they had the opportunity. I studied the photos one more time and mentally picked Kaisley, Charlotte, Lyanna, and Ava. Charlotte was a blogger with a daughter, so she and Kaisley would have something to talk about, and Lyanna and Ava had the medical field in common. Not that I was trying to play matchmaker with my own contestants, but it was important to make sure everyone had similarities so they would be friendly when I was off with somebody else. That left Alix for the dinner date and Emma, Frankie, Madison, and Thea for the other group date. In three days, I would start eliminating sparkettes. I didn't care what Denise said. Madison wasn't getting my flame.

"I'm ready," I said.

The knock on the front door didn't surprise me, but I was startled. It was almost midnight, and I was just about to retire for the night. I was tired of always having to be aware of how I stood, what I said, who I said it to, how I sat, how my hair looked, and keeping my hands away from my face so I didn't ruin my makeup. All those little details wound me up tight. By the end of the night, I needed a hot shower to relax me. I was wearing an oversized T-shirt and thin pajama shorts when I opened the door. A part of me knew it was Lauren, but another thought it might be somebody from the crew leaving me the itinerary for tomorrow. That happened sometimes.

"Hi." I stood to the side and invited her in with a sweep of my hand.

"I'm sorry I couldn't do dinner. I had another engagement," she said.

She stood just inside the door, waiting for permission or something. "Come in. Don't worry about it. I forget your job is more demanding than mine. I just need to show up and either show emotion or not, depending on what they tell me." Our conversation continued as we walked up the stairs to the only private room in the entire mansion.

"Is it worse than you thought?"

"No. I'm just feeling sorry for myself. It's different for sure. I hate that I don't really have anybody to talk to. I miss Jane, my best friend. She would have so much fun here discussing the contestants. Not in a bad way, but in a supportive way." I didn't want Jane to come off as snobby or mean, because she wasn't.

"I will try to make more of an effort," Lauren said.

I touched her arm. "No. I don't mean it like that. You aren't responsible for entertaining me. It's just hard for me to be idle." I crawled into bed and propped a pillow behind me so I was at least sitting up.

"But I do consider you a friend, and since you are shielded from the rest of the world, it's important to have somebody to talk to. Let me be that person."

Tonight, Lauren was dressed more like me, in shorts and a T-shirt. Her sandals were still fancier than my flip-flops, but these little glimpses of the real her were a treat. "Tell me anything going on in the world. Tell me something important that's happening out there." I was used to scrolling on my phone, reading the news or on social media, and being away from it was killing me.

"Someone is setting a lot of churches on fire in the South. Most of the news is still bad, but some good things are happening." At my nod of encouragement, she continued. I needed good news. "A photo of a canine soldier from World War I wearing dog tags is circulating. More people are signed up as organ donors than ever before. Oh, and we got your beeswax candles, which Denise plans to use. She ordered two hundred and fifty."

I sat up straighter. "What? How?"

"Denise loved the candles you had delivered. She called Jane. Well, somebody from the show called Jane, and she sent them to us."

That wiped out our inventory. I did some quick math. At twelve dollars a pop with seven gross-margin dollars per stick, we'd made close to eighteen hundred dollars. "That's great news." I was beyond excited.

"And I'm sure once people figure out your store, your fans will buy out your stock. Do you make your own product?" Lauren asked.

I nodded. "Most of our inventory is handmade. We buy some items, but I'm such a stickler that I spend most of my weekends making candles." She looked as though she felt sorry for me because I worked every day. "I love it though. I'm an olfactory-type person, and I'm doing something I love. I have a whole setup in my garage, so I can knock out about a hundred candles a week. I put them in different-sized mason jars and in some of them press herbs and flower petals into the top of the wax."

"I love that you're passionate about it. And everybody loves candles. I checked your website, and you have some really nice things for sale."

I blushed because Lauren took time to learn more about me, whether she was instructed to or not. "Thanks. I'm pretty proud of my shop. I'd like for it to be more successful, but I know it'll take time."

"The show will generate business for sure. Trust me," she said.

"What about you? What do you do for fun?"

She laughed. Immediately I knew she didn't have time for anything other than *When Sparks Fly*. She was everywhere. Sometimes I'd see her in the video village and other times with her head down and chatting with Denise. I never saw her sitting still unless it was time for us to chat on camera. "When you're not filming. I'm sure this job requires twenty-four seven, three hundred and sixty-five days a year."

"I get Christmas and New Year's off."

My jaw dropped. "That's it?"

"I'm teasing. It's not that bad. When we're not in production, I'm home. I like the beach, and I enjoy reading."

"Let me guess. Nonfiction, most likely political autobiographies," I said, certain politics was her niche.

"You're right. It's hard to walk away from that part of my life," she said.

"Why did you?"

"Lots of reasons, but mainly I did it for love." She leaned back in the chair and sighed. "And it was totally not worth it."

# CHAPTER EIGHT

Even though I was sitting at a table for two in a very romantic setting decorated with flower petals and candles, I couldn't get my mind off Lauren and what she'd said last night. We didn't get a chance to discuss any of it. She shut down and excused herself almost immediately.

"You're not eating your dinner," Alix said.

I sighed. "I'm sorry. The heat got to me today, and I'm not very hungry." I left off that I'd just eaten a salad and breadsticks, heavy on the breadsticks, an hour before. "How are you enjoying Florida?" Alix was from Portland, Oregon, and although Oregon had beaches, they weren't hot and sexy like the ones in the Florida Keys.

"It's nice to be in the heat. I love the sun. And I'm making new friends and hopefully on my journey to find true love." They lifted their glass and clinked it against mine. Alix was awesome, and I needed to focus on them, not my behind-the-scenes life.

"I was nervous being on this show again, but for the most part, everyone seems to be here for the right reason."

"I watched the first season live. I was in high school. My friends and I would text during it. There wasn't a lot of queer representation on television back then. A kiss here and there and maybe a queer person on another reality show, but *When Sparks Fly* was a game changer," they said.

I skipped over the part about Alix still being in high school when I was on the show the first time. They were five years younger, which was the youngest I said I would date. "The show has come a long way. It's exciting that you're the first nonbinary person on it."

A shy smile spread across their lips. "It is. If seventeen-year-old me could see me now, they would be really impressed."

"That's so cool. You've already accomplished a lot, owning your own tattoo shop and all." Alix was a flirt, but I think they really wanted a relationship. "Portland seems to be one of the hot places for artists. I can't believe you're single." Well, that was an awful thing to say. "What I mean is, what are you looking for in a relationship? Why are you—captivating, sexy, charming you— still single?" We were both given questions ahead of time so if the conversation fizzled, we could fall back on standardized, safe ones.

"I'm young, so I'm taking my time looking for somebody who gets me, who's just as comfortable going out as they are staying in. Sometimes I want to burn energy doing something like paddleboarding, and sometimes I want to veg in front of the television."

"Do you have a type? Are there people you won't date?"

"I won't date cis men, and I might be too young to date somebody with a kid. Nothing against them at all. I love kids, but I have a lot to do before I settle into a relationship bigger than just two people." Their eyes grew huge in alarm. "Oh, my God. You don't have any children, do you?"

It was too easy not to tease. "I have twin boys. They're eight. And a daughter who's four." I looked them straight in the eyes. "All different fathers." Then I winked.

They slapped their napkin on the side of the table and burst out laughing. We laughed for a solid minute before finding our voices again. I dabbed the tears away with the corner of my napkin.

"Do you want children?" they asked.

"I like them, and maybe one day I'll start a family, but if I don't, I know I'll be a wonderful godmother or fake aunt to a ton of children out there. I don't feel strongly one way or another. My best friend has children, and they're great. I don't want parenting to become a need. I first want to find my soul mate. What follows is fate." I sounded so cheesy, but I didn't lean one way or another on kids. If I loved somebody and they already had them, I would love them. If my person wanted children, we'd have them. If they didn't, that was good, too. But the hard part was finding that special person, and I didn't want to settle.

"That's a great philosophy. I help my brother coach kids' softball, so if I need a fix, I just throw in a few extra practices."

Right then, one of the curtained walls fell and exposed a small stage, where Willow McAdams stood with a guitar and a microphone. Both Alix and I gasped. Willow was huge. Her debut pop album had just hit number one. That *Sparks* got her to appear on the show was incredible. "Hello, Savannah and Alix. I hope you don't mind that I'm here, but I wanted to play a few songs. And if you want to dance, well, there's a small dance floor right here." She pointed to a little area in front of the stage, and Alix didn't waste any time.

"Do you want to?" They reached for my hand.

I stood out of fright because I was a horrible dancer but pasted on a smile as though it was the best idea ever. "Of course." I prayed Alix was as smooth on the dance floor as they were in life.

They carefully pulled me close and wrapped one of their arms around my waist while they grasped my hand with their other one and held it out about shoulder level. It was easy to slip into a slow dance. Alix was incredibly smooth on their feet, and it felt nice to be held.

"I can't believe Willow McAdams is singing to us," I said.

"Right. This is incredible. Everyone is going to be so jealous."

I relaxed in their arms and closed my eyes for a moment to enjoy the music and try to forget the four cameras trained on us. When was the last time I danced? It had to have been at my cousin's wedding two years ago. "I can't remember live music ever sounding this good."

"I love concerts. It's one of the things I adore about Portland. All the fresh music and venues everywhere. And I'm right in the middle of all of it."

"Is Willow's the kind of music you like?" Alix struck me as someone who appreciated faster, rawer music.

"I love it all. Except maybe country. It's not my favorite."

"Same." I kept my response short because Willow was singing, and it was rude to talk over her. Alix got the hint and danced me around the small dance floor and dipped me when the song ended.

"Any requests from the happy couple?" Willow asked.

I didn't hesitate. "How about 'Don't Go'?" It was my favorite song on the album.

"Excellent choice," she said. She adjusted the capo on the neck of her guitar and strummed a few times. "It's my most requested song at concerts."

I didn't care that the show was using her and she was using the show. I was thrilled to have this experience and a moment with Alix. Both of us applauded when she started the first chord. Rather than dance, Alix stood behind me and wrapped their arms around my waist. We swayed to the gentle lull of the sad love song, and Alix kissed my temple when it was over. It felt like a real first date. When Willow finished playing, Norman quickly took photos of the three of us, then of just me and Willow, and finally me and Alix. By the end of the night, I was elated and not tired.

When Alix pulled me into their arms and kissed me, it was a gentle kiss, not awkward, and I felt their controlled passion on the tip of their tongue. Before the show started, we were advised to keep the open-mouth kisses to a minimum. This one was a hell of a lot better than the one with Ophelia. To be fair, though, Alix and I were standing on dry land.

"I had an amazing night. Thank you for saving your dinner date for me."

I kissed them two more times, forgetting that we were on camera. "I did, too."

"I'll see you tomorrow." They brought my hands up to their mouth and kissed them before slipping into the car waiting to take them back to the sparkette mansion.

Denise didn't even have to tell me to smile. I was grinning so hard my cheeks hurt.

A new person I hadn't seen before approached me. "Lauren's waiting for you outside."

"Okay, thanks." I walked through the mansion and out to the deck, where Lauren and Willow were drinking wine and laughing. I put my hand up to my chest in surprise. "Hi. What's going on here?"

Lauren patted the cushion beside her. "It didn't make sense for Willow to leave us yet, so I thought we could hang out for a bit."

"That sounds great." My stomach quivered with excitement as I sat beside Lauren and across from Willow. I was sharing a bottle of pinot with two famous people, and cameras weren't even on us. I could be myself and not worry about sitting up straight or getting lipstick on my teeth.

"Congratulations on being the new flame. I really enjoy this show, and I'm glad you're getting a second chance," Willow said.

"Thanks." I didn't know how to respond when someone said that. I hated my first season, but people like Willow and a few of the contestants told me they were cheering me on. I didn't get any negative vibes from her. "Two completely different experiences."

"I bet. My mom and I were upset that the pit viper didn't pick you, but at the same time, I'm glad, because look at you now." Willow pointed to me as if I'd made something of myself.

"She's going to be a hit," Lauren said.

I waved them off. "Let's just hope it all goes well and doesn't end in another catastrophe."

Willow leaned forward and touched my arm. "I hope so, too."

"What's next for you? I love your music, by the way. It was such a surprise to see you tonight," I said.

"Thank you. I'm so surprised at how fast all this happened."

"Definitely well deserved," I said.

We spent the next two hours talking, eating fruit and crackers, and drinking wine. At some point we switched to water, at Lauren's request, because I had a big day. When Willow's manager interrupted us, we all groaned.

"No. It's not fair," I said.

"I know. I'm sorry. I've had so much fun tonight. Please keep in touch." Willow laughed. "Well, when they give you back your phone."

I was trying not to freak out as I told her my phone number. Willow freaking McAdams! We took a selfie that she promised to send me and said she wouldn't share it with anyone until after the episode aired.

"What a night, huh?" Lauren asked after Willow left.

I plopped down next to her on the couch and laughed. "One for the books. I had so much fun tonight. I mean, Willow McAdams? Come on. That was so cool. Did you know about her?" I smacked my forehead with my palm. "Of course, you did. This is your show."

"The show reaches out to different artists. Some of them are up-and-coming, and some just need a little boost," Lauren said.

At some point during the chat, Lauren had shucked her suit jacket and let her hair down. It rested in waves over her shoulders, and she pulled it back with one hand, fanning herself with the other. Even though it was two in the morning, the humidity was almost unbearable.

"I like it when you wear your hair like that. It's so pretty," I said. She slowly dropped it and smiled at me.

"Thank you. I was going to say the same about yours. I'd kill for naturally curly hair."

"Your hair isn't normally wavy?" I touched a piece of it but quickly pulled my hand back when I realized I'd overstepped. "I'm so sorry. I don't know why I did that." Flames of embarrassment ignited me. I wasn't even drunk, so I couldn't use that as my excuse.

"It's fine, but thank you for apologizing. My hair is super straight. Mandee spends more time on my hair than on yours every day."

"Does she ever sleep?" My unruly mop kept her busy for a good portion of the time. Add Lauren to the mix and I doubted it.

"Probably not. Speaking of sleep, we both need to get some rest before your date in exactly seven hours." She looked at the thin watch on her wrist. "You have a big day today."

I did a small cheer. "I'm so excited. Who gets to swim with dolphins in their lifetime?"

"You'd be surprised how many people are scared to," she said.

"Really? I think it's a great group date."

"I do, too."

She stood and slipped her shoes and jacket back on. "Sleep well, Savannah. Today was enjoyable."

"You, too, Lauren. I'll see you later."

I wanted to spend a few minutes alone to think about my night. Alix was so much fun. First kisses were either spot-on or awkward as hell. Most fell into the latter category, but our first one was nice. I felt something with them I didn't feel with Ophelia. That made Alix the front-runner, which could change as early as tomorrow, but at least I had hope again.

# CHAPTER NINE

After five minutes in the limo with the four women I'd picked for the group date, I knew we were going to enjoy ourselves. All four were laid-back and didn't fight to sit next to me or monopolize the conversation. Cameras were wired everywhere to capture our conversations, and after about a minute, we forgot about them.

"Has anyone swum with dolphins before?" Lyanna asked.

"I did in Mexico once," Ava said.

"No, but I love swimming," I said.

"So do I." Lyanna opened her beach bag, pulled out a blue swimming cap with a dolphin pattern, and twirled it on her finger. "But I'm going to have to wear this."

Ava playfully took it from her. "How can you even get this on your head? It seems so tight."

"Not all of us have wash-and-wear hair, so I'm going to need help getting all mine into this." We laughed as she mimed putting her hair up. Lyanna was the only Black sparkette, and her hair was straightened and styled every time I saw her. It had never occurred to me that swimming would be a problem for her or any of the sparkettes, which seemed naive now that I thought about it.

"Oh, I'm sure we can all pitch in," I said. I should have asked the contestants if they were okay getting in the ocean before I put them on the spot on national television. "Are you good swimming with dolphins?" I turned to the whole group. "Is everybody? I sometimes forget people don't have the same interests I do."

Lyanna smiled and nodded. "I'm in. I mean, it's not every day a person gets to swim with them."

"Right? That's what I said." My voice was a bit high.

"I'm a little scared because I think they'll probably be the size of horses once we get into the water," Charlotte said.

"They're more like Great Danes," Ava said.

I breathed a sigh of relief that not everyone was against the idea. I really should have asked, but I assumed everyone would be up for it. The show was located in Florida. Marine life was part of the experience. "It's not necessary for everyone to get into the water. We'll have a picnic at the center, and I'm sure they have other things we can do privately or as a group."

"Well, even if I have to wear this stupid cap in front of the world, I don't care. I'm going swimming with them," Lyanna said.

I high-fived her because she had the adventurous spirit I was looking for. The ninety-minute drive flew by as we talked about where we lived, what we did for a living, and what we did for fun. I felt like we had all known each other for a long time. We just clicked. By the end of the trip, I had an idea of who I wanted some alone time with first.

"Welcome, ladies. How's everyone doing today?"

Lauren greeted the limo and waited until we all stood to the side of her. She had her hair back in a French braid and wore a fitted white-and-navy summer dress with thick shoulder straps that hit the sweet spot right above her knee. She looked great and refreshed, whereas I needed all the help I could get to look alive. Mandee had slapped cucumber slices on my eyes this morning to minimize the puffiness around them from lack of sleep. Showbiz wasn't a life I wanted.

"Great," I said and meant it.

"Wonderful. Are you ready to find out about your group date?" she asked.

At our nods, she introduced us to Danielle, a marine biologist who worked at the center. I watched Lauren disappear inside the center and wondered if she would get to have fun today, too.

"Are you ready, Savannah?" Danielle asked.

I refocused on my group. Hopefully, it wasn't obvious that I was staring at Lauren. "I am so ready. The minute I heard we were swimming with dolphins, I was thrilled."

"Then let's go." Danielle waved for us to follow.

I didn't want to come off as cheesy for the camera, but it was hard not to smile. Most of us were eager to get into the water, where two dolphins were doing laps in one of the large pools.

"I want you to meet Toga and Toffee."

As a group, we collectively sighed at how adorable they were. "How old are they?" I asked.

"Toga is about eight, and Toffee was born here. He's almost five and very friendly. He's kind of a ham around people and loves attention."

"We're willing to provide that," Charlotte said.

Danielle walked us through the safety measures and taught us several hand commands we could use with the dolphins. I was the first one in the water and had a playful splash fight with them. Then I got to do a dorsal pull, where both dolphins pulled me around the pool. I understood why we were told to wear full bathing suits. Had I been wearing a bikini, the top would have disappeared after my ride with Toga and Toffee. I didn't want to get out, but it was important to share, so reluctantly I climbed out while Lyanna jumped in.

"How was it?" she said.

"Incredible! You'll love it." I hadn't smiled that much since I started the show. If my candle store tanked, I was going to be a dolphin handler. Ava handed me a towel and my cover-up.

"I can't wait. It looks like so much fun."

We sat together on a bench and watched as Lyanna gave hand signals to Toga and Toffee. "She's really good with them," I said.

"I like her and the group you picked for this date. I'm enjoying myself, which I don't think would be the case if different people were here," Ava said.

I picked up on her hint. "Are there people you don't like in the house? Should I be wary of someone?"

"I don't want to say anything because we're here to have a good time. I'm sorry I brought it up."

I took a deep breath. I knew she wanted to say something about somebody in the house but didn't want to come across as a snitch. "I'd like to know if somebody isn't here for the right reasons."

"I'm not sure if that's the case. I just know she rubs people wrong," Ava said.

"I'd appreciate it if you told me." I kept my voice even and threw in a smile to establish trust and a safe space.

"It's Madison. She's very…commanding," Ava said.

"What do you mean?" None of this surprised me.

"Nothing. Never mind. Forget I said anything."

Ava shook her head and waved her hands. I couldn't let it go. I was curious, and the fans would never forgive me if I didn't ask.

"Come on. You can tell me. Has she said or done anything?"

"No. She's just really vocal about things. She's nice, just kind of bossy."

Ava nervously tucked her bob behind her ear several times.

"Is she mean to anybody?"

"Oh, no. She just told us she was going to spend the most time with you on the group dates and would throw a fit if anyone interrupted. She laughed, but a few of us didn't like that comment. I'm so glad she's not on this date."

Great. We might have our first bully. Nobody liked bullies. "Thank you for telling me. I'll keep that in mind. Let's forget about her and focus on today. I want to have fun. Are you excited to get in the water?"

"For sure. Like we said in the limo, how often do people get the chance to do this?"

"I agree. What else do you like to do besides hang around and wait for dolphins to show up? You're from New Hampshire, right?" I remembered that fact from the first night.

She nodded. "I like hanging out with my friends. I watch movies nonstop. If I'm bored, I pick up extra shifts at the hospital. I also volunteer at the local animal shelter."

She sounded too good to be true. I was sure a lot of people fell in love with her, with her smoldering eyes and tight body, but I wasn't attracted to her in the least. My pulse was steady, even though she was in my personal space. Our arms touched as we talked, and I knew right then Ava wasn't the girl for me. We looked great on paper, and she was unbelievably sweet, but we had zero chemistry. "It looks like it's your turn in the water." I pointed to Lyanna, who was sitting on the edge of the dock drying off. Ava squeezed my hand.

"Wish me luck," she said.

She wasn't gone ten seconds before Charlotte slid onto the bench next to me.

"Hi there," she said.

Charlotte was the type of woman who was so nice and kind that I felt guilty around her. Not that I didn't have a good heart, but she seemed angelic. "Hi. What do you think so far? Are you going to brave the waters?"

She shrugged. "I don't know yet."

"It's so fun. I promise."

"If you ladies want, you can come with me, and I'll introduce you to Walter," Danielle said.

"Oh. I'd like to meet Walter," I said. I didn't know who Walter was, but if he lived at the center, I knew I wanted to meet him.

"Follow me," Danielle said.

And that was how Charlotte got the first official one-on-one time with me. We crossed a footbridge over to another building with two cameramen in tow. Somehow, by the time we entered the building, we were holding hands. Danielle stood by the door.

"Are you ready?"

"Should we be worried?" Charlotte asked.

"It'll be fine." I couldn't imagine the show would put us in danger. The liability would be too high.

Charlotte stopped. "Wait. You aren't taking us to swim with a shark in one of those cages, are you?"

"Thankfully, we're not part of Shark Week. Besides that being cruel, I don't think they want us to get hurt," I said.

Walter ended up being a ginormous sea lion. An injury when he was little had prevented him from being released back into the ocean, so he had lived most of his life at the Dolphin Research Center.

"Say hi, Walter," Danielle said.

He leaned his thick, smooth body to the left and raised his tiny, misshapen flipper. I squealed and waved back, completely caught up in the moment. Even Charlotte didn't act as excited as I did.

"Sorry. Apparently, I need to get out more."

Charlotte put her hand on my arm. "I think you're wonderful with the animals here."

"I've already decided that if things don't work with my business, I'm going to come down here and become a trainer."

"We could always use the help," Danielle said.

We gave Walter small fish treats and laughed when he barked and roared. Even though he weighed five hundred pounds, his little barks and whiff noises were adorable. Danielle informed us that the dolphin pool was open if Charlotte was willing to swim with Toga and Toffee, and to my surprise, she went for it. I started to go and support her, but Lyanna entered the pool area and wanted to meet Walter and hang out with me.

"That swim was incredible. The dolphins are so smooth and have such large personalities," she said.

Even though she was still in her bathing suit, she wore a modest cover-up, and her hair looked great after being crammed in a tight cap. "And you were worried about the swimming cap for nothing."

She patted down her hair and smiled. "I'm used to managing it."

"You look lovely. Would you like to meet Walter?"

"I thought I heard some strange noises in here. Is Walter a seal?"

"A sea lion. He was wounded when he was a baby, so most of his life has been here. Full disclosure, he kissed me on the cheek after eating a lot of fish, so sit next to me at your own risk." Lyanna had a nice laugh. I knew some people on reality shows were mean behind the scenes but super nice to the person they were trying to impress. I didn't get that vibe with Lyanna, but my track record wasn't great.

"This falls under the 'things I need to do before I die' category."

"Like a bucket list," I said.

She bumped my shoulder with hers before following Danielle to Walter's oasis, where she gave him treats and talked to him. The show was a well-oiled machine because Kaisley rounded the corner five seconds after Lyanna left me. Her hair was wet, and she was wearing a thin cover-up that wasn't doing a very good job, but I didn't mind. It was hard to keep eye contact.

"Did you swim with Toga and Toffee?"

Kaisley had a beautiful smile. Her teeth were perfectly straight, and she had such a calm demeanor.

"It was better than I imagined. Why are you here by yourself? Are you up for some company?" she asked.

"How about we take a walk and hang out for a bit?"

"I'd love that," Kaisley said.

I knew there was a picnic somewhere for us. The cameraman pointed to another footbridge away from the dolphin pool and Walter's oasis, so we headed that way, stopping to wash up first. Mandee did a quick makeup check and hair fluff. The picnic table was covered with an array of fruit, sandwiches, vegetables, desserts, and bottles of water and lemonade. No alcohol, at my request, because I was done with it.

"Oh, this is nice," Kaisley said. We fixed plates and sat next to each other at an adjoining table. It was easier for the camera people to film us side-by-side.

"How did you enjoy your dolphin time?" I asked.

"It was great. I always try to get to the ocean at least once a year. To see them in the wild is exciting, but to swim with them is an entirely different and thrilling experience. You live in Arizona. Do you get to the ocean a lot?"

"No. I spend a lot of time working. My mom lives in California, and I sometimes visit her." Not enough, I silently added. "I read, watch television, and come up with new scents for my store."

"That's right. You own a candle shop."

"I started a candle business in college, so when the show approached me the first time, I figured it was a sign. I mean, candles and candles, right?"

"Amazing coincidence," she said.

"Let's talk about you." I hated myself for saying that, but I wanted to know about Kaisley, and time was valuable. Also, I was aware the other sparkettes would find us sooner rather than later.

"I love to cook. I try to keep it healthy since I'm thirty now, and pounds stick around longer than they did when I was in my twenties."

"What's your favorite thing to cook?"

"I like grilling, so I make my own rubs and seasonings. Sometimes I compete in barbecue competitions," she said.

"That's great. I never really got into cooking, but I love cooking shows. *Top Chef, Master Chef, Chopped.* I even watch *Nailed It* because I like to pretend I would bake better than they do, but I know that's probably not true."

"That show makes me laugh," Kaisley said.

We spent about five minutes talking about food and other television shows we enjoyed before the others found us.

"Oh, is this lunch?" Ava slid across from us with a plate of fruit and two vegetable kebabs.

"It's a great spread," I said and blushed immediately at my unintentional double entendre. "It's nice to have so many options."

Within five minutes, the table was full, and we spent a solid hour talking about our experience at the center. I didn't experience anything but politeness and genuine fun. When we got back to the contestants' mansion, everyone hugged me and said they were excited to see me later at the happy-hour event.

Alone in the limo, I smiled, not because I knew the cameras were on me, but because I was happy. Last night and today had been great. I was looking forward to a nice happy hour but was stressed about the candle ceremony. Somebody was going to have to go home tonight, and even though I knew who it would be, I remembered the heartache of seeing the flame snuffed out on my candle.

## CHAPTER TEN

Through the haze, I heard light tapping but ignored it because I was tired, and a glance at the clock told me it was only six. I snuggled deeper into the covers and drifted back into my dream, where I was riding horses on a beach somewhere. I frowned when the light tapping of their hooves on the sand turned into thunderous hooves on the boardwalk.

"Savannah? Are you awake? Savannah?"

I groaned when I realized my dream was ending and the horses' hooves beating on the boardwalk was really somebody knocking harder on my door. What the hell? "Go away."

"Savannah, it's Mandee. We need to get you ready for the party. It starts in an hour."

What? I looked at the clock again. It was six at night, and I had been asleep for only an hour. My arms and legs felt heavy. I wanted to stay in bed, but I was contractually obligated to get up and participate. "Come in," I mumbled.

"I'm already here."

A voice right beside the bed startled me. "You scared me."

"You scared me. I thought something had happened to you," she said.

I sat up and wiped my eyes. "I'm so tired."

"Do you want me to order an energy drink or energy-boosting smoothie?"

I needed calories, and a smoothie sounded delicious. "Yes, please. Add a shot or two of B-12."

Mandee gave my order to whoever was on the other end of her headset. "Let's get you in the chair and work on hair and makeup. Buzzy's making an appearance later with a few dresses. I think you're going to like their options."

I hadn't seen Buzzy in almost a week, and a tiny part of me missed them. Mandee was easy to be around, but she didn't talk a lot. Even when I tried to engage with her, her answers were short and sometimes forced. "Is it formal attire?"

"Yes, but not over the top. You'll like the selection."

We didn't talk until she finished my makeup, not even when an assistant brought my smoothie in. She was spraying my hair when Buzzy breezed in carrying two dresses.

"Perfect timing. I heard about your sunburn fiasco, so I have a few options that will cover up tan lines."

Fiasco seemed a bit dramatic, but my shoulders had developed some awkward tan lines. Buzzy showed me a red dress with thick shoulder straps that would definitely cover the lines, but it wasn't very dressy, so I would have to accessorize with jewelry. The other was a black evening gown that shimmered under the lights, but Buzzy was concerned I wouldn't like the slit so high up my leg. It was a dress made for somebody a lot taller, but they would be able to throw a stitch or two in strategic places to keep it modest. "Let me try both on." Buzzy huffed but followed me into the dressing room just off the bedroom. I dropped my robe, so I was wearing nothing but black panties. The red dress was tight, but the material had enough elasticity that I was able to move comfortably.

"How's it going in here? Oh, I like that dress, Savannah." Lauren breezed in as though she knew I was fully dressed, when just thirty seconds ago I'd stood almost naked in front of Buzzy. She was wearing a three-quarter-length-sleeved black dress with a conservative neckline. She had on a small bracelet and her hair partially down.

"You look great yourself."

Lauren cleared her throat and looked down. "Thanks, but this is about you."

"Let's try the black one on." Buzzy unzipped the dress I was wearing.

"I'll wait out here," Lauren said since I was going to be naked in about five seconds. She disappeared behind the door, much to my relief. Attractive women made me nervous. Buzzy zipped up the dress, tucked in my breasts, and took a step back. They pressed their forefinger against their lips and studied me.

"I like this. I can close this gap a few inches and raise the dress several inches, so you don't have to worry about twisting your ankles in high heels. These should work." They held out a pair of strappy heels that were only about two and a half inches tall.

I slipped them on and immediately felt like I was headed for the red carpet. "Finally. Heels that won't make me twist my ankle." I looked in the mirror and struck a pose. I was showing a bit more boob than I wanted to, but the dress would stay decent if Buzzy used fabric tape. It was a risk.

"Let's get Lauren's opinion," I said.

Buzzy called for Lauren, who walked in the room and gave a slow clap. "I liked the red dress but love this one," she said.

I looked at my shoulders. "Can you see any tan lines?"

She took a few steps closer and inspected me. "There's a slight line here where I can see a difference in color, but Mandee should be able to touch that up."

"What do you think?" As much as I appreciated Buzzy's talents, they weren't who I was here to impress, and I trusted Lauren.

"You look very sexy in that dress."

"Too sexy? Because that's not really my vibe."

"I don't think so. It's still classy, and your hair looks amazing," she said.

Her compliment gave me chills, as did the way she gazed up and down me appreciatively. A hint of something in her smile gave her power over me. Lauren, for as sweet and kind as she was, struck me as a high-femme top. I didn't realize I was attracted to high femmes until now. One day I would ask her about her love life and what had happened in her past, but that would have to wait until after camera time. I was getting used to our late-night conversations in my room. "Thank you. As long as I don't pop out of this dress, I'll wear it."

"How much of the side slit do you want me to close?" Buzzy's hands on my thighs barely registered.

"Maybe three inches. My legs aren't long enough to pull off this look."

"I think they're fine," Lauren said. She pulled up the dress high enough that it barely grazed the floor. "You think about right here?"

Buzzy nodded their approval and pinned the bottom. "Okay. Take it off. I'll have it back to you in a few minutes."

Lauren turned around and left before I peeled the dress off and slipped into the robe. I went back into my bedroom, but she wasn't there either. Slightly frowning, I realized I wouldn't see her until the end of happy hour.

"Have a seat so you don't mess up your hair and makeup before they start filming." Mandee pointed to the couch while she straightened her makeup brushes and colors. It was incredible seeing how much foundation, bronzer, concealer, blush, eye shadow, mascara, and lip gloss she used on me. It seemed pointless to put everything away because she touched me up several times throughout the night.

Tonight's happy hour was at my place. While the contestants' mansion was bigger, mine was cozier and warmer. I sat for five minutes and waited for Buzzy and their assistant to finish my dress. Mandee said a few things to somebody in her headset, and I sat there doing nothing. I had no phone to scroll through, no television to turn on, no books to read. My only option was to watch Mandee. "So, do you ever get away from the show?"

"What do you mean?" she asked.

"Like are you tied down to the show or are you allowed to leave the sets?" I didn't care. I just wanted to have a conversation with somebody without the cameras rolling. The psychology of the show was starting to get to me. I wasn't a social butterfly at all, but I needed something.

"Nobody knows me out there in the real world, but I stay pretty busy on set, so I don't get out much," she said.

It felt like an eternity before Buzzy came back with the dress. I met them halfway across the room and dropped the robe. Buzzy handed me the dress and disappeared into the dressing room at the exact moment Lauren entered my suite.

"Oh, my God. I'm so sorry." Lauren froze.

The shocked look on Lauren's face probably mirrored my own. I wasn't used to other people seeing me naked. Sure, Buzzy and Mandee had seen me that way at least a dozen times. I was used to them around me fluffing up my boobs or fixing my straps, but they were very discreet and professional. I pulled the dress close to my chest to afford me some cover before turning my back. Heat exploded on my cheeks. "No, it's okay." Who says that? I was dying inside. I wasn't okay, and I tensed until I heard the sharp clip of her heels fade.

"What's the holdup?" Buzzy, who had missed the entire exchange, clucked at me to get dressed. "And why are you so red?" They tilted my chin from side to side. "Did Mandee put too much makeup on you?"

"No. I'm fine." They zipped me up and admired their quick stitchwork. I took deep breaths to slow the rapid thumping in my chest while they taped the dress to my skin to avoid any wardrobe malfunction. One a night was enough.

"Stop by Mandee to see if she needs to make any adjustments."

I knew my makeup was spot-on. I just needed to cool down. Things were going to be awkward on camera, and I needed to shake off my discomfort. It wasn't a big deal. I repeated that sentence over and over until Denise asked for me. My stress level shot up, but I managed to push my embarrassment to the side and force a smile.

"Are you ready?" Denise asked.

The knot of tension between my shoulder blades loosened when I scanned the room and saw only crew members. Lauren wouldn't join us until the end of the evening, and by then I would have had at least one glass of wine to relax me. I nodded. "I'm ready."

❖

I felt a jolt of excitement when I saw Alix edge toward where Charlotte and I were sitting. After they asked if they could interrupt,

Alix sat in the spot vacated by a very unhappy Charlotte. The rule was to give the contestant at least five minutes, but interruptions were expected.

"How was the dolphin date? Also can I say how beautiful you look tonight? When you came out, I forgot how to breathe."

"Thank you. You look pretty incredible yourself." Alix wore a navy suit with a white shirt open at the collar. They must have been spending all day poolside because they were tanner today than the other night. "It was so much fun. Well, the dolphin part was. Oh, and I met Walter."

Dimples popped out on their cheeks, and their face exploded into a brilliant smile. "Do tell."

I wanted to kiss Alix right now. They were exciting and fresh, but too many sparkettes could see us, and the show was still in the beginning stages. I didn't want to be the girl who kissed everybody. Too many bachelorettes on all the reality shows got roasted on social media for kissing a lot.

"Walter is a sea lion with a hurt flipper. He lives at the center and is super sweet."

"Walter sounds like a lucky guy. I'm not jealous, because I had the best time with you on our date. Thank you again for inviting me."

"I had so much fun, too. Willow McAdams."

"I still can't get over it," Alix said.

"Right? Did you tell the others about it?"

They lowered their voice. "I told them I had an amazing time and that she sang to us, but I don't kiss and tell. And believe me, they asked."

"That's the tough part about dating more than one person at a time. I'm not a fan."

Alix held their palms up. "Agreed. Yet here we are."

Alix's words didn't offend me. They were right. The show was a catch-22. "I hope to show the viewers that you can find love on the show. I'm not here for anything other than trying to find somebody. I don't want to be an actress, or a model, or look for another job. I just want to find love."

Alix playfully stretched out their arms. "Here I am."

"Such a ham," I said, playfully shaking my head but secretly thrilled that I wasn't the only one who felt something.

"Can I interrupt?" Madison sneaked up behind Alix without me noticing, and Alix rolled their eyes at Madison's voice.

I pasted on a smile. "Of course."

Alix stood and winked at me. "I'll see you later."

It took a moment for Madison to get comfortable on the rattan sofa next to me. Her dress rivaled mine for cleavage attention, but I kept my eyes on her face the entire time. She was attractive, but something about her rubbed me wrong.

She grabbed my hand and said, "Hi. It's good to see you again."

Her palm felt clammy, and I resisted the urge to pull my hand free. "You, too." I didn't know what to say to her. "How has it been around here for you? I know you're usually busy with work. The adjustment must be difficult."

She nodded. "I trust my employees though. We knew it was going to be a challenge."

I pushed through the awkward silence that followed. "What hobbies do you have?"

"Work." She smiled to detract from the short answer.

There was the connection. I knew they wouldn't just throw somebody on the show for kicks. Lauren said they vetted each person. "Ah, yes. I know that hobby well. Nothing else? Binge-watcher of bad television? Do you play any sports? What about pets? Do you have any?" I was grasping for anything to keep the conversation going.

"I have fish."

Something I knew nothing about. Jane had a pond with koi, but that was the extent of my knowledge. "Like a koi pond?"

"No. I have a hundred-and-thirty-five-gallon tank with puffer fish, African butterflyfish, and some others. They're peaceful to watch after a grueling day in court or at the office."

Her answer personified her, made her seem like less of a shark, pun intended. "I need something soothing. That sounds perfect," I said.

"Maintenance is low. Plus, they don't get mad if you're late."

"And you don't have to race home to let them out." Pets were tough for me. I loved them, but I was too busy to give an animal the attention it deserved. Madison and I had a civil conversation for about another minute before the conversation stalled again. Thankfully, Emma popped into our private bubble, breaking up our choppy conversation. She, along with Madison, would be on the group date tomorrow. I liked Emma. She was bubbly and extremely focused on me. My ego always got a boost when she was around. I needed to pay more attention to her. She was confident but not overtly, attractive, and slightly flirty.

"Can I have everyone's attention, please?"

My stomach clenched when Lauren slipped into the room. I wanted her to see me, but at the same time, I wanted to hide behind people so she couldn't. Because of so much sudden commotion with the camera people at Lauren's surprise appearance, everyone quieted quickly.

"Good news. We won't have a candle ceremony tonight. We want Savannah to get one-on-one time with everyone, so we're postponing until after the second group date tomorrow." Everyone clapped and smiled. Lauren cocked her head and held up her finger. "Hold on before you celebrate too much. Tomorrow will be a double elimination."

Eleven pairs of eyes looked at me. I raised my eyebrows in surprise. I'd thought we'd have an elimination tonight and one tomorrow. "Then that means we should have a really good night tonight." I hated that my answers sounded scripted. I wanted to say, what the actual fuck, but *When Sparks Fly* wasn't that kind of show.

# CHAPTER ELEVEN

S avannah, I'll leave the evening up to you."
When Lauren finally looked at me, I felt like I was burning from the inside out. It wasn't just from embarrassment. She was an attractive, intelligent woman, and the more I got to know her, the more she ticked my boxes, even though she wasn't an option. On top of that, I was mortified at what had happened earlier this evening. I managed to force a smile. "Thanks, Lauren." She gave me a soft nod and left the room. I exhaled. That had gone better than expected, but then I knew Lauren would be professional regardless of what happened behind the scenes.

Emma, the preschool teacher who would be on tomorrow's group date, tapped my shoulder. "Would you like to go for a walk?"

"Definitely," I said. I couldn't remember a lot about her other than her occupation. She was quiet, like Kaisley, but older. We went inside because it was too loud outside. The contestants didn't have a lot of places to go since we were at my mansion, and most rooms were off-limits. We found a small study off the foyer.

"How was the group date today?" she asked.

"It was very entertaining. But don't worry. We have fun things planned for tomorrow's date, too."

"I'm kind of sad I didn't get to hang out with dolphins, but I trust that whatever you have planned tomorrow will be perfect." Her Kentucky accent only added to her charm.

"What do you do for fun?"

"I hike with my family and friends. We have a ton of national parks in Kentucky."

Everyone's hobbies made me realize what a joke my life was. I didn't do anything. I'd been camping maybe a few times with friends during my twenties, but most of them had drifted to other friends because I was a dud. Jane was my ride-or-die friend. She was the only one who got me to do things outside of work. "Hiking's a good way to stay in shape." I nodded as though I hiked all the time.

"Do you like it? It's too bad we can't hike around here."

"I know what you mean. What else do you do when you're not working?" I took a moment to study Emma. She had gorgeous dark-brown, straight hair that fell past her shoulders and chestnut-brown eyes. She wore a conservative cream-colored dress that made my outfit look skimpy. It was the only time I regretted picking it over the more conservative red dress.

"I like puzzles and creating things. I love coming up with art ideas for my preschoolers. You can learn a lot on Etsy and Pinterest," she said.

She ran her finger back and forth across the ribbed pattern of the sofa. She clearly wasn't used to cameras a few feet away from her face and averted her eyes several times. Or maybe she was shy. "I bet there's a lot for teachers on Pinterest." Her eyes lit up, and I knew immediately that the rest of our chat would be about craft projects for children under five. Emma wanted to settle down and have kids. I could almost hear her biological clock ticking.

"Like you, I love making things. I have a small store on Etsy. I've learned so much from the internet."

I had a love-hate relationship with the internet. I loved the resources but hated when I came across memes or gifs of myself. It didn't happen a lot, but when it did, it hurt. "It's been a blessing for the most part." A knock on the door interrupted our bland conversation as Lyanna peeked into the room.

"Here you are. Can I interrupt?" she asked.

Emma visibly bristled at Lyanna's sudden appearance. "We just sat down, and since you had time with Savannah earlier, I'm going to have to politely decline your interruption. I need some one-on-one time." And then she turned her back on Lyanna and gave me all her attention. "You were saying?"

I smiled apologetically over Emma's shoulder. "I'll find you in a bit." Lyanna nodded at me and slipped out of the room. I focused back on Emma. "I like how you stood up for yourself."

"It's so hard to get to know you when I have to share," she said. She touched my arm softly. "I spend so many hours with them, and it gets catty sometimes."

That remark piqued my interest. "Is there any house drama that I need to know about?"

She hesitated so I pressed. "I remember being in your place and wanting to tell Katie what was going on but didn't want to snitch on my housemates either. I get that you're in a tough spot." Like every other show, the drama was overinflated. But I also wanted to protect the sparkettes. If nine out of ten people told me one person was being an ass, I should probably investigate.

"Sometimes I don't think Madison is in it for the right reasons."

I couldn't stop the surprise from registering on my face. Emma had picked up on Madison's vibe, too. "Interesting. What makes you think that?"

She shrugged. "It's just a feeling. She's very standoffish with the rest of the housemates. The only person she ever spends any time with is Thea. They always have their heads together and laugh when somebody walks in. I mean, it's probably just high school antics, but it's hard being outside of a clique, even if it's just two people. You can't help but think they're making fun of you or at least talking about you."

I knew too well. "Have you heard her be mean directly to anyone?"

"No. It's just a feeling. It's nothing. I shouldn't have said anything."

I touched her hand. "Thank you for telling me. It's always good to know what goes on over there. I only get to see everyone's best side, and I'm making one of the biggest decisions of my life. I'd like to know that other people feel the same way."

Her fingers locked with mine. "I'm here for the right reasons. I think you're charming and beautiful and sweet. I know this journey might be hard for you, but you're doing the right thing."

My list of top five kept changing. This was going to get tougher, and I was going to hurt good people along the way, but I had to remember this was about me and what was best for my life. "Thank you. I've enjoyed getting to know you better, too. As unfortunate as this sounds, I probably need to get back out there, but I promise that tomorrow I'll pull you aside first for some one-on-one time."

"That would be great," Emma said.

Her gaze darted down to my cleavage before she stood in front of me for a hug. I followed her back outside, where the rest of the contestants held fruity cocktails and were in the middle of some sort of dance-off. I couldn't help but laugh at adults doing old-school dances like the Cabbage Patch and the Sprinkler and Alix teaching three women the Running Man. Under no circumstances was I going to dance in this dress. I grabbed a cocktail and worked my way around to everyone. After an hour of making pointless small talk, I was done.

The sparkettes were finally shuttled off, and I dragged myself up the stairs to my room. The crew was still shuffling about, but I closed my door and ignored any mumblings from headsets or beeps off in the distance. I hung the dress up, showered, and slipped into a 10,000 Maniacs concert T-shirt and a pair of boy shorts. I wasn't expecting Lauren tonight, or any night for that matter, after what had happened earlier.

It was after one, and I had to be up at ten for the next group date. Another day at the beach. We were scheduled to go sailing. That made for a small environment, and I hoped I had paired the groups well. I almost yelped when I heard a soft knock at my door.

"Savannah? Are you still up?"

Oh, fuck. It was Lauren. I looked at my pajamas and grabbed a robe. "Come in." I sounded hoarse and desperate. I cleared my throat. "It's unlocked. And I'm dressed this time."

She dropped her head into her hands. "I'm so sorry about that."

I forced out a laugh and waved her off like it wasn't a big deal, though my pulse was throbbing under my skin, and my heart felt light now that she was here. Suddenly I wasn't tired. "It's no big deal. So many people here have seen me naked." That wasn't true, but I was trying to make her feel better.

"I really should have knocked."

I shrugged and ignored her. We had both apologized, and it was time to move on. "Have a seat. Tell me about your night." She sat in the chair farthest from me.

"It was kind of boring. I had a late dinner, looked at some earlier footage from your group date, and got some rest. Tell me about yours."

"It was fun to relax with all the contestants tonight. Why didn't we have a candle ceremony?" Not that I was looking forward to sending anyone packing, but that ritual had to start soon.

"We're working some things out first. Look at it this way. It gives you more time with the contestants. That's a good thing, right?"

I crinkled my nose at her. "What if I already know who I want to leave first?"

"This is our cone of silence." She waved her hands around the room. "You can trust me."

I looked into her eyes. "I know." My voice was lower than I wanted. "I trust you." She glanced away. We were having a moment, and I couldn't let that happen. Lauren was a professional, and I was tripping over my emotions because of my lack of sleep during the last three weeks. "I'm not super fond of Madison. Hopefully, that reaction doesn't come across." I raised my eyebrows and smiled. "I mean, you can tell me that, right? You aren't my therapist or under any contractual obligation not to talk to me, are you?"

Her first genuine smile of the night. "My job is to help you. I can talk to you on camera, off camera, whenever you want."

"Except I can't call you or text you."

"No, but we have a staff of about thirty people who do know how to reach me."

She pointed to the doors behind her as if people were lined up out there to help. Most of the time they ignored me and acted as though I didn't exist. "I'm tired of talking. I don't know how you do it. I've had to be on point for hours. Tell me something. I don't care what. Tell me one thing that most people don't know about you."

"Brace yourself." She held her hands out and pressed them down as though keeping herself from falling. "I want a dog, but my career doesn't really allow me the time for one."

I sat up straighter. "Get one. And bring it on the set. Having a dog on staff would be amazing for all the flames and sparkettes. Dogs are so good at making people happy, if you have the right kind."

She frowned at me. "Is there such a thing as the wrong kind of dog?"

"Good point, but I mean a big ole golden retriever or Labrador on set would be so much fun. They're too big to trip over, and people can't help but want to snuggle with them or pet them. Oh, and they're great therapy dogs, too."

"Sounds like I'm not the only one who wants a dog," she said.

I shook my head. "I wish I could have one, but my store is in a strip mall without any grassy areas, so the poor pup couldn't come to work with me. Trust me. I've thought about it. Plus, I work stupid hours."

"The joys of working in a desert," Lauren said.

"I'm rethinking my location. My lease is up at the end of the year. I'm considering Windsong. Same size space but cheaper, closer to my house and grassy areas."

"Do you get a lot of foot traffic? Could your business be strictly online?"

"It was, and then I decided I wanted a store. I do okay, but maybe I should go back to online only."

Lauren moved closer. "Listen, don't listen to me."

"Listen, but don't listen?" I smiled when the dimple popped out.

"You know what I mean. Sometimes I get ahead of myself. If having a store is your dream, don't let me talk you out of it."

I sighed. "It's tough. Dreams aren't always great or right. I'm sure with the money from the show, I'll rethink the business. I like making candles. I know that sounds boring and not challenging, but it's what I'm good at."

Lauren touched my hand. I watched as my fingers held hers. Neither of us let go. "You are thirty-two years old and running your own business. That's admirable."

"No, you're—wait. I don't even know how old you are." I blushed at not only her nearness but my embarrassing ramble. "It's none of my business, but you have done so much with your life. You've worked for CNN, traveled the world, done at least two news shows, and have taken on a pretty crappy show and made it one of the network's biggest successes. You're amazing and have probably surpassed all your dreams." She blushed, but I meant every word. "Your family must be so proud."

The noise she made was a cross between a sigh and a bitter laugh. "My dad is a hard-core Republican. My mother hangs on his every word. We don't talk much."

"No. That's awful." Our fingers were now entwined. My sluggish heart kicked up several notches at the contact, and I was begging myself not to sweat or freak out. She needed a friend. That's what was happening here. "I'm sorry. Most people take their family for granted. Even though it's just my mom and I, we try to stay in touch as much as possible." That wasn't entirely true. I could do better. "Do you have any brothers or sisters?"

"I have a twin."

"Shut up. Identical?"

"Fraternal. A brother."

"How am I just learning about this now? That's very cool."

My shoulders dropped when she let go of my hand and got more comfortable on the couch. "He's a lot like my parents. He's definitely their favorite."

"I don't believe that for one moment. I mean, unless he's in the NFL or a doctor who discovered a cure for cancer, and I highly doubt that statement." I couldn't imagine anyone being disappointed in Lauren.

"He's a firefighter with a wife and two young children."

"Is this a guy thing?" I knew parents who loved their sons because they were boys and would carry on the name and all that patriarchal bullshit.

"Not a guy thing, but a gay thing."

And just like that, Lauren officially outed herself and changed the game for me.

## CHAPTER TWELVE

H ow do you manage to make something as ugly as a life
vest look sexy?"

Frankie, a professional soccer player now coach, raised her
voice even though she was sitting right beside me. I could still
barely hear her over the boat slapping against the waves and the
wind snapping the sails.

Most of us took motion-sickness medication. Only Madison
refused, and she was the one below deck trying to calm her stomach.
Thea was down there, too, probably holding her hair back. That left
Frankie and Emma above-deck with me. Because we had limited
space, several cameras were hidden around us. The camera people
showed us where and asked us to be aware of them and try to have
conversations as close to them as possible for the best sound and
picture. Reshooting scenes on a sailboat was tricky.

"I don't want to drown," I said.

She nodded. "It's a great day for sailing, but not so great for
talking."

I turned my head away from her because the wind was blowing
my hair into her face. "And we can't go downstairs because Madison
is down there getting sick."

Frankie tapped my shoulder.

"I can't hear you," she said.

I pulled my hair back the best I could and repeated myself.

Frankie shook her head. "Not a place I want to be."

"Let's just enjoy the ride, and we'll talk once we get to the island." We were sailing to a small, private island about an hour from Key West, where we would dock, picnic, and spend the afternoon getting to know one another better.

She put her arm around me and casually played with my hair. Because of her career and just basic human decency, I would have thought Frankie was aware of consent rules. I pulled away. "I'm not very comfortable with that. Plus, Emma is right there."

"Oh. I'm sorry. I forget that we're on a show." She removed her arm and put space between us.

I smiled to soften the blow for Frankie and for the viewers. It wasn't that Frankie rubbed me wrong. She was just too eager, and I didn't think it was because of me. Every interaction we had made me feel like a prop instead of someone she was genuinely interested in. I had a list of at least four contestants who made me feel like they were here because of me. Frankie didn't make that list.

When we docked, we all slowly made our way off the boat. I grabbed Emma's elbow as she stumbled on the dock.

"Are your legs shaking, or am I just a wuss?" Emma asked.

"No. That was a hard trip. I heard they're taking us back by normal boat." I looked behind us to see medics helping a very ashen Madison off. "Wow, she really had it rough, didn't she?" I tried to look concerned, but I didn't have much sympathy. Thankfully, she had Thea, who did, in fact, hold her hair back.

"At least I can hear you, and we can have a conversation now," Emma said.

Her voice was so calming that I managed to push the last uncomfortable thirty minutes from my mind and focus on her. "Sorry about back there on the boat."

"About Frankie?" She waved it off. "I'm not worried about her. I don't think she's your type."

I bumped my shoulder into hers. "She can probably hear you. Shh." I lowered my voice. "Why do you say that?" I quickened my step to put distance between us and Frankie.

"She tries too hard. Everything she does is full steam ahead. Nobody likes a full-court press."

The way she dragged out the word press because of her accent made me smile. "I totally get it. She's trying to be seen in a room full of eligible women. I did the same thing years ago." Emma kept talking about what Frankie was doing wrong and something about me when I was on the show before, but I completely tuned her out when I saw Lauren waiting for us. She was standing on a patio in front of the resort. The wind pressed her dress against her, sculpting the outline of her feminine curves. Even though her hair was back in a bun, a few tendrils escaped and completed the sexy-as-fuck look. She was all I could see.

"Kind of a rough day for sailing," she said as we approached.

Madison and Thea were sitting on a bench near Lauren. Madison was nibbling a cracker and taking small sips from a water bottle.

"Are you feeling better?" I asked.

Madison smiled through her misery, but she looked one deep breath away from throwing up again. "I'll make it. And take motion-sickness pills."

"I'd ask how the ride was over here, but from the looks on everyone's faces, I'd say it was bumpy," Lauren said.

We nodded.

"It was hard to talk on the sailboat. I hope lunch is in a quieter place," Frankie said.

"You're in luck. We have a very private spot for the five of you to enjoy lunch and get used to being on solid ground again."

She led us down a stone path to a beautiful shaded and cooled area with four picnic tables and a buffet full of fruit, vegetables, barbecue, breads, and desserts that made me lick my lips in anticipation. I was going to eat food that wasn't healthy, and I had no regrets. Normally we ate before shooting, which would have been on our way to the island, but the choppy sailboat ride had made everyone balk at the idea.

"Savannah, when you're done, Mandee is behind those doors to fix your hair and makeup. Eat up," Lauren said. She shot me a brief smile on her way out. I wanted her to stay and sit with us since we hadn't started filming, but there was a line that couldn't be crossed.

"I don't know about you two, but I'm famished." Frankie set a beer and her full plate on the table. Her food was the kind I wanted—a cheeseburger, a hot dog, chips, and a brownie. She worked out feverishly, so her caloric intake would disappear by the next day. I was too lazy to work out since I couldn't do my usual runs. I was limited to a treadmill and other equipment I feared using because it was top-of-the-line, and I didn't want to break anything. Besides, running in place was boring.

Maybe I should start swimming in the evenings. We had a giant pool on the estate that I hadn't taken advantage of. It had a beautiful waterfall and a hot tub. Swimming was an allover body workout and would help keep the pounds off. I convinced myself to take a swim tonight after the first candle ceremony. I was extremely nervous and needed comfort food. Brownies would definitely keep me content.

"I need one of those." I pointed to the brownie on Frankie's plate.

"Do you want mine?"

"Thanks, but I should get my own. Where's everybody else?"

Frankie thumbed at the door behind her. "Madison's somewhere in there to lie down for a minute. Seeing her on her ass is kind of funny."

"I feel so bad for her though," Emma said.

I was split. I felt sorry for Madison, but it was kind of funny. She'd get over motion sickness. It wasn't like a cold or a broken bone. She just got shaken up a bit. "Yeah, to both of those." I quickly looked around, hoping that cameras weren't on me. Most of the crew were eating off in the distance, so I figured nobody but Frankie and Emma heard what I said. "On that note, I better get some food in me." I would definitely want a glass of wine to settle my nerves during the ceremony.

"I'll go with you," Emma said.

The look on Frankie's face told me she wished she'd waited. "We'll be right back." I didn't want alone time to start now. I wanted to eat. I grabbed a cheeseburger because I'd been craving one since day one, a handful of vegetables and dip, and the biggest brownie I could find without digging through them all.

"I want to eat everything," Emma said.

I looked at her dismal plate of cut veggies and two pieces of honeydew melon. "That's it? Are you a vegetarian? Because we can have them make anything you want." I looked around for someone from the kitchen staff to whip up a veggie burger, but she stopped me.

"No. I just want to stay trim."

"Tonight's a big night. You'll want something in your system before the ceremony," I said. Her hand lightly touched the small of my back, and I was surprised at the little jolt I felt.

"I want to be able to fit into my dress, too. I think you'll like it." Her voice got a little huskier as she looked into my eyes, then down to my lips. She bit her bottom lip in a way that wasn't overly sexual, but I knew exactly what she was thinking. It was time to step up my game.

"I'm sure I'm going to like it." It was the first time I'd looked her up and down without having to worry about being caught on camera. Emma was beautiful. She had a nice body and kept it hidden under modest clothing that was a bit reserved for Florida, but I respected her for her choice. She was slowly climbing into my top three.

We took our plates back to the table and were chatting pleasantly with Frankie when Thea joined us.

"Did you get sick, too?" I asked Thea when she sat.

"Not really. I just felt bad for Maddie."

"You should try to eat something," Frankie said. She slid over the cheese-and-cracker tray she'd fixed during her last trip to the buffet.

Thea nibbled on a cracker. "I didn't think I'd be hungry after all that, but I am."

"Grab something quick. I'm guessing they want to start filming, because Mandee's walking this way." That meant hair and makeup touch-up. "I'd say you have about fifteen minutes." I grabbed the last half of my brownie and shoveled it into my mouth on my way to her.

"Are you done?" Mandee asked.

I nodded as I chewed. I could have gone back for a second plate, but that would have been uncomfortable. Eating in the heat wasn't my favorite thing, but I needed something in my stomach for all the toasts later tonight.

❖

"I'm so sorry I missed the sail over here."

Madison looked better than she had an hour ago. Either the color was back in her cheeks, or Mandee's crew did an excellent job with her makeup. "You were probably better off where you were because it was so loud it was impossible to have a conversation. The view was nice though."

"Ugh. I never thought I'd get motion sickness."

Having Madison knocked down a peg made her more human. She wasn't on point like she normally was—wondering where the cameras were and how to expose her best side. She was friendly and low-key. Gone was the high-strung lawyer whose heels clicked sharply everywhere we went. "You seem to be doing well now. Did you get something to eat? Tonight's a big night." But I didn't need to remind her of the double elimination.

"I ate a bagel."

"That's good to hear. It's nice that Thea was around to help. She's a good egg," I said. I looked around. "I haven't seen her today hardly at all, and we're boarding in an hour." We had just joined the group after our obligatory one-on-one time walking through the aquarium on the private island. I'd never seen so many colorful fish. It was hard to keep a conversation going when I really just wanted to sit down and watch the different fish float by the glass. It was so peaceful, and being with Madison was anything but.

Madison looked at me in terror and shook her head. "I won't be going back on the sailboat."

I laughed at her expression. "None of us are. We're taking a small ferry. It'll still be rough, but not nearly as rough as our ride here."

"I mean, I still have to walk in heels tonight."

"Or maybe it can be a shoe-optional night," I said.

She touched my hand. "That's the best thing I've heard all day."

This was the longest amount of time I'd spent with Madison. Since she owned exotic fish, she enjoyed educating me on the different ones. Time shared together wasn't awful. Emma and Frankie were more like me. We pointed and oohed and aahed at the ones that got our attention because they were either colorful or different. We didn't know a thing about them.

"Hi. Here you both are."

Thea came up behind us and sat beside Madison. "How are you feeling?"

Madison smiled at her, then guiltily at me. "So much better. Savannah and I were just discussing the ride back. It should be a lot easier."

"Plus, the wind has died down," Thea said.

Madison held up her glass of Gatorade. "I'll drink to that."

Small talk was easy as we discussed mishaps around water. Emma and Frankie told me a story from the fifth season where one of the sparkettes pushed the flame into the pool, who was so pissed off she excused herself for the night.

"Not really my idea of fun by the pool. So, nobody here push me in. It might make for good television, but I'm still a no on that," I said.

Frankie smiled. "The rest of the contestants gasped, and she eventually got sent home, but why would anybody risk it? Unless she knew she was going home and just wanted to make a big splash, pun intended."

"You really haven't watched any of the other seasons?" Emma asked.

I shook my head and rolled my empty glass between my hands to settle my nerves. "No. I mean, I've seen bits of the show here and there, but it was hard to watch knowing what the sparkettes were going through. I've been where you are, so I promise to be gentle."

"Unlike Katie Parson. I wonder what's she's doing now. Last I heard, she was doing some morning show in Atlanta," Thea said.

"Did she ever find anyone? I hope not. She was awful," Emma said.

She was still single. At least that's what the internet had said a few months ago. I shrugged like I didn't care, and I didn't, but if I said something, they would know that I'd looked into it. I didn't want to appear pathetic. "I don't know."

"This is all for the better. We're here now, and that's what's important," Madison said. She was getting her spunk back.

"Ladies, I hate to interrupt, but the boat will leave in twenty minutes."

Lauren drifted into my view, and I sighed. She was so pretty and sweet and a lesbian. I sat up straighter and nodded at her. "Okay. Thank you."

"I wonder if Lauren is single." Frankie looked at us and waved her hands. "I don't know a lot about her private life."

"That's because it's private," I said, running to Lauren's defense. "And even though she's the hostess, she's not required to tell us anything about her life." That was probably more for myself as a reminder to leave her alone.

"I know. I was just curious. She seems so mysterious and unapproachable. She's nice and all, but she never talks to us unless she's doing it for the show. She uses assistants to get us whatever we need if we ask for something."

"Isn't that what the assistants are for? Besides, what do you need that you don't already have?" I had a stocked bar, stocked refrigerator, bathroom full of anything I could possibly want.

Frankie shrugged. "I don't know. Maybe sunscreen or lip balm with SPF."

Thea nudged her with her elbow. "You're just too lazy to get it."

When I was in the first season, we had six rooms, with four contestants to a room. With only ten this season, I wondered how the setup was, especially since it was a mansion with tons of space. "Do you room together, or do you have your own space?"

"We have roommates. I bunk with Lyanna. Thea and Madison share a room, Frankie and Charlotte are next door to me, Ava and Kaisley are across the hall, and Alix and Ophelia are next to them. Every room has an en suite, so basically we're back in college," Emma said.

Everyone laughed. "I thought I was done with sororities, but apparently not," Madison said. The look on her face said she wasn't happy with the setup.

I stopped my eyes from rolling. "It's an adjustment, for sure, but thank you all for sacrificing just for the chance to get to know me better. We should probably head to the dock. I'd like to get back and relax after eating all this food." The audience didn't see us eat. They only saw what we put on our plates and pretended to eat.

"Are you nervous about the candle ceremony tonight?" Thea asked.

"Definitely. It's a tough process. We know this doesn't always go smoothly, and I'm afraid I might let the wrong person go, especially this early."

"Hey, we aren't supposed to talk about this," Emma said.

She helped me up from the bench even though I didn't need it, but my hand in hers felt nice. I let go before anyone got suspicious. I knew for sure one person who I wanted to go home, but I wasn't one hundred percent on the other. I was already stressed, and we'd just begun.

❖

"Excuse me, but I need to borrow Savannah for a moment." Lauren glided into view, wearing a conservative black, sleeveless dress with her hair pulled back and held together with an ornate clip. She wore a silver ring on her thumb and another on her middle finger. Pearl earrings dangled from her lobes. She was lovely. "Savannah?" she asked again.

"Oh, of course." I stood after Alix bumped me with their elbow and followed Lauren into the private room with everyone's pictures and stats. This time it was set up with two chairs and two cameras, so I knew we were going to discuss the ceremony that was to begin after our chat. We sat, and Lauren nodded at the cameramen.

"Are you having a nice evening?" she asked.

"I get pulled in different directions, as expected, but I'm having a good time." I liked being around most of the women, and so far, the gossip had been minimal. Most of it came from me.

"I need to tell you something." Her expression told me it wasn't good news. Her jaw clenched once, but her smile was soft.

"Oh?"

"I'm sorry to have to say this, but two of the contestants have been found in compromising positions. More than once," she said.

She stared at me, waiting for my reaction. I sat back in my chair, hoping it wasn't somebody I liked. "Who? And what do we do about it?" I held my breath and prayed it wasn't anybody I liked.

"Madison and Thea," she said.

I nodded slowly and kept my emotions in check. I felt my face relax and hoped the change didn't come across on television. I'm sure they wanted a stronger reaction, but I was relieved. Madison was going to be the first to go, and Thea wasn't that far behind. "Interesting." I couldn't wait to discuss it with Lauren after the cameras stopped rolling.

"We can handle it several different ways, but it really depends if you want them to leave or stay."

"If I want them to stay?" I was confused.

"I can make an educated guess based on your personality, but I don't want to assume anything." She was giving the power to me. After Madison and Thea's behavior, it was a nice reminder that I was in control.

"I want them gone. People shouldn't be using the show as an excuse to hook up."

Lauren smiled, and warmth flooded my system. "In that case, the show can ask them to leave now, or we can have the ceremony." She squeezed my hand. "We want you to be as comfortable as possible."

I hoped my determination registered. "I'm perfectly fine asking them to leave."

"Are you ready to do that now, or would you like a few moments?" she asked.

The right answer was to ask for a moment, but I was eager to get them out of the house. "I'm ready now," I said.

She stood. "Let's do this."

When they turned off the cameras, I stood and exhaled. I couldn't sit still. "You've got to be shitting me."

"This isn't the first time this has happened, and I'm sorry they hurt you." Lauren looked at me not with pity, but with understanding.

"Oh, I'm only pissed because it's embarrassing for me. Coming on the show a second time was hard enough."

Lauren stood and rubbed her hands up and down my upper arms. "I know, and all of it sucks, but keep your head up. I really think the rest of the people are here for the right reasons. I've combed through so much footage of extremely boring and safe conversations. And I came across some very nice chats about you."

I heard the words, but the only thing I could think about was her hands on my arms and her face only inches from mine. My knees felt wobbly, and I smiled weakly. "At least that's something, right?"

"I'll gather the contestants in the ceremony room. I can tell Madison and Thea they are off the show, or you can, whatever you want."

I wanted to lay into them and tell them to fuck off, but I had an almost squeaky-clean reputation. "I'll tell them, but I can't promise I'll be nice about it."

"Same goes for me." Lauren stood there with her fists on her hips, as though ready to fight. Her nostrils flared, and her chest heaved with every breath. I found her passion arousing. "Thank you, Lauren."

She took a final deep breath. "What are friends for if they don't have your back? Let's take a moment and cool down a bit before we head in there."

We sat and took the ice waters that Mandee's brother quickly and quietly delivered. He made us both smile at his awkwardness and speed. He reminded me of Andrew at the flower shop and his inability to slow down.

"When did you know? Or at least suspect about them?"

Lauren leaned forward and rested her elbows on her lap. "It's been a grueling day going through all the footage. It appears they felt a connection the first day. Maybe rooming queers together is a bad idea."

"Nobody really knows what's going to happen. It probably occurred on my show, and I was completely clueless." I couldn't recall any hookups, but I was also very young and naive and either drunk or trying to woo Katie. "Maybe that's what happens when you're bored?"

"What did you do when you were bored or had downtime?"

"Swam, drank margaritas poolside, and played dress-up most of the time. The dates were fun. At least I got to hang out in British Columbia, although Mexico is going to be a hell of a lot nicer."

"I'm sorry you're so restricted here. In other news that's good, the first episode drops next week. The world and social media went nuts when they found out you're the flame."

It was hard not to smile when Lauren did. Her eyes sparkled, and her entire face lit up. "Really? Oh, that makes me so happy." I wanted to press and know everything that was being said about my return, but even though we were alone and the microphones were technically off, we were probably still being watched. I would save my questions for after the ceremony if Lauren stopped by. It was becoming a welcome habit.

"It's good that you've already been revealed, because even though Madison and Thea signed nondisclosures, you never really know what's going to get out."

"After I read and signed the contract, I was scared to death. No way was I going to talk to anybody about anything," I said. I finished my water and headed for the door. "I'm so ready to get this over with."

# CHAPTER THIRTEEN

It has come to our attention that two of you aren't here for the right reasons. This is a dating show, not a dating service," Lauren said. I stood beside her and tried to look angry, because a part of me was, but I was so over them and this problem. I hoped I would be seen as the victim instead of undatable. She looked at me, and I nodded, indicating she could continue. "Madison and Thea, can you please come forward."

Every single person in the house looked shocked, except for Frankie, who rolled her eyes and gently shook her head. Madison approached first, with Thea trailing her.

"To say I'm disappointed is an understatement. I agreed to this show because I'm looking for someone to build a relationship with. I'm here for the right reasons. You both signed up to get to know me, but from the moment you arrived, you were only interested in each other." I paused because I needed to catch my breath. Confrontations weren't my thing, and my anxiety was making me squeeze the muscles in my chest and tighten the ones around my neck. I cleared my throat. I didn't need to have a panic attack now. The color drained from Thea's face, but Madison didn't flinch. She didn't even move as I spoke. "I hope it was worth it. Needless to say, I don't feel a spark with either of you."

All the contestants were holding candles because we were at the ceremony. True to form, Madison smirked, dropped the candle at my feet, and walked past me. Thea mumbled a weak apology and quickened her step to catch up to Madison. An assistant herded

Thea into a room for her exit interview, but Madison ignored him. A producer followed her, and they had a short argument before Madison went into the room he pointed at. We wouldn't see them again until the "Secrets Revealed" episode right before the finale. I had dreaded it ten years ago and only missed it because I was in the hospital with appendicitis. Now I was dreading it even more, since all the dejected contestants would be talking about me.

Lauren turned to the remaining contestants. "As I'm sure you guessed, Madison and Thea were more than friendly with each other." She waited for the gasps and sharp whispers to die down. "Hopefully they found what they were looking for and the relationship they had here will carry over into their lives. Unfortunately, it was at the expense of Savannah." She looked at me, not with pity, but with confidence. Her expression boosted me a little, but I was still shaking from the entire ordeal.

"Because of the heaviness of the evening, I'm going to retire. I will see you tomorrow. Have a good night," I said.

We were having a low-key pool party and barbecue tomorrow. I needed to wrap my head around what had happened. Thankfully, I wasn't emotionally invested in either woman, but it was still a betrayal.

"Savannah, wait a minute. Please?" Alix jogged after me, a cameraman racing behind them. They took my hands and held them gently.

"I'm sorry that happened. I'm in shock about it really, but please don't let their shitty actions make you feel sad. You've pulled the bad weeds out, and all that's left are people who really do want to get to know you. I wanted you to hear that before you retired for the evening." They opened their arms, offering a hug. I walked into their embrace and relaxed when they gave me a tight squeeze.

"Thank you, Alix. I needed to hear that." I stood there for a few moments, then broke the contact. "I'll remember your words when my mind overthinks tonight. I'll see you tomorrow. Have fun tonight."

Lauren was nowhere to be found when I walked outside and slipped into the limo. I didn't really want to leave, but I needed a break from everything. Only a small crew would be at my place tonight since the ceremony had happened at the contestants' mansion. It was only ten, so that gave me plenty of time to chill, maybe go for a swim, and get to bed early. I carried my heels up to my room and hung my dress. It would be gone by morning, replaced by something just as sexy for tomorrow night's cocktail party.

Being on this show was exhausting. No wonder Katie Parson was so bitchy. She had virtually no privacy, no link to the outside world, and probably nobody to talk to. I found the one-piece bathing suit from when I swam with the dolphins and grabbed a robe. It was a shame to let that beautiful pool go to waste. I quickly braided my hair and dived into the cool water, which felt wonderfully refreshing. If I had any money left after this, I was going to get a pool. I doubted it, though, as I wanted to move my business, order more equipment, and buy an SUV. One hundred and fifty thousand was nice, but it wouldn't cover all my selfish wants.

"Here you are."

I looked up to find Lauren sitting on the side of the pool with her long legs dangling in the water.

"You should come in," I said.

She shrugged. "I don't have a swimsuit."

I treaded water a few feet from her. She'd changed from her evening gown to linen shorts and a sleeveless blouse. Her arms were toned, and I wondered if she worked out every day.

"Oh, please. There's a mansion fifty feet away with about two hundred new bathing suits, bikinis, board shorts, or whatever you want or need to swim in. Come on in. We both deserve a break." She stood and wiped the back of her shorts as though she had sat in dirt. The pool and everything about it were cleaner than my house. "And bring back a bottle of wine. Then we can talk about Madison and Thea, who made me look like an ass." We also needed to discuss the bomb she'd dropped on me last night.

"They didn't, but I'll be right back."

Of course, I watched her walk away. She was a beautiful woman, it was a hot summer night, and I was barely dressed in a pool swimming with very few lights on. I hummed all over with excitement and needed release. I couldn't remember my last self-induced orgasm, but it had been at least two months. I had a solid seven minutes before Lauren returned. The pool was too open, and I would have more privacy in the hot tub, so I jumped out of the pool and sank into the warm water of the Jacuzzi. The jets felt good on my tense muscles, but that wasn't why I was there.

I closed my eyes and swallowed a gasp as one of the jets rocketed warm water all over my pussy. The rush of blood pounded in my ears and made every part of me throb. I tried to remain stoic because I was sure somebody somewhere had a camera on me, even though the area was dimly lit. The bubbles made it impossible to see what was happening below the surface though. I floated my arms on top of the water and tilted my hips slightly, so the pressure was right on my clit, but I didn't have a chance to enjoy the buildup. The explosion happened in less than thirty seconds. I dropped deeper into the water so only my head was above the surface as I shook out the orgasm I desperately needed. After a few minutes of controlled breathing, I jumped back into the pool—relaxed, refreshed, and not so damn tense.

Lauren showed up a few minutes later wearing black board shorts and a white tankini. "I can't believe you talked me into this."

I smiled when I saw the wine bottle and a stack of paper cups. I smiled even harder when she walked around the pool area and covered discreetly hidden cameras with the paper cups. Thankfully, there was only one by the hot tub, and it was behind where I sat, so the only action the crew would see, if they were looking over the video, was the back of my head.

"Genius."

She poured wine into the two remaining paper cups. "Paper because I don't want to get glass in or around the pool. The last thing we need is the grounds crew pissed at us." She slipped into the water and gasped at its coolness. Then she pulled herself along the pool's edge over to me with one hand, holding our cups high and out of the water. "I'm sorry about Madison and Thea." She took a sip of wine and licked her bottom lip. I couldn't stop staring at her mouth.

I shrugged. "They weren't top-five material, so I wasn't too heartbroken. Let's not talk about that."

"What do you want to talk about?"

Without thinking, I blurted out, "I want to talk about the bomb you dropped on me last night. The one where you came out to me and then disappeared."

Lauren laughed. "I never tell people anything too personal about myself, but something about you makes me trust you."

I tingled with excitement at her confession, or maybe it was the buzz of my orgasm from a few minutes ago, but her words made my heart soar. I drank more of my wine. It was liquid courage, and I needed to calm my nerves. "I'm pretty trustworthy and definitely private. I guess that's hard to find when you're famous."

"It is. I don't know how you have the courage to come on a show like *Sparks*."

"You must think I'm a sucker." I frowned for effect.

She gasped and put her hand on my upper arm. "No. I didn't mean anything like that. I know you and other flames have to question the integrity of the contestants. You're putting your heart out there, and then you have to hope you don't hurt somebody and they don't hurt you. We try to weed out the people who want to be television sensations or models. It's a rigorous process. How to prevent them from hooking up inside the mansion is hard."

"If nothing else, that episode will make for good television."

She sighed. "Unfortunately, you're right. Denise will make that a 'coming up on this special season of *When Sparks Fly*' dangler to hook people in."

"How come they're dropping the first episode so soon? Usually, we see clips of the entire season in the intro video. What's that called?"

"The title sequence?" she asked. I nodded. "The title sequence is short because it's a bonus season, and we're running during the summer months. When *Sparks* decided to do this, they knew going in it would be fast and furious. The intro is very vague. They'll add the drama during the promo snips to generate interest for the show instead of revealing too much upfront. Does that make sense?"

I nodded and finished my cup. "Do you like the title sequence?"

"It's wonderful," she said.

"Wait. We were just talking about you and dating, and somehow it got back to me. Who was the last person you dated that I would know?" I grinned and hoped that question wasn't offensive. I held up my hand and waved it between us. "This is a cone of silence, remember?" I made a dramatic wave of my arm to create an arc.

She laughed and drained the rest of her cup, too. "Do you know Ashton Baker from *Date Me?*"

My jaw dropped. "Really? I had no idea she's queer." The show was about four college students who created a dating app and spent every episode trying to prove their secret formula worked. Ashton was a thirty-year-old playing the part of a twenty-one-year-old student and completely believable, according to Jane, who watched it every week.

"Yep. We dated for a year. It was pretty intense. I had just taken a leave of absence with CNN, and she pushed me to find something to do in Hollywood so we could be together. In the end, it was too hard because she was in the closet and trying to make a name for herself. Once she got a huge following and tons of fans, she came out. It was about two months after we broke up."

"That's shitty," I said.

Lauren shrugged as if it wasn't a big deal. "I think she waited until she had enough attention and made a grand gesture. Everybody has a coming-out story. She wanted hers to be public."

She pulled herself out of the pool to refill our glasses. The water weighed down her board shorts, and I saw several inches of flat, muscular stomach. Even though it was dark and the tankini had a thin padding, her nipples were erect. I swallowed hard. She handed me my cup, and I took a large gulp to help suppress the feelings that threatened to push through the blockade in my head. I was there to meet other people. Lauren was off-limits. I was already forming relationships with a couple of the contestants. Lauren wasn't interested in me. I was totally into her. Shit. I took another drink.

"You might want to slow down," she said.

Her voice was soft and nonjudgmental. She had no idea the thoughts that were spinning in my head. "Just trying to forget certain things." I tried to keep my response vague.

"They aren't worth it."

"My thoughts?" I asked. She was confusing me.

"No. Madison and Thea."

I snorted for the second time in front of her. "Oh, I'm so over them."

She nodded slowly, as though she understood, and I prayed that she didn't. That would make the next two months awkward.

"Is this your first time in your pool?" she asked.

"Yes. I'm sure we'll have a pool party here at some point. Or maybe a one-on-one date." The word date tasted bad in my mouth. I changed the topic. "Do you have a pool in real life?"

"Me? No. It's hard to have alone time and enjoy it. I stay pretty busy," she said.

She placed her cup next to mine and dived into the pool, popping up ten feet from me. "Although I really love swimming. It's the best exercise."

"I just had a great idea. Why don't we make a pact to come down here every night and do laps? I can't go for runs, and I hate exercise equipment. A swim buddy would help me focus and curb my drinking. What do you say?"

"That's a great idea. Are you saying no more doughnuts and no more wine bottles by the pool?" she asked.

"Let's not do anything drastic. I don't think we should take doughnuts off the table."

She laughed. "Okay. How about doughnuts only the day after a candle ceremony?"

"Yes. That's perfect. But no more wine. I'll use the calories that I would have consumed in alcohol and apply them toward my doughnut intake."

She giggled, which was adorable. "And we shouldn't start laps tonight because we've both been drinking. We shouldn't even be in the pool. I won't be able to save you, and we've hidden the cameras so nobody would find us for days."

"Excellent point. Let's get out and raid the kitchen," I said. I decided to use the stairs because I was sure watching me struggle to get out of a pool wouldn't be nearly as sexy and smooth as Lauren getting out of it. I noticed she gave me a quick up-and-down glance, and I smiled at catching her. Maybe I was on her radar after all.

"I should probably go," Lauren said and handed me a towel.

"We have an easy day tomorrow. I'm pretty sure anything goes after the shit show that was today. Come on. I think I remember seeing ice cream. Besides, you need to dry off." She wrapped the white, fluffy towel around her waist. On her, the towel landed at her knees, and she looked sexy and carefree. On me, the towel hit mid-shin, and I felt anything but that. I grabbed my robe instead and followed her into the house, enjoying this casual and relaxed side of Lauren more than I should.

I walked into the contestants' mansion, and every single person approached me and apologized for Madison and Thea within the first five minutes. I knew I had to make an announcement to stop the rush of people who were stumbling over one another to get in front of me. "Thank you so much for making me feel better about last night's disaster. I'm doing fine, and I know we have a great group of people who are here for the right reasons. I say we forget about all that nastiness and have a fun day at the pool."

"I second that," Charlotte said and handed me a lemonade.

It was refreshingly nonalcoholic. After last night, I needed to hydrate.

"Come sit over here." Alix waved me over to where they, Lyanna, and Frankie sat. "How was the rest of your evening?"

I smiled, thinking about my night with Lauren. "I fell asleep early and slept hard. Thank you for asking."

"You look amazing," Alix said.

"Give it a rest, charmer." Lyanna shoulder-bumped them. A blush crept over Alix's features that even their deep tan couldn't hide.

"Well, it's true."

I chose to change the subject to save Alix from further discomfort. "Thank you. What did you all do since we ended the night early?"

"Ophelia and I played a rousing game of Scrabble," Lyanna said.

"Oh. Who won?" I liked to play it on my phone with random people when I couldn't sleep at night.

"I did." Lyanna smirked. Then she sat back and crossed her legs. "Truthfully, only because O fell asleep."

"Most of us just chilled. Last night was sobering," Alix said.

"I'm sorry that all happened," I said.

Three people immediately spoke at once.

"It's not your fault," Alix said.

"They suck," Lyanna said.

"I thought something was going on," Frankie said.

We all turned to her.

"Really?" Lyanna asked.

She shrugged. "I mean they were always together. Besides rooming, they came down to breakfast together, sat together out here, even hung out together during our cocktail parties."

"I thought we weren't going to talk about them," I said. It didn't bother me, but I knew the cameras were on us, and I didn't want to seem more worked up about it than I was.

"Of course. What's next for us all? Do you have any dates planned?" Alix asked.

"Starting Monday, you all plan the dates." I was excited to see how creative everyone could be when given unlimited resources. "But we have something special planned for the group date coming up."

"I'm way more excited about individual dates." Lyanna fist-pumped to show her enthusiasm.

I had a feeling she was creative. I was looking forward to her idea of the perfect date.

"Think art." I covered my mouth like I'd revealed a big secret. The video message I had recorded earlier this morning would hit their video message board in two days and told them to open their mind to explore their creative side. We were going to paint a nude model. The show wanted us to do a body-paint session, where we would roll around in paint and use body parts to create art, but both Lauren and I nixed it. The compromise was painting somebody naked with the whole group.

"Sounds like something right up my alley," Alix said. Of course, they were going to rock the assignment.

I knew it was apparent that I was into Alix. I needed to downplay my interest and get to know others, or else Denise would have a chat with me. "So, now that you have me here for this barbecue, what are we going to do for fun?"

That question riled them up.

"How are you with water basketball?" Frankie asked.

I had the coordination of a toddler, but I smiled because I knew everyone would let me win. That was the fun part about being the most popular girl in the room. "I'm horrible at most sports, but I'm willing to give it a try." Immediately two teams formed. Frankie picked Alix, Lyanna, and Ophelia. The other team consisted of Emma, Charlotte, Ava, and Kaisley. I already felt sorry for them. Frankie's team was heavily loaded with tattooed hard bodies who obviously worked out, while the other team seemed more like fit but soft cheerleaders. They were bikini-clad and dressed for attention, not a rousing game of water basketball. I agreed to play between the two since we had an odd number.

"What does the winning team get?" Ophelia asked.

She batted the inflatable basketball between her hands and waited for my answer. I'd forgotten how stunning she was. Her long, dark hair was piled high up on her head, and the look in her eyes told me she would stop at nothing to win. She wore a black cropped tankini and French-cut bikini bottoms.

Kaisley piped up. "Why can't it just be for fun? Savannah is here all day, so we'll have plenty of time to hang out."

"Aw, pumpkin, are you scared?" Frankie called.

"Nope. We're not doing that. No shit-talking while I'm here." I liked Frankie, but I didn't like the way she goaded people. I got that she probably did that coaching her team, but this really wasn't a competition. It was just a simple day at the pool. "I'm giving Kaisley's team a ten-point lead."

"What? You can't do that," Frankie said.

"I just did." I stood by the side of the pool with my hands on my hips and raised an eyebrow at her.

She threw her head back and laughed. "Okay, okay. We can handle that, can't we, team? Also, what's our name?" she asked.

"Oh, that's easy. We are the Badasses. Are we playing to twenty-one?" Ophelia asked.

I smiled at the name, wondering if they were going to have to bleep it. "Sure, but I don't want anybody to get hurt." I took off my wrap and walked down the stairs into the shallow end. I wasn't super comfortable wearing a bikini because I didn't have a hard body like everyone else, but I had curves, and that got me a lot of attention. "And I get the ball first. Kaisley, do you have a team name yet?" I watched as they put their heads together and whispered among themselves as though it were a big secret.

"We're the Sparklers," Emma said.

I could almost see Denise rolling her eyes from behind the camera. The other team groaned with either regret or disapproval. I couldn't tell for sure. I twirled the ball in my hand surprisingly gracefully and announced the start of the game. "Sparklers ten, Badasses zero." Then I tossed the ball to Kaisley. She passed it to Ava, who was immediately tackled by Frankie, who dunked her and stole the ball. Ava rose coughing and stuttering.

"Foul!" I yelled. Everyone stopped. "Okay, let's set some ground rules. No dunking and no getting on anyone's back. Let's try to keep it like the actual game."

"Fine." Frankie expertly sank the ball into the basket from where she was, then floated it to Ava. "Do-over." She clapped and told her team who to cover on the other team.

Even with a ten-point lead, the Sparklers lost sixteen to twenty-one. I scored three points for them and only one for the Badasses. I breathed a sigh of relief when the food was ready because the game was getting rowdy. Ava got elbowed in the face by Lyanna by mistake, and Alix hit their head on the side of the pool when they were trying to dunk the ball. I mostly stayed out of the way. "Great game, everybody. I don't know about you, but I'm hungry." I was the first out of the pool, followed by the Sparklers. The Badasses were still horsing around.

"That was brutal." Kaisley grabbed a plate and stood next to me as I fixed mine.

"Agreed. I was hoping it wouldn't get so physical. I'm going to be sore tomorrow." Even though I'd stated rules, there was still more bodily contact than I wanted. I was sure it made for good television though.

"Same here. I scraped my side." She showed me an angry welt on her ribs.

"You need to put something on that."

She eyed her injury and waved me off. "It's not that bad."

I took her plate from her. "I'll save you a seat next to me. Now go."

"Thank you."

She hustled inside, but I knew she would be back quickly. Real estate next to me was prime. I sat at the table with four chairs and was immediately joined by Charlotte and Ava. I gave Emma an apologetic smile when she pointed to the empty seat next to me and I had to tell her Kaisley would be joining us soon.

"I'll just sit here," she said and spread out on a chaise lounge next to the table.

"Look at them still in the pool trying to figure out who's the best at water basketball. You should have seen their eyes when Denise's assistant dropped the game off this morning," Charlotte said.

"For some reason, I thought you already had it here," I said.

"Nope. They gave it to us earlier with specific instructions not to play it until you got here."

"I think the Sparklers did well. I mean, yes, this is a competition, but I don't care about water basketball. I care about getting to know each of you better," I said. It sounded so rehearsed, but it was the truth. "Let's talk about movies or cars or what you miss most because you're sequestered."

"I'm back. What did I miss?" Kaisley slipped into the chair next to me, wearing a shirt that covered her ribs.

"Everything okay?" I asked.

"Yes. They treated it and told me not to go in the water for the rest of the day. What's everyone talking about?"

"Savannah just asked what we missed most," Charlotte said.

"My son. I've never been away from him for so long," Kaisley said.

Charlotte nodded. "Yeah. I miss my daughter. I didn't realize how hard it would be."

"That is hard. And now I feel shallow for saying social media. I miss my phone," Ava said.

"I do, too. It's not like I was on it a lot, but I had immediate information anytime I wanted," I said.

"I miss talking on the phone. I mean, yes, I can talk to all of you, but I miss chatting with my parents and my family," Charlotte said.

"That's sweet. Are you close with them?" I couldn't remember everything about Charlotte other than she was the mom blogger.

"Yes. I spend most of my day on my computer, so it's nice to actually converse with people. My daughter always wants to FaceTime with her grandparents. I know most people our age don't like talking on the phone, but I do."

I was one of those people who didn't like it. I attributed it to my job. I didn't like answering the company phone because I didn't know who was calling. "I answer the phone a lot during the day, so I don't like to be on it after hours. I'll talk to my friend Jane, but that's about it."

"What about your parents?" Ava asked.

"It's only my mom, and I need to do better with her. She doesn't even know I'm back on the show."

"What? How could she not know? Isn't she going to be worried when she can't reach you?" Charlotte asked.

"It all happened so fast. I left her a couple of voice mails and emailed her. It wasn't the best way to tell her, but I didn't want a back-and-forth with her. She saw what happened the first time, and I knew she would talk me out of it."

Everyone burst out laughing, and I covered my face with my hands in embarrassment.

"That's bad, Savannah," Kaisley said.

"I know. I feel bad about it because she hated it the first time I was on the show, and now she's going to have to go through it all again," I said.

"Maybe this time you'll walk away with somebody who wants the same things as you, and your mother will be happy and supportive," Kaisley said.

"I certainly hope so," I said.

I spent another hour hanging with the sparkettes before I asked to go back to my place. Being in the sun only made me tired, and I was overwhelmed. Tonight was the first official candle ceremony, and that would probably take hours to film until we all knew our places, what to say, how to act, and how it was going to play out. Ava, the nurse practitioner, and Frankie were on the chopping block. I liked them both, but I just didn't feel any chemistry with Ava, and Frankie was too much. She required a lot of attention and was loud. I was her polar opposite. She was fun but somebody I could take only in small doses.

Mandee greeted me at the door and handed me a water. "You have three hours until we need to get you ready for the cocktail party." She pressed her lips together tightly as she looked me up and down. I knew she didn't see me but noticed slightly sunburnt skin and tan lines. I guessed tonight's dress wouldn't work, and she would have to hit up wardrobe for different options.

"In absolutely no surprise to anybody, I'm going to nap. I'll set the alarm on the clock, but you might want to check on me. I can't guarantee I'll hear it," I said. I shut my door and crawled onto the bed fully clothed, forgetting to set the alarm.

## CHAPTER FOURTEEN

Yᵒu look so beautiful. Are you ready for tonight?" Lauren
asked.

I reached out and smiled when she grabbed my hands. We were
alone in my room, so I knew the gesture was sincere. "I'm more
nervous than anything."

"You'll be fine, I promise. I'll pull you into the information
room before we get started and ask you a few simple questions,
like 'do you have an idea of the contestants you want to keep?' and
things like that. Very direct and to the point. Then you'll spend a
few hours talking with them, and I'll announce that it's time for the
ceremony."

"I've got this." I knew to save my answers for the cameras.
I caught myself from frowning when she let go of my hands. She
touched my cheek. I almost leaned into her hand but stopped myself.

"You got a lot of sun today. It's a good thing we have indoor
activities coming up so you can heal," she said.

I touched my other cheek. My entire face felt like it was on fire.
"No matter how much sunscreen Mandee puts on me, I seem to get
burned. It's like she thinks it's my fault."

"Even with a sunburn, you look amazing. Don't let her berate
you. How's Buzzy? Are you working through your differences
okay?"

"I haven't seen them lately."

"You ready to head down?" She took a step toward the door.
Tonight she wore a red, full-length, sleeveless dress with a slit that

showed off only a tiny bit of her sexy legs. The collar rested right below her neck. I had never seen the soft swell of her breasts in any piece of clothing. Even the tankini the other night was modest. Maybe my dress was too much, but the way she looked at me told me otherwise.

"Are we still on for tonight? I can't wait to work off all the carbs I ate at the barbecue." I needed to qualify my question. If I made it as simple as wanting to see her, she might bail.

"Depends on how fast the ceremony goes. Sometimes they can last for hours. If you drag it out to four in the morning, then no. But tomorrow is a blackout day, which means everyone gets the day off. You, me, the crew," Lauren said.

"A day off sounds heavenly. What are you going to do?"

"Relax. Maybe watch a movie. Sleep in. Not wear makeup. Eat junk food. Scroll on my phone."

"Stop teasing me. I'm totally jealous. What am I going to do here in this big mansion all by myself without any of that? What's scrolling? Is that what you do on a cell phone? I've forgotten how. I don't even know what's going on in the world. Plus, I'll be all alone in the kitchen, which means lots of sugar and no supervision." I sighed playfully and pouted.

"Maybe I can arrange it so we can see a movie."

"Oh, is the new Victoria Crib movie out yet? I'd check on my phone, but I don't have one," I said.

"I don't think it's out yet. I'm good, but not that good." At my pout, she sighed. "I'll see what I can do."

"Thank you." I wanted to tease her about doughnuts in the morning and the fun we could have tomorrow, but I had a ceremony tonight, and I needed to remember that somebody was going home who maybe didn't want to. We were still early in the process, but I didn't feel any strong emotions for the contestants yet. Several made my heart speed up, but I hadn't had enough alone time with them. Group dates and cocktail parties were tough.

"Are you ready?"

"Let's do this."

After the five-minute ride to the mansion and Mandee double-checking that every hair was in place and my makeup hadn't smudged, Lauren and I slipped into the information room.

"Big night, right?"

I held my hand over my heart. "Very big night."

"Are you nervous or scared?"

I liked the way Lauren gave me her total attention. It mesmerized and unnerved me at the same time. She was still professional, but I detected something a little more personal in the way she looked at me now than she did on day one. "Both. I hate the thought of sending somebody home early who could be the perfect person for me. It's a risk I have to take. I have to trust my instincts and my heart."

She nodded and smiled. "Do you know who is going home tonight, or do you have an idea?"

"I know who I want to stay, but I don't know for sure who I want to go home," I said and shrugged. "That's why tonight is so important. I need to talk to several contestants privately to get a better feel for where they are in the process and about their feelings for me."

"Well, let's get you to the cocktail party that sounds like it's already in full swing," she said.

I could hear murmurs and laughter from the great room. "I'm ready."

I knew who was in the clear: Alix, Ophelia, Emma, Lyanna, Kaisley, and Charlotte. That left Frankie and Ava. I felt so hot and cold about Frankie. Sometimes she was disrespectful, and other times she was hilarious. She struck me as a hot mess, but also that person who people enjoyed being around at parties, just not real life. Ava, the other person in the bottom two, was fine. Nothing was wrong with her. I just didn't feel flutters in my stomach when we spent time together.

"Hi, everyone," I said when I walked into the room. It felt incredible to have eight people smile and raise their glasses to me. "This is a big night for all of us. I'd like to spend the time with a lot of one-on-one moments. Ava, I'll begin with you. Would you like to go for a walk?"

"Of course." She gracefully put down her drink and followed me outside. We could go only a few places to have complete privacy. I didn't want to make out, but I wanted to ask some questions and couldn't do that with other contestants milling about. Tonight, Ava wore a dark green, strapless jumpsuit with bell-bottom legs. With her long, straight hair, she looked like a woman on an album cover that I remember seeing in my mother's vinyl collection. What was her name? Was it Cher? No. Cher was too iconic not to know immediately.

"Crystal Gayle!" I yelled and snapped my fingers.

"What?" she asked as she flipped her long hair back and sat beside me on a small bench hidden in an alcove of hedges.

I blushed and pressed my lips together, silently scolding myself for my outburst. "Oh, your look reminds me of a singer from the seventies. My mom always played her music, and I memorized all the album covers. She had long, beautiful hair like yours." Ava stared blankly at me. "What kind of music do you listen to?"

"I don't have time to listen to music. I work quite a bit."

"So, wait. When you're driving to work, what do you do?" I couldn't imagine not cranking up the volume and singing to whatever was playing through the speakers.

She shrugged. "I usually listen to podcasts, or I talk on the phone."

Nope, but I played along. "I catch up with my mother on the way home some nights."

"Does she live far away?"

"She's about a four-hour drive for me. Somewhat close, but not close enough to pop in without an announcement first. Tell me about your family. Siblings, parents, nieces, and nephews?"

Ava was from a large family—two older brothers and two younger sisters. She was the only one without kids and wasn't sure how she felt about them. She was always babysitting her nieces and nephews, so having a child of her own wasn't high on her list. I respected that preference.

"What do you do for fun in New Hampshire?" I hope I got that right. Didn't I already ask her this question? "Do you ski, ice-skate, sled with the kids?"

She had a sweet laugh. "Yes. We're an outdoorsy family. We have a cabin up in the woods with a pond, and it gets cold enough so we can skate on it. My brothers ice-fish, and my sisters and I cross-country ski."

"How's the wildlife? As terrifying as I think?"

She nodded. "Worse."

I playfully gasped. "Bears? Elk? I hear moose are pretty mean."

"They're terrifying and huge. Black bears are common, too, but they usually leave us alone since we never go out by ourselves," Ava said.

We had a decent conversation, and I got a better background on Ava and what life with her would be like. She wasn't completely out, but I still didn't get the warm fuzzies. I also wasn't a fan of cold weather. "Thank you for spending time with me. I should probably head back inside and talk to a few more people."

"Can I give you a hug?" she asked.

"Definitely," I said. It was quick, and instead of walking with me back inside, she raced ahead. I couldn't disguise my confused expression. I even looked behind me to see if anything was chasing us or if somebody had sneaked up on us. Nope. Just me and four camera people. I walked into the room and found Frankie with Lyanna, sitting on a couch, drinking and laughing. She was wearing a black suit that fit her well. The T-shirt underneath boasted the Captain Marvel logo. Her black velvet loafers were under the coffee table, and her legs were stretched out, showing her bare feet. She was too comfortable in front of me, the other contestants, and the camera.

"Hi, ladies. Frankie, can I have a moment, please?" I felt rude bypassing the other contestants, but I wanted to get through this first ceremony. I was a bundle of nerves.

"Sure."

Frankie slipped on her loafers and followed me to the pool area. I knew people could see us from the window, but I didn't care. "Tell me about the rest of your day."

She took my hand, which was awkward because she didn't ask, and we were too far apart. One of us was going to have to scoot over, but it wasn't going to be me. She got the hint and slid so our hands rested on the bench.

"Well, we won the basketball game, but I was never told what we actually won," she said.

I didn't take the bait. I couldn't flirt with Frankie. She wasn't the one, and I didn't have the heart to string her along. "I guess next time we'll have to figure that out ahead of time."

"Okay, okay. I can do that," she said. She smirked at me, and even though she was very attractive and made me laugh, I knew that any sort of relationship would be all about her and about me only when I complained I wasn't getting enough attention. It was an unfair assumption, but I wasn't invested enough in Frankie to see if I was wrong. Frankie would be going home at the end of the night.

"Let's see if I remember correctly. You're from Kansas City, you like lake life with your friends, and you have a dog named Boomer. He's a big dog, right?" I remember one night we were chatting about pets, and Frankie and Kaisley were the only ones who had dogs. The rest either had cats or were petless.

"Yeah. He's part bloodhound and part Labrador retriever. He's my boy. I miss him."

"Who's watching him while you're here?" I couldn't imagine he was easy to pass off to people who weren't used to large dogs. Judging from the way she described him, he filled the entire couch when he napped. Not to mention the drool factor.

"The team. Everyone gets him for a week. He's kind of the mascot anyway. I take him to all the practices and games," she said.

"Aww. That's so sweet. Does he have a team jersey?"

She laughed. "He actually does. He's number one."

"Why the name Boomer?"

She looked at me as though she couldn't believe I'd just asked that question. I smiled and blinked at her.

"Have you ever heard a bloodhound bay? It's booming. It's so loud."

As interesting as this conversation was, I knew I had to steer it back to relationships. Denise would need plenty of material to work with. "Has it been a problem with dating? Having a large dog?" It was a stupid question but a valid one.

"Yes. Some people can't handle him. He's too big, and he takes up a lot of space," she said. She stirred the whiskey in her glass with a tiny red straw. "But I won't date somebody who doesn't love him or is afraid of him. How are you with dogs?"

"I love animals. I always had dogs growing up. I don't have one now because I work long hours, and it would be selfish to get one and keep it locked up in the house all day." The size of Boomer was a deal-breaker for me, but I knew Frankie was out, and it didn't make sense to bring the issue up now.

"You could take one to work, right? You own your own business," she said.

"Yes, but it's in a strip mall that has zero grass. Trust me, I've thought this through." Why did I keep having that conversation? It was time to move on. "Thank you for spending time with me. We should get back inside and see what we're missing."

"Good idea. Thanks for inviting me. It's nice to get away from all the energy of the other contestants."

After another hour of getting whisked away by contestants who were going to survive the candle ceremony, I asked for Lauren, who was by my side in less than a minute.

"I'm going to steal Savannah for a few minutes. When we come back, we'll start the candle ceremony in the great hall," she said.

My energy ramped up when I saw her. It was hard not to stare. I followed her into the information room, ready to get this night over with. My anxiety was at a full ten.

"Are you ready?" At my nod, Lauren continued. "I'm going to ask you about each contestant, and when I'm done, I'll leave you alone with your thoughts. Just take a quiet stroll around the room. Pick up photos and look at them. Denise will have production play a snip of what you said about each person, so we need a little time between each photo you pick up. Does that make sense?"

My mouth was dry and my stomach unsettled. This was the part I hated, then and now. "It does."

"Let's have a seat, and I'll name each contestant, and you just tell me something good or bad about them." She leaned forward and whispered, "It's better if you say good things."

Lauren's subtle perfume was floral and sweet. As an olfactory person who had a business based on smells, I really enjoyed it. Cologne and perfume candles were making a comeback. And a lot of perfumers were inventing creative ways to get their scent out there in candles, car air fresheners, room sprays, and even oils. I would kill for a business opportunity like that.

"Savannah?"

Lauren's soft voice kicked me out of my daydream. "Yes?"

She pointed to the chair in front of her. "Would you like to sit down?"

I shook my head. "I'm sorry. I got lost in a thought." I sat and carefully crossed my ankles. Lauren's gaze dropped to my legs for a moment. A tiny burst of energy exploded inside me because she'd looked and wasn't even shy about it. We slowly went through each contestant until I said nice things about them all. She left when I picked up each frame and stared at each person for a few moments. I was done and out of the room in ten minutes, only to be accosted by Mandee, who primped me in record time.

"That was fast. Are you ready?" Lauren asked.

I took a deep breath and nodded. She handed me one of my own candles, and I almost wept for joy. "So, I'm supposed to say 'I feel a spark with you. Do you feel it, too?' and if they respond, I light their candle with my flame. Is that correct?"

"Yes. It's terrible, but production likes consistency throughout the seasons."

I looked at her. "It's awful."

"I completely agree."

"I still have to say it?"

"My hands are tied, but you can make it sound good. You're a natural in front of the camera. You won't make it sound cheesy."

She gave me a quick wink and left. I did exactly what they wanted, with some direction from Denise. By the time I was to meet everyone in the great hall, I was exhausted. Mandee took care of the shine and added body to my limp hair. It was almost eleven when I lit my candle and stood in front of the sparkettes. They were quiet.

"Welcome to the first official ceremony," Lauren said.

She was greeted with nervous smiles. Somebody dropped their candle, and we had to reset. Denise changed the arrangement of the contestants and adjusted them so the camera could capture their reactions better. I was getting tired of standing around.

Lauren softly touched my lower back, and I stiffened at the unexpected contact.

"Whenever you're ready, Savannah," Lauren said. She tapped my back with her finger and slid to the side of the room.

I took a deep breath and addressed the room. "I want to thank you all for taking time out of your lives to see if we can find a connection. I know it was a big sacrifice, and I appreciate it. I've been in your shoes, and I understand it's not easy." I called the first contestant forward. "Alix." They put their hand on their heart and approached. "I feel a spark with you. Do you feel it, too?"

They nodded and held their candle against mine. We had to be very still because camera person number four was focusing on the flame being lit. It was a hard task, given we were both incredibly nervous and shaking. The wicks were the perfect length to spark when lit, but then they settled immediately. I was so proud. "Light my fire," they whispered. I tried to stifle my giggle when they hugged me.

"So cheesy," I whispered and watched as they walked over to the designated area next to Lauren, where sparkettes were to stand after receiving a flame.

"Let's cut for a minute and get wardrobe and makeup in here," Denise announced.

That meant I was shiny and sweaty. I followed Mandee to a private room, where the temperature was at least ten degrees cooler. It felt wonderful in there.

"Have a seat. Let's take a look at you." She blotted my upper lip and my temples and applied more powder.

"That bad?"

She pursed her lips and shrugged. "Not really. The camera picks up everything. Plus, it's hot under the lights. We might have to do this after each contestant."

That's why Lauren had told me it could take up to four hours. I sighed. As predicted, we had to stop after every contestant was selected. When it got down to Frankie and Ava, I tried to look like I was struggling with the decision.

"This is your last flame for the night," Lauren said from her spot beside the sparkettes.

I felt the entire room hold their breath as they waited for me to decide. "This is a hard choice. I like you both for different reasons. I hope you know that I have to do this for me."

"Ava." Frankie hung her head but nodded at us. I focused on Ava. "Ava, I feel a spark with you. Do you feel it, too?" I sounded so ridiculous, but Lauren was right. What else could one say with a candle?

"Thank you, yes." She put her candle against mine until the wick sparked and a flame appeared on hers.

Lauren smiled at Ava after she stood on the mark with the other sparkettes who received flames. "Frankie, I'm sorry, but please say your good-byes."

I stood and anxiously waited for Frankie to work her way over to me. When she did, I reached for her hands and gave her fingers a supportive squeeze. "I hope you find somebody who can appreciate your humor and your charms."

"Good luck," she said and walked away with a chorus of "bye, Frankie," "talk soon," and "take care" trailing her out the door.

I didn't feel bad or sad about my decision. Frankie wasn't for me, but hopefully the right person would snatch her up. Kaisley handed me a glass of champagne, and we toasted with the others as the cameras swirled around us. I was so ready to be off my feet. When the glasses were empty, I excused myself for the evening and wearily crawled into the limo to take me back. Thankfully, no cameras were filming me. Nobody wanted to see me rub my sore feet or shake my hair loose.

It was after two in the morning. I decided to swim a few laps because I missed exercising, and I still hoped Lauren would drop by. With the crew having the day off, I honestly didn't know if anybody was in the house with me. I still closed the bedroom door to change. I pulled out a two-piece sports bikini to show that I was serious about staying in shape in case Lauren made it. If she didn't, this was still the best one to swim laps in and not lose either piece. I went out to the pool, and Lauren scared the shit out of me.

"I wasn't sure if we were still on or not," she said.

I was so worked up about the possibility of her being there, I wasn't prepared to actually see her. She was lying in a lounge chair staring up at the stars.

"I've been looking forward to it—um…to a good swim all day. Splashing around in a pool while stationary doesn't give me what I need." I cringed at how obviously excited I was to see her. "What did you think about tonight?" I sat on the lounge next to her and stared up at the night sky too.

"You did a good job. And Frankie was the best choice."

"It wasn't tough. She's nice, but we're just in different places. I'm too old to party, and I think she's a long way from retiring from it. She's not my forever person." I noticed Lauren had covered the cameras with paper cups again.

"This is the easy part. Before feelings get in the way," Lauren said.

Had anyone offered to talk to Katie on her journey? At the time, the host was Michael Coors, and he was as douchey as could be. I didn't think he was in television anymore. He was the epitome of cis white entitled men who sexualized women. He was never inappropriate with me, but several lawsuits followed him after the first two seasons of the show. His reputation took quite the hit, and I couldn't imagine anyone wanting to hire him again. Katie had to do this on her own, and I felt a tinge of something that could be empathy. But she was fully in charge of her shitty words, so the feeling passed quickly.

"You've been with the show for three seasons, right?"

Lauren turned to face me. "Yes. Why do you ask?" It was hard to see her in the dark, but the soft glow of a nearby solar light gave me just enough light to make out her features. She looked relaxed and beautiful.

I had a mini crush on Lauren. She was way out of my league, so the tiny fantasy of us was too far-fetched for me to believe in. I was a small-business owner who had never been to any red carpet event and drove a car that limped along. I wasn't a catch. I was just someone who had evoked sympathy when she was dumped in front of millions of viewers. Television was going to make me out to be somebody I wasn't. Jane had told me not to worry about it so much. She said I was worthy of anything good that came out of this show, even if it meant being single at the end of it. I would have enough money to keep my business alive, and more people would know I was available. That meant more app dating.

"Ugh."

"What?" Lauren asked.

"Sorry. I was just thinking about something. So, the last two flames, what were they like?"

"They were both really sweet. One was a captain of a cruise ship, and the other was a marketing director," she said.

"Did they both find love?" I asked.

"The captain did. The marketing director did at first, but she didn't find her forever person. I like how you said that. Forever person."

"I'm thirty-two, and I feel like if I don't find my forever person soon, I'm not going to have one. I'm not just saying that to make you feel sorry for me. I have a good life. I have a best friend, a house, and a business I love."

"Savannah, that's why you're here. To find your forever person. We have a good mix of personalities that are still compatible with yours. I know you have frontrunners, and that makes me happy. But as we both know, first impressions are important, yet they aren't everything." She stood and unbuttoned her shirt as I sat and watched her. "Are you going to join me?"

*You mean quit staring at you?* I jumped up and dropped my robe onto the lounge chair. "Yes. Let's get some laps in before sunrise. Words I never thought I'd say." She was wearing a full bathing suit with a sleeveless rash-guard shirt. "You know, I don't think you have to worry about the sun shining." I pointed to her shirt.

"It's my safety blanket," she said and dived into the water.

For somebody who didn't have a pool, she was extremely graceful in the water. I quickly slid in and gritted my teeth when the coolness hit my back. Lauren surfaced almost at the other end of the pool. "What are you? Part seal? Dolphin? Wait. Mermaid?"

Her hearty laughter echoed.

I swam over to her. "That's your secret, right? Single because you're a mermaid and you haven't been able to trust anybody with that information. I mean, I get it. People would want to keep you in a lab if the truth came out." Her smile warmed every part of me. It made me want to entertain her, but I didn't want to push.

"I swam in college."

"Now you tell me? After you've seen me nearly drown a few times? I'm the world's worst swimmer, just so you know."

"I promise to just do laps and not make it a race," she said.

"Did you swim all four years?"

"Yes."

"That explains the discipline around junk food," I said.

"Except doughnuts."

"The perfect food."

We swam quietly up and down the length of the pool several times until I couldn't feel my arms and had to surrender. We were slipping into the sweet spot right before dawn when the world was quiet. I'd never felt so alive.

"I'll come over later, if you want. I managed to get my hands on a copy of the movie you wanted to see," Lauren said.

"That would be great!" I sounded too excited about seeing her again, so I quickly added, "I miss television and movies."

She shook a finger at me. "Sorry, kitten. Only the movie."

My eyes widened at her term of endearment. So did hers.

"Obviously, I'm sleep deprived." She gathered her things quickly after slipping into her shorts. "I'll see you later."

She was gone before I had a chance to say good-bye.

## CHAPTER FIFTEEN

I slept for eight hours and woke up only because I was hungry. We didn't set a time for Lauren to come over, so I ran a bath and grabbed half a bagel and a small bottle of orange juice from downstairs. I ravenously ate the bagel as I waited for the Jacuzzi tub to fill.

I was warned not to put bubbles in it because the jets would multiply them and send them all over the room, but I could add a few drops of oil. I settled on a de-stress muscle bath and shower oil that included a blend of rosemary, black pepper, lavender, and ginger. The water was hot, but the room was cool, so I snuggled down and leaned my head back. I could get used to this pampered lifestyle.

I turned the jets on medium and let the water blast over my shoulders. Who the hell did I think I was, swimming a zillion laps with a professional swimmer? Okay, maybe not professional, but a really good one. I was sore everywhere. I moved so I was facing the door and the jets were on my lower back. My stomach jumped and my clit twitched when I remembered the hot tub by the pool and my incredibly fast and hard orgasm. This time I could control it, and I wasn't in a hurry. I had the whole day.

I folded my arms over the side of the tub and rested my chin where they crossed. I slowed the jets with the remote and carefully ran my pussy across the forced water. Gasping with pleasure, I moved away. I wanted to take my time. The remote had a pulse button, and I almost wept with joy at how perfect it was. I slowly moved my hips up and down and let the water roll over my slit, careful to avoid my clit for now. This felt too good to have a rushed orgasm. I pushed against the jets, then pulled back. I did that several times until I allowed myself to start the climb. I moaned softly as the force of water licked my entire pussy fast and hard. I wasn't going to last. I didn't have to be quiet. Nobody was here.

Another moan and I gripped the sides of the tub harder. The fact that I was naked and didn't have bikini bottoms that covered me like last time was decadent. Never mind the pool I was thinking of getting. My big purchase was going to be a bathroom remodel for a Jacuzzi tub. I closed my eyes, surprised that Lauren's image floated into my mind. Not from this morning, but from the candle ceremony when she was wearing a red dress. She had a nice body but was very conservative with what she wore. Thankfully, my imagination was incredible. I bit my bottom lip and pushed out a guttural groan that turned into a shout as I came. My chest heaved up and down as I gulped in air. When I opened my eyes and saw Lauren standing in doorway, I froze.

Panic spread across her features. "Oh, my God. I'm so sorry." She turned and left.

"Wait." My voice was a whisper. What was I thinking? I didn't want her to wait. I wanted her to put as much space between us as she could. Fuck. I jumped out of the tub and dried off quickly. I threw on a pair of yoga pants and a sweatshirt. Makeup wasn't an option. My face was too red from embarrassment.

I jogged down the stairs and stopped when I saw the back of her head. She was sitting on the sofa that faced the ocean. What the fuck was I going to say? What do you say to somebody who caught you masturbating? I didn't even masturbate in front of my ex-girlfriends. I quietly padded over to where she was sitting and sat down next to her, leaving plenty of space between us.

"So…" I really couldn't think of anything else to say. "So, that happened," I said.

She looked at me and burst out laughing. I joined in after covering my face with my hands. "I'm so embarrassed." I felt her fingers on my hands.

"Don't apologize. That'll teach me to barge in unannounced. You'd think I would have learned after last time."

"Ugh. I'm still embarrassed."

She squeezed my hands. "It's normal. We all do it. It's a great stress reliever, and you've been under a lot of stress."

She didn't let go, and I didn't pull my hands back. Technically, I'd just masturbated in front of her, and now we were holding hands. "It's been pretty hard. Also, I don't have a Jacuzzi tub at home."

"I truly feel bad for interrupting."

"At least I finished." We fell into fits of laughter again. Other than die of embarrassment, my other options were to pack up and leave, not a viable option, or never see Lauren again, also not a viable option.

"In other news, are you hungry? I brought pizza and Chinese food. They don't go together, but I wasn't sure what you were in the mood for, so I ordered both."

I wasn't about to tell her I'd just eaten half a bagel because I was still hungry. "Chinese sounds perfect."

"I'll fix us plates. Stay here and...well, rest."

We laughed again. If this had happened at home and Jane walked in, we would forever laugh about it. I wouldn't have been this mortified, but I wasn't attracted to Jane. I was attracted to Lauren, and I'd just masturbated to a vision of her in last night's evening gown. She was never going to know that part. We would leave it as a stress reliever and hopefully never talk about it again.

"I got fried rice, Kung Pao, egg rolls, and crab Rangoon."

Lauren raised her voice so I could hear the menu from the kitchen. I almost playfully told her I loved her for bringing greasy food over, but after what just happened, I decided against it. "That sounds delish." I had to give it to her. Lauren acted completely normal around me. Maybe that was her professional training, but she didn't make me feel uncomfortable at all.

"Anything crazy going on in the world that I should know about?" I asked when she handed me a plate piled high with takeout.

"Are you asking if you can see my phone? The answer is no. And also, no. Locally, I mean. The usual catastrophic events are happening worldwide, like climate change. But as far as here? Some local crime, a few cars were stolen, and it's going to rain every day this week," she said.

"It always rains here. That's not news."

"That's all you get."

"What was it like reporting on the other stuff?" I bit into an egg roll and dribbled cabbage and carrots down my chin before catching them in my napkin.

Lauren looked poised as she ate her fried rice and answered my question after she swallowed her food.

"It was a very difficult job. Rewarding, but difficult. Reporting tough news is hard on the heart, and I didn't want to lose who I was as a person, so I resigned. I don't care that people think I sold out by doing *When Sparks Fly*," she said.

"Was this what you had in mind when you quit CNN?"

"Not really. I couldn't find a news station locally or nationwide that suited my needs, so I wallowed in self-pity for a few months. When I was done, I decided to try a television show and approached this one with a new plan."

"Obviously you've done great things, but how do you feel about where you are? Did you go to school for journalism?"

"I did. I've always wanted to bring the truth to people. I think everyone starts out that way. But networks don't necessarily want you to tell the truth. They want you to report a sensationalized version of it, and I refused to. I made a choice." She'd eaten half of what was on her plate and set the rest on the coffee table in front of us. "My story is boring. It really is. I work too hard. I don't make enough time for me. Maybe after this shortened season, I'll take a vacation somewhere. Get away from everything and everyone."

"This place would be ideal if it wasn't part of the set. You have everything you need. The ocean, a lap pool with a hot tub. A huge kitchen if you like to cook. And privacy. You must hate the lack of privacy," I said. I remember how reporters swarmed my apartment and my mother's house. Eventually, it died down, but privacy wasn't a thing for months.

"How about we stop talking about our lives, because it's bringing me down, and watch the movie instead?"

I excused myself for a quick moment and raced upstairs to brush my teeth and freshen up. I couldn't do anything about my hair, so I left it down. I brushed mascara across my lashes and put on socks. It's not a date, I repeated to myself.

"Can we watch the movie upstairs in your room? I can't relax knowing how many cameras are in here," she said.

I nodded. "Sure. Let me grab a few sodas. What do you want to drink?"

"Sparkling water would be great."

"Do you want me to pop some popcorn?"

Lauren held her stomach and shook her head. "Not after everything I just ate. I'm already slightly miserable from being so full."

Even after a bagel and a plate of Chinese food, I was down for popcorn, but I followed her upstairs instead. We could worry about snacks later. "Do you want to sit on the couch or lie on the bed?" She kicked off her loafers and crawled onto the bed.

"I'm sorry it's not made."

She waved me off. "Don't worry about it."

I piled pillows behind us and let her connect her iPad to the TV. It was a smart TV, but all access was cut off for me. She typed in something I couldn't see.

I gasped. "You know the Wi-Fi password?"

She laughed at my antics. "Don't get any wild ideas."

"I guess this is better than watching on the iPad."

"I don't know about the quality of it. Mirroring tends to lose quality."

I looked at her. "Is this a pirated copy?"

"No. It's an advanced-screening copy. This was a favor from one of the producers."

"You're an impressive woman, Lauren Lucas. And you must have a lot of contacts in the business. Thank you for humoring me. Now hit play," I said.

"Yes, ma'am."

Being this close to Lauren made it super hard to focus on the story. She was in my bed, fully clothed, and smelled like fresh linen and vanilla. I couldn't imagine this behavior was appropriate, but I wasn't going to question it. Her body was warm next to mine, and I could hear her soft breathing when the movie got quiet in parts. What was the film about? Something about a girl fighting against all odds. I laughed when she did because it was expected. I was hyper-aware of her closeness and closed my eyes for a moment because I was overwhelmed. What was happening? Her shoulder bumped mine.

"Hey. Stay awake."

I didn't turn my head because I would have kissed her. One major mistake a day. "I'm awake. I just had to close my eyes. Sometimes I forget to blink, and it dries my contacts out."

"I didn't know you wore contacts. Look at me," she said.

The very thing I didn't want to do. I turned and gazed immediately at her lips. "You don't wear any."

"How do you know? You aren't looking at my eyes." Her voice was low and husky.

When I finally looked at her, I saw unguarded emotions swirl and darken the blue. "Nope. No contacts." I cleared my throat and looked back at the TV.

The pounding I heard in my ears was coming from inside me as my pulse quickened. She wasn't looking at me like I was a friend. At that moment, I realized things were different between us. I wanted to create space, but the need to be next to her won. I didn't move. I watched the movie but couldn't focus because all I could think about was how close Lauren was to me and how wonderful she smelled and how warm her body was next to mine. Every time our arms brushed because we moved to reach for our drinks or get situated, the jolt of her skin against mine was almost unbearable. When the movie finally ended, I almost wept with relief and disappointment.

"What did you think?" Lauren disconnected and closed the cover to her iPad. She climbed off the bed.

*You mean the movie I barely remember*? "It was great. Thank you so much for sneaking it over. I know it was a risk." I slid off the bed. "Do you feel like taking a walk or something?"

She hesitated when she dropped her iPad into her bag. "Well, we can't be seen together, or people will know who you are."

"I thought the commercials had already dropped so the secret was out?" When I realized maybe she needed space, too, I balked. "Sorry. I know your job isn't to entertain me. Josef with an 'ef' should be here in about an hour to cook something healthy, so I can chat with him. I can still go for a walk on the beach, right? I know. Just not far, wear a floppy hat and sunglasses, and don't talk to strangers."

"If somebody approaches you about the show, you'll have to say 'no comment' or 'I can't discuss it.' A lot of shady reporters pretend to live here so they can build trust. Just be careful," she said.

She slipped on her shoes and slung her bag over her shoulder. My heart dropped when I realized she was leaving. "Ten-four, boss. I'll be quiet and keep my head down." Hopefully, my voice didn't sound shaky. I followed her down the stairs and opened the door. "Have a nice afternoon off." She stopped before she crossed the threshold and gave me a hug. It was over before I had the chance to put my arms around her and hug her back. "Thanks for lunch and the movie. Bye."

I watched her drive away. What had just happened? Did she feel the energy between us? Or was it one-sided, and after catching me in the Jacuzzi tub, was she afraid I was going to hit on her? We seemed to have moved past it. But why did she bolt? The movie had barely ended before she shut her iPad off and bounced off the bed. We had probably been too intimate. We should have stayed downstairs and watched it on the couch. Or just talked. I was so frustrated and confused. Note to self. *Lock the fucking doors when I feel the need to touch myself again.*

## CHAPTER SIXTEEN

K aisley, I still feel a flame with you. Do you feel it, too?" I fucking hated that phrase but smiled patiently as I started the elimination process again. I picked Kaisley first because we had the best one-on-one time today during the model painting experience. Only one artist's painting remotely resembled the nude model. Alix winning didn't surprise anybody. It was almost too easy for them.

It was a fun afternoon with zero alcohol and quiet enough to have a good group discussion about love and funny stories about life. I whittled down the list until Charlotte and Ava were the only ones standing in front of me. It was still easy to say good-bye. My top four, Alix, Kaisley, Ophelia, and Lyanna were solid. I wasn't as close with the bottom three, which was just as much my fault as theirs. First impressions were clouded by reality, and true colors were starting to show. They weren't bad; they just weren't for me.

"Ava and Charlotte. This is the last flame of the night. Good luck." Lauren made eye contact with me, and her smile grounded me after she had barely spoken to me on set today. It gave me a little boost. I hid my own smile. This was a serious moment.

I didn't think either Ava or Charlotte was super into me. To date, I had kissed only Ophelia and Alix. Kaisley and I'd had a long hug earlier today, and I thought she was going to kiss me, but she pulled away and blushed.

"Ladies, thank you so much for all the experiences we've had so far on this journey together. You're both incredible. We've had so much fun today, so it's hard." I paused for dramatic effect. "Charlotte." I waited until she stood in front of me. "I still feel a spark with you. Do you feel it, too?"

She nodded happily. "I do. Thank you."

She one-arm hugged me and stood with the others. Lauren stepped forward. "Ava, I'm sorry, but please say your good-byes."

I waited for Ava to make her way to me. "Thank you so much for everything. I wish you the best luck at finding somebody," I said.

She hugged me hard and left the room. I saw one of the producers issue her into a room for her exit interview. It looked like she was wiping away tears, but I wasn't one hundred percent. Sadness pinged me because, even though I didn't feel a connection, it didn't mean that she didn't. That's why I hated this process.

"How are you holding up?" Lauren asked.

I was standing in the doorway away from the celebratory contestants, who held glasses of champagne and were in a large group talking. "I'm okay. I guess the deeper we get, the more people are going to get hurt. I don't want to cause anyone pain, and honestly, I'm surprised at Ava's reaction."

"I know it's hard for you, and it's only going to get harder. Why don't you head over to the group so we can finish filming and call it a night?" she asked.

She was so sincere, and I was so tired and drained that I wanted to lean into her and just breathe. I wanted to feel her strength and have her arms around me again. "That sounds perfect." Mandee quickly powdered my face so it wasn't shiny for the cameras and straightened the straps of my evening dress. Tonight I was wearing a sapphire-blue, full-length dress with spaghetti straps and no bra. Mandee used pasties to cover my nipples in case they decided to make an appearance. I did my obligatory cheering with the remaining six and spent an additional half hour talking to Denise about the day and where I was emotionally in the process.

"I have to focus on what's best for me and who's best for me. When you meet somebody and start dating, their best foot is always forward. I want to get down to the nitty-gritty with the remaining contestants and see what they're like when their walls are down. I want to know who they are when they're just being their genuine self."

"Do you think you'll find that with somebody in the other room?" Denise asked.

The rule was to repeat the question and answer it so that Denise's voice, or whoever was handling the camera at the time, wouldn't be heard. "Do I think I'll find that with somebody here? I think I will. I have very high hopes."

❖

Lauren knocked this time, which was weird yet completely understandable. "I thought today went well. You seemed to be enjoying yourself."

"It was fun. We probably should have had Alix paint with their other hand to make it an even playing field, but at least everyone tried. Come on in." I stepped aside so Lauren could enter. She was wearing board shorts and another sleeveless rash guard. I guess the laps were still on. I had planned to swim even if she hadn't shown up.

"At least nobody fell into a fit of giggles at seeing the model."

"Oh, for sure, Frankie would have. And it would have snowballed from there," I said. I stopped and smiled at her. "Thanks for coming. I wasn't sure if you were, since it's so late."

"We had a deal. Doughnuts on candle night."

"Wait. You have doughnuts? Where are they?" I playfully held her arms out and gave her a look-over to see where she was hiding them.

She laughed and pulled away from me. "They're in the car. For after our laps."

I groaned and sighed. "You're right. Two laps for every doughnut." I headed out the sliding door to the pool area.

"Two laps for every bite of every doughnut."

She kicked her shoes off and threw her hair back in a ponytail.

I looked at her in disbelief. "You're about to see me eat a doughnut in two bites. Six laps, here I come." I quickly removed my shirt and shorts and dove into the water. She was beside me in a matter of seconds.

"Let's shoot for ten laps. That shouldn't take too long," she said.

"Says the Olympian," I said.

"The Olympics would have been nice, but I wasn't that good. Come on. The sooner we swim, the sooner we eat."

We swam in silence until we finished all ten laps. It felt good to stretch my body in the water. I wasn't a great swimmer and wondered if I flailed as badly as I thought.

"I hope you're not judging my form," I said. We were leaning back against the edge of the pool resting. Lauren didn't look winded at all. I felt the burn all over.

Lauren smiled. "Your form is fine. Are you open to tips?"

"Yes, of course."

"Breathe in through your mouth when your head is to the side and breathe out through your nose when your head is in the water. Eventually you'll find a rhythm, and you won't be so breathless at the end of a lap."

"To be fair, this is a pretty good-size pool. It's not something you'd find in the backyards of Scottsdale, Arizona."

"This is a beautiful pool. I love that you want to take advantage of it and invited me, too. I really appreciate your generosity," she said.

"If it wasn't for you, I wouldn't be here, so thank you. And you're welcome anytime. I've learned to lock doors."

"And I've learned to not barge through them."

She was smiling so I knew she wasn't appalled or upset by seeing me masturbate. Secretly, I wanted to know how much she saw and if it turned her on. I'd touched myself this morning and thought about her the entire time. I didn't know if the lust in her eyes was from that moment or because I fantasized that was her reaction. Either way, I came hard and fast.

"Are you ready for a doughnut? We can sit out here and wait until it gets light out."

"That sounds nice. Coffee? I think I can figure out the machine. I can make it while you get the doughnuts."

"Coffee and doughnuts sound like the perfect start to this day," she said.

The machine proved to be too much for me, and I couldn't find the manual in any of the drawers. Ordinarily, I'd YouTube instructions, but I didn't have a phone or the internet. I was at Lauren's mercy. What was taking her so long? As if we were recording, she popped into the kitchen on cue, wearing dry clothes and carrying a pink box with a white ribbon.

"It beat me." I leaned against the counter looking as pathetic as I possibly could.

"You're in luck. Because of my coffee obsession, addiction, whatever you want to call it, I've got this. I've used this machine many times." She added the grounds to the machine, flipped the "on" switch located on the back, and hit a combination of buttons that I wouldn't remember tomorrow. After a hiss and a gurgle, coffee started dripping into the pot. Lauren turned, and I put my hand up. She slightly smacked hers against mine in an awkward high five.

"How do you take your coffee?" I asked.

"There's only one way when eating doughnuts. Black," she said.

I looked at her in disgust. "What? It's way too bitter for that."

She shook her head. "There's way too much sugar in the doughnuts to drink something sweet, too. Black coffee or unsweetened almond milk."

"I need cream to cut the bitterness. We'll have to agree to disagree." I opened the box and inhaled the sweet scent that made my mouth water. "Also, thank you for bringing them. I'm eating two." I grabbed a cinnamon twist and a glazed and put them on a napkin while I waited for the coffee. "What time do we have to report for duty?"

Several crew members were milling about. I knew I would be interviewed today about last night's elimination. They would get camera angles of me saying very generic yet heartfelt things about my emotions or what I was looking for in a partner. It was hard to keep myself entertained during the in-between times when the crew was busy doing its thing. Since my skin was sensitive, and Mandee and Buzzy hated tan lines, I couldn't go poolside. I had started a paper-and-pen journal on day one, but that had fizzled after the first two weeks. My journey was important, so I vowed to write more today. I wished it was digital so my thoughts weren't just laying around in a book that could be picked up and read by anyone walking by. At least I had passwords on a laptop or iPad.

"Closer to sunset so the lighting is softer and more romantic."

"I can't tell you how boring my life is here. But at least I have doughnuts."

"I'm sorry you're bored. Can I do anything to help?"

I brushed crumbs off my cheek and swallowed before answering. "I could use some books. The contestants at least have one another to talk to and can play games and go in the pool. As beautiful as this place is, without a book, a phone, or cable, I can't really enjoy the sunroom or the big fluffy chairs by the window or the patio furniture outside. I'm alone with my thoughts, and then I question every decision in my life. I need something to get my mind off things. I need to decompress." During my first season, the only book in the entire apartment was the Bible.

Lauren nodded. "Totally understandable. There's no reason you can't have a stack of books. What's your favorite genre?"

I hadn't read a book in forever, but with my downtime between shoots and dates and interviews, I could get caught up on a series. I smiled as I conjured up a list of books from the last three years I was dying to read. "Any lesfic or lesbian romance or, oh, Dolly Parton's book, no political books, but anything else on the *New York Times'* bestseller list." I grabbed her hands. "Anything is fine. Janet Evanovich, Gillian Flynn, Stephen King, James Patterson—even though everybody hates him personally. Anything. I'm kind of losing my mind here all by myself, even though I'm not by myself." I heard the desperation. "See? I'm losing it."

"I get it, and I'll see what I can do."

The determined look in her eyes gave me hope. "What did the other flames do when they weren't on camera? I can't be the only bored one."

"The last flame was poolside most of the time. And drank a lot. You are definitely low maintenance. Josef with an 'ef' isn't used to cooking whatever he wants. Most of the flames have taken full advantage of this place and the amenities."

"I guess I forgot I could put in requests. I usually just stay out of the way and come running when he rings the bell. I should be eating healthy anyway." I swallowed the irony with a bite of the tasty cinnamon twist.

"Listen, I have to run, but have a good day, and I'll see if I can't get you some reading material for boring days," she said.

I frowned because she was leaving already, but she had a job to do. "That would be wonderful, because I look forward to our visits way too much." I froze at my confession. We were just getting over our last awkward moment. The last thing we needed was another one.

She quickly masked her surprise at my words. "I know it's hard having only me as a friend during this time. Stay hydrated, and be careful if you go out on the beach."

"I will. Thanks for the doughnuts."

I grabbed the box and knocked on the video-village door, where the crew members were all smiles at receiving the leftover sugary treats. Lauren had given me the okay to get out from behind these walls. I covered myself in 50 SPF before slipping into shorts and a full-length UV sun shirt to protect my arms and chest from burning. I braided my hair and tucked it up under a wide-brim hat. After putting on sunglasses, I didn't even recognize myself when I looked in the mirror. It was quite the transformation. I looked like I did back home, not the sexy, high-femme bachelorette that was on television.

Why didn't I live near a beach? I stared out at the ocean and smiled as diamond sunbursts reflected off the water. The water felt refreshing on my feet and calves, and I smiled again when small rocks and shells rolled over my toes as the waves pushed their way ashore. This was a beautiful place. Never in a million years could I afford to live here. It was private, quiet, and great for my anxiety.

I walked for about twenty minutes without seeing a single person. I pocketed a few pretty shells and pieces of sea glass and sat in the soft sand for a break. I heard shouts and laughter off in the distance that I assumed came from the contestants. Their mansion wasn't too far away. Maybe I could sneak over and not be seen. I was virtually unrecognizable. I got up from my quick break and headed that way. I needed shade and something cold to drink.

I smiled when I heard they were playing chicken in the pool. Getting up to them proved to be quite the challenge. On a whim, I pulled on the gate and smiled again when I found it unlocked. Whoever forgot to secure the latch was going to get into trouble. Or maybe the show saw me coming and unlocked it for my impromptu visit. I was torn between playing lost beach wanderer or tearing off my hat and obnoxiously large sunglasses and revealing myself immediately. Sneaking sounded like more fun, so I slipped into the garden and slowly made my way to the gazebo. Kaisley lay on a lounge chair and sat up in alarm when she saw me. I put my forefinger up to my lips and removed my sunglasses. Her smile lifted my heart, and she softly patted the seat beside her. She held up her hand to stop me when people were close. When the coast was clear, she flagged me over, and I sat on a small table beside the chair, where others would have a hard time seeing me.

"What are you doing here?" she whispered softly and touched my face.

It was the first time I'd wanted to make the first move and kiss somebody on the show. "I went for a walk and followed the laughter. My place is surprisingly close."

"I'm going to sneak you inside." She looked around for our escape route. "If you're okay with it."

I nodded, knowing full well that even though the crew wasn't around filming now, every single camera in the house would easily pick us up.

"Okay. Wait here. I'm going to the side patio door, and I'll wave you over when it's safe. I need to find Lyanna. She's the only one not out here with us."

I couldn't help but smile as I hid behind the chair. I was pretty sure this was okay behavior, something Denise would definitely love and hate. She would be pissed that she'd missed it but delighted that she had footage of me skulking around the mansion. Maybe. We'd find out soon enough. After three very long minutes, Kaisley appeared at the door and waved me over after she ensured nobody was paying her any attention.

"Lyanna is asleep. We can hang out in the study. It's private and away from the noise," she said.

She grabbed my hand and pulled me inside. Surely somebody saw us, but nobody jumped out at us with a camera on their shoulder. We were in the clear. "Do you want something to eat or drink? You feel hot."

"I would love something cold and nonalcoholic, please." I slipped off my hat and sunglasses and sat on the leather couch. This felt like a university president's study, with oversized leather couches, high wingback chairs, and a mahogany bar built into the credenza behind the desk loaded with more brandy and whiskey than I'd seen at several bars. I assumed the bookcases housed tons of books but were placed elsewhere when the show took over. This arrangement forced people to communicate. Kaisley was back and quickly closed the door with a giggle.

"You look so lovely without makeup."

Cue the embarrassment. At least I knew the cameras wouldn't be able to catch me in super high-definition. "Thank you. That shows you I wasn't expecting to come here. I literally was going for a walk and made my way."

She locked her fingers with mine. "Is this okay?"

I nodded. Her emotions at seeing me felt so genuine that it was hard not to believe her excitement.

"I'm sorry last night was hard."

It wasn't, but I nodded. "It's getting harder."

"I'm glad you kept me."

"I'm glad, too."

To kiss her seemed completely natural, so I did. Her lips were full, and she tasted like sugar and lemons. My stomach dropped for a second when her tongue softly brushed against mine. It was a nice first kiss that was organic and without an audience. She slid her hands up my arms and locked her fingers behind my neck. This wasn't just a kiss. She planned to make out with me. Everything about the situation was exciting. Kaisley was beautiful, fun, and totally into me. She had sneaked me in so she could have alone time without the others knowing and without cameras three feet from our faces.

"I'm having such a great time with you, and I can't wait until it's our date night. I have the best date planned," she said.

Her lips were back on mine before I had a chance to respond. Tomorrow night was the start of date week. I had six sparkettes left, and by the end of the week, another casualty would pack her bags and head home. As a group, we would have lunch together every day, and then, the date of the day and I would head out for several hours of uninterrupted time. She got to plan the date with unlimited funds. Or at least within reason.

When Kaisley deepened the kiss and straddled me, I panicked. She didn't strike me as an aggressor, and while it was a bold move, I wasn't offended, but I was concerned that another contestant would find us in this intimate position.

"We can't do this here. I'm sorry," I said. She frowned but nodded and crawled off my lap.

"I understand. I didn't mean to make you uncomfortable. Sneaking you in here is just so decadent, and I couldn't help myself," she said.

"I appreciate your enthusiasm." I touched my lips. They still tingled from hers. "But we should probably keep it chill in case somebody finds us." Guilt washed over me when I thought about how the other contestants might feel at us hiding behind closed doors. "Actually, why don't I sneak in and surprise everyone at the pool?"

She squeezed my hand. "Okay, but thank you for giving me a few private moments."

I brushed a soft kiss over her lips. "Thank you." She quietly opened the heavy mahogany door and waved me over.

"The coast is clear."

I tiptoed to the kitchen and grabbed an apple before opening the sliding door, then walked out to the pool.

"Oh, my gosh! You're here," Alix said. They playfully splashed their hand on the water and left the water game they were in the middle of to jump out of the pool and pull me into a hug. I didn't even mind that they were getting me wet. "What are you doing here? Was there something on the schedule?" They looked around. "Did we know about this?"

I laughed. "No. I went for a walk on the beach and ended up here. By the way, I could hear your pool party from four houses down." I sat under the umbrella and waited as everyone climbed out of the water. I didn't even care that I didn't have any makeup on or that my hair wasn't perfect. The smiling faces of everyone surrounding me confirmed that I'd made the right decision. Who cared if I got into trouble?

"You sneaked out?" Lyanna high-fived me. The squeals from the contestants must have woken her up.

"I don't have anything to do there. I'm bored. All alone in a huge house and nobody to talk to. Even though this is a day off for everyone, I thought it might be fun to hang out and not worry about cameras." I was winging it.

"Do you have a suit on underneath?" Alix gave my sun shirt a soft tug.

"No, but I can sit on the side and dip my feet in. What game did I interrupt?"

Charlotte, who was sharing a chair with Kaisley, waved me off. "We were practicing our synchronized Olympic swimming."

"Oh, so we have Olympians here, huh?"

"Look, we're just as bored here as you are there. We have board and card games, if you want to go inside and get out of the sun," Lyanna said.

It felt so good to just be myself. Because the cameras weren't rolling, everyone was casual about their attitude and their appearance. This was a great way to see how people were going to be when and if it was just the two of us later down the road. Alix's personality was large and confident. They were wearing a swim tank and a pair of mid-thigh shorts. While they had an athletic body, the look was laid-back. Lyanna and Ophelia were the only ones who appeared camera-ready. Was it a good idea to hang out here? Probably not. Was I going to leave and go back to an empty house? Probably not.

"Do you have Trivial Pursuit? Let's play a game." I mean, what was the worst thing that could happen?

## CHAPTER SEVENTEEN

W hat the hell were you thinking, Savannah?" Denise stood in front of me with her arms crossed. Her thin, bony fingers squeezed her biceps.

"I'm sorry, but I don't see what the problem is. I just went for a walk and spent a few hours with the contestants. It was a lot of fun, and I think we got to know one another a lot better without all the cameras there." I didn't like being scolded. I was an adult, and nowhere in the contract did it say I couldn't fraternize with the contestants on our black-out days. I'd checked. Sure, I hadn't checked until after I'd done it, but I still checked.

"We have to rely on our house cameras for your visit."

I threw my hands up and stood. "It wasn't planned. That's the whole idea."

"We missed some pretty important moments yesterday."

I refused to feel bad about my decision. "And we have plenty more 'important moments' to come." I felt bitchy, but I didn't like her coming at me.

She sighed and turned away. "We're trying to show all the important connections on *When Sparks Fly*, and you had one yesterday. That's the whole premise of the show."

"This very thing has happened on other reality shows. Besides, you still have footage. And to be truthful, it's more realistic on hidden cameras than on cameras two feet from our faces."

Denise's shoulders slumped. "Can we just put it on the record now that we don't want you to do it again? Please."

"Fine." I shrugged. I wasn't going to apologize for having fun. I got that they didn't want us on social media or watching television shows that might discuss us, like *Entertainment Tonight* or *Access Hollywood*, but there wasn't anything wrong with a collection of movies on an iPad without access to the internet. "I don't know how the other flames did it, but on the days when we aren't filming or we have gaping hours of time between filming, I don't have anything to do. I didn't sign up for the show *Alone*. I signed up for *When Sparks Fly*. I need something. Let me make candles, or give me some movies or a stack of books to read." I clenched my teeth to keep them from chattering. I'd been at the mansion for six weeks, and without Lauren's recent visits, I would have cried myself to sleep every night. I was desperate for any kind of entertainment.

"Lauren mentioned you wanted books. I will make sure that by the end of the day you have that and some movies. I don't know what goes into candle making, and we don't want you to burn yourself, but I can agree to books and movies," Denise said.

Mandee knocked and entered after Denise barked. "I'm sorry for interrupting, but I need Savannah. Ellie Stevens from *Reality Bits* will be here in two hours, and I need time to get her ready."

"We're done here. She's yours." Denise dismissed me and stormed out of the room.

Lauren slipped in behind Mandee. I was fuming and turned to Lauren. The tender look she gave me was guarded but there. My anger evaporated. "I hope I didn't get you into trouble."

Lauren gave me a sad smile. "I'm sorry it's been so hard for you. I should have asked you sooner if you needed anything."

"Look, I know I'm interrupting, but I really need the time with Savannah." Mandee shifted her weight from one foot to the other as she waited for somebody to answer her.

"We'll both go. I want to tell you what to expect with Ellie."

We followed Mandee to the vanity in my bedroom. Buzzy had picked out a cream pantsuit with gold trim that looked better on me than the hanger. Mandee did her magic while Lauren asked me possible questions that Ellie might come up with.

"What do you hope to gain from this show?"

"That's too basic. Love, a relationship, a partnership."

"Partnership? That sounds like a business plan," Lauren said and crinkled her nose.

"You're right. That's a horrible answer. How about I hope to find the person who makes me laugh and gives me butterflies and makes me believe in things I've forgotten about, like love and tenderness and compassion," I said. Lauren stared at me. "What?"

"That's a beautiful answer. You don't need me to help you with this." She tossed the list of questions onto the desk near the chair she was sitting in.

"I do. You're my rock here. Without you, I would have lost my mind weeks ago," I said. Lauren really was the glue that held me together.

"You're doing great. The world is over-the-moon excited that you are the flame. We are getting so much fan mail. You're even more popular than you were before, and for all the right reasons," she said.

"Quit smiling," Mandee said. She was working on my lipstick and had to fix a smudge because I'd moved.

"Okay. I'll keep talking," Lauren said. "We're in the top ten for Wednesday night shows. Granted, it is the summer, but a lot of people are tuning in to see you find somebody."

"Oh, that is good," Mandee said.

I hated that I couldn't talk yet. I wanted more information. Six shows had already been recorded, and two had aired, so to be in the top ten was monumental. Denise had warned me that it would be a fast season. We were down to six people, and honestly, I already knew who my top four were—Alix, Kaisley, Ophelia, and Lyanna. I'd already decided they were going to Mexico with me. Charlotte and Emma were the bottom two. Unless a miracle happened, they would leave in the next week and a half.

Mandee sprayed my hair and put a final matte finish on my face to keep my makeup from smearing or sweating off since I would be in an interview and at the mercy of *Reality Bits*'s camera crew.

"Okay, you can have her," Mandee said to Lauren.

"You look stunning. I was hesitant about the outfit, but Buzzy was spot-on again. Ellie is setting up downstairs. She wants to do a walking interview, so make sure you're comfortable in those shoes."

The three-inch heels were a bit much. Mandee pulled out a pair of shorter heels that worked with the outfit, and I quickly made the switch. I followed Lauren down the stairs and was greeted warmly by Ellie. She grabbed both of my hands and squeezed them.

"I'm so excited to meet you, Savannah, and see how your journey ends."

I liked Ellie's show because she seemed to enjoy the reality-television world and watched everything. She always found the good and exciting and revealed shitty things only if the shows were over-the-top fake. She seemed genuine and didn't give a fuck about what people said about her. She gave curvy women an unapologetic voice. I liked her immediately. "Thank you for talking to me today. I enjoy your show. Too bad I don't have a television, or I'd watch it now."

She shook her head. "They still aren't letting you watch TV? How do you stay sane in this large place all by yourself?"

"It's really tough. I begged for books, so they're at least going to humor me."

"Let's take a walk and get away from everyone who's trying to listen to what we say."

Her boom operator carefully pinned a cordless microphone on the strap of my shell and did a quick check, followed by a thumbs-up. "Do you want a tour of the place?" I asked.

"That would be great. We'll start at the front door. I'll knock, and you'll open and let us in," she said.

I couldn't tell if I was excited because somebody was here visiting, or that it was Ellie because I admired her so much. Probably both. Two camera techs were in the house behind me, and several were outside, but far enough away to not be in the shot. I waited for the knock on the door. "Ellie Stevens. What a nice surprise. Come in." I stepped back and let her enter the mansion.

"This is such a beautiful house."

"Would you like a tour?" I asked.

She looked at the camera and smirked. "That's why I'm here. America wants to know how the new flame of *When Sparks Fly* is doing. I'd say, by the look of this place, pretty well."

"At least for the next few months." I wasn't sure when Ellie planned to air this segment, but she was quick, and I assumed it would be on this week's episode. I bypassed the video village, saying it was the production room, and moved her and the crew to the massive kitchen. We walked side by side outside to the pool area and the gardens, where a pop-up interview spot appeared. Their makeup professionals gave us a quick brush-over before we sat.

"How has this journey been so far? Do you think you'll find your perfect match?"

"Being on this side of things is an entirely different experience."

"What makes it so different?" she asked.

"This time, I'm sending people home, and that's hard and only getting more difficult."

"We've seen the first episode already, and the trailer for the second looks like a whopper. What can you tell me about the upcoming episode?"

I shrugged. "I don't know what to tell you because I don't get to see the episodes. Although this shortened season starts with a bang."

She squeezed my forearm with excitement. "It's what we love," she said.

"I can't give anything away, but if you intend to watch a reality show this summer, *When Sparks Fly* is the one."

Ellie rubbed her hands together with gossipy excitement. "Some people out there don't know this is your second time on the show. Can you tell us all about your first time on *When Sparks Fly*?"

"I was a sparkette during the first season. The show was so new, and it didn't go well for me."

"So, being the flame is a lot better than being a sparkette?" she asked.

"Were you the one who coined the phrase sparkette?" I asked. I couldn't remember how long Ellie had been in the reality-show world.

"I'm going to take the credit, although when the first season was on, I was on a radio talk show, before podcasts were the rage, with three other personalities. I'm not sure who said it first, but we were all thinking of it."

"And to answer your question, I don't know that it's better. I have so much pressure and responsibility on this side. What if I get rid of the wrong person? Maybe they were having an off day or were just nervous in front of the cameras? It's not easy having a camera in my face all the time."

She nodded while I answered, but I knew she wanted more. "Have you found the one yet?" she asked.

"It's still really early, but a few are in the running." I smiled, knowing she wanted me to name names, but Denise would kill me if I did.

"Like two? Three? Give us and the viewers something."

I counted in my head Alix, Kaisley, Lauren. Wait. Lauren wasn't available, but I counted her anyway because who was going to know? "Three. I've bonded with three, and hopefully by the time we get to the final two, I'll know for sure."

"So the whole thing about other shows where the person struggles between two people is fake?"

How was I going to dig myself out of this one? "Not fake by any means. Some people take their time making a decision this big, and rightfully so. I tend to jump in feet first and then struggle with massive regret. I'm determined to take my time. I'm thirty-two, and I want to find my person. Hopefully, they are on this show."

"They, huh? You're talking about Alix, aren't you? The first episode has aired, so we know you have a soft spot for them." She smirked and nodded, as though goading me to slip up and name-drop.

"I do, but for other contestants as well. That's why this takes so long. I'm dating several people, and time is necessary. First impressions can be completely wrong. I learned that from season one." I looked at the camera and raised my eyebrow. Ellie howled with delight.

"I think you'll be happy to know that Katie Parson is still single after several crash-and-burn relationships," she said.

I wasn't about to shit talk on national television. That would ruin my squeaky-clean reputation. "Trust me, I have a new appreciation for Katie and what she had to go through on this side of the show. It's not easy, and I really hope she finds somebody." Katie was pushing forty, and I remembered that she wanted kids. That was one of the questions I balked at. I was twenty-two and just getting started in life. I froze when Katie asked the question, and when I answered, I said something lame like I'm not there yet. At least I was truthful.

"Thank you so much, Savannah, for inviting us into your life and showing us the behind-the-scenes world. I wish you nothing but the best, and hopefully when this is all over, you will find somebody worthy enough of your heart." She took my hands and squeezed them softly. "You deserve the best."

When the cameras stopped, Ellie hugged me. "Thank you so much for agreeing to do this. I know you're pulled in so many directions. This will really boost *Reality Bits*."

"Are you kidding me? Thank you for having me on your show. I've watched it for years and have always appreciated your determination to get to the truth of reality TV." I didn't tell her that I blew past any segments about *Sparks*. That would've been rude.

She leaned forward and whispered, "You can tell me now. Anybody special yet?"

I leaned forward so that our faces were only inches apart. "You're going to have to keep watching."

## CHAPTER EIGHTEEN

My first date night was with Lyanna. I had thought I got to choose the order, but Denise didn't want me to play favorites. It didn't matter, because Lyanna was in my top four. I was looking forward to seeing what she came up with, which made the evening even more disappointing. She didn't go all out like I thought she would. She picked a private dinner prepared by Scooter Wilmes, a James Beard award-winning chef located about twenty minutes from the mansion. During the limo drive, we went back and forth about how good the other person looked. She was stunning, and apparently, so was I.

The show had rented out a small restaurant overlooking the ocean. We had to move the romantic dinner indoors because the waves were too loud, and the wind kept blowing out the candles. They were on the table and meant for a romantic vibe, but the dying flames accurately represented how the night was going

"This is the most delicious beef Wellington I've ever tasted," Lyanna said.

She took another bite and moaned her approval. While it was tasty, I'd had better. This was too salty, and the pastry wasn't crisp and light. But the mashed potatoes served with it were incredible. I missed carbs.

"Who does the cooking at the house?" I asked her, thinking the contestants had a chef.

"We take turns. I fix salads and a protein. So many people at the house are vegan or vegetarians. It's nice to be with somebody who isn't afraid to eat meat. That's what makes this night special," she said.

Did she just use me for an indulgent meal? "I don't eat a lot of red meat, but every once in a while, I crave a steak or a burger. Do you like to cook?"

"Not really. I did the cooking for my siblings, so it was more of a chore than a delight. But I love to eat. Know that going in," she said.

"I love it, too." I really tried to move the conversation. We toasted to finding the right person, which ten different cameras captured, and spent the rest of our night talking about college and how much we'd changed since. Lyanna was two years younger and, as a sales rep, had a lifestyle well beyond what I had back home or could offer another person. As nice as she was, I knew after the date that she wasn't the one either. Hopefully we could at least salvage a friendship after the show.

"Do you want to go back to your place for a bit?" she asked.

It was only ten and I was done. I felt lethargic, because of the food, and bored. I bowed out as graciously as I could. "This was such a nice dinner, but after spending the afternoon with everyone and having a date, I'm exhausted."

"I'm so glad you said that. I'm tired, too. We don't get a lot of sleep at the mansion."

The limo ride back was comfortably quiet. It didn't become awkward until the limo pulled through the gate to my house and parked. "I had a very nice evening with you, Lyanna. It was good to get to know you better."

She hugged me and kissed my cheek. "Have a great night, Savannah. Don't stay up too late."

The date didn't seem to affect her either. Maybe that was a good thing. I didn't want people to fall for me if I would only have to break their hearts in a matter of weeks or days. Lyanna and I seemed to be on the same page.

I kicked my heels off and hung up the dress. After a meal of fatty food, I wanted a swim whether Lauren showed up or not. I changed and headed down to the pool.

"How was dinner?" Lauren asked.

I yelped and threw my towel down. "Why are you forever scaring me?"

Her laugh was charismatic and washed away the fear that had settled in my chest. "I'm sorry."

"No, you're not."

"You're so fun to scare." She sat up and kicked off her shoes. "Are you ready?"

"I'm in a food coma, but yes. Just make sure I stay afloat." I dove in after her and matched her strokes in the water. Her tip about breathing helped, and I wasn't as winded after ten laps.

"You stayed right with me the whole time. That's impressive."

She was wearing a bathing suit and a rash guard again.

"Why do you always wear a shirt when we swim? Isn't it cumbersome in the water?" I looked down at my modest bathing suit with a scoop neck that landed right at my collarbone.

"I'd rather not talk about it. I hope you don't mind."

"Oh, my gosh. I'm so sorry. I didn't mean to pry. I was just curious, and sometimes I say dumb things when I'm nervous." Fuck. Now she knew I was not only nervous around her, but I was an insensitive jerk, too. She pulled herself out of the water and flipped around so that she was sitting with her legs dangling next to me.

"One day I'll talk about it, but not today," she said. Her voice was quiet, and the sadness in her words made my chest constrict.

"So, do you want to hear about my date?"

"Sure. How was it?"

I hopped up next to her and squeezed the excess water from my braid before tossing it behind me. "I felt like I was with a friend. I'd thought we had chemistry, but we don't. We have almost nothing in common." I grimaced. "Honestly, the date she chose was kind of lame. Dinner? With all the resources available, she picks dinner? All I do here is eat and hide from the sun."

"Let's start with the positive."

"She looked beautiful, and the food was decent. I prefer Josef with an ef's cooking over Scooter's, but at least I got to eat a potato."

"How was the conversation?"

I watched as she wrung the water out of her shirt. It still clung to her, even though she pulled it away from her. I didn't know why she was covering up, but I found her so incredibly sexy whether she sat next to me soaking wet under the stars or wore an elegant evening gown with full makeup and styling.

"Hello? Earth to Savannah? What are you thinking about?"

Obviously, I wasn't thinking, or I would have pulled a canned answer out of my repertoire of boring things to say. I blamed my exhaustion. "How nice your lips are and how you're so beautiful regardless of what you're wearing."

She leaned away from me and quickly stood.

"Fuck," I whispered. Way to fuck everything up. "Wait, Lauren. I meant that in the nicest way possible."

"It's probably best if I go. It's been a long day for both of us."

I stood with my hands on my hips and stared at her. I refused to apologize for being honest. "You're always telling me how beautiful or nice I look, and nothing's wrong with me telling you the same thing. How is it different?"

She walked over to me. "It's different, and you know it."

I swallowed hard. Confrontational Lauren was hot and frightening. Her light eyes flashed with anger, but I saw something else. She was scared. "How is it different?" My voice was low, and I bit my bottom lip to keep from saying another stupid thing. She shook her head and turned. I repeated myself. "How is it different?"

She ran her fingers through her wet hair and stopped. "This can't happen, Savannah."

"I knew it. You feel it, too."

She held her hands up and walked backward. "You are the star of this show, and you're looking for a relationship with contestants who have been screened and are perfect for you. I have nothing to do with it. This is not a thing." She motioned her finger between us.

"That's not true. Something's here, and I want to explore it."

She huffed and made a noise of disbelief. "There's nothing between us. You need to focus on the six people who are here for you. I'm not one of the six."

Her words were crushing, but she was right. I was here to do a show, and she wasn't a part of it the way I wanted her to be. I held my hands up. "Okay."

"Okay, what?"

I shrugged like I didn't care. "I'll stay focused on the people who are here for me. You aren't here for me. You're here for a career."

She shook her head. "Don't be like that."

I took a deep breath. "You're right. I'm sorry. That was uncalled for."

"I'm going now. I'll see you tomorrow."

I watched her gather her sandals and car keys and disappear into the darkness. I heard the low throttle of her car starting and driving off until the night was silent again. I sat on the lounge chair and dropped my head into my hands. What had I just done? We weren't even halfway through the season, and I'd just fucked everything up.

## CHAPTER NINETEEN

I panicked when I didn't see Lauren on set. Denise told me Lauren wasn't feeling well and was getting checked out by a doctor and that I shouldn't worry. She would be back tomorrow, but they would improvise for tonight's date.

"Tell us how your date went last night." Denise was asking me the questions off camera.

As if things weren't fucked up enough, my one-on-one date tonight was with Alix. I needed to clear the air with Lauren first, but I wouldn't get that chance. Alix was here for me, because of me, and wanted to be with me. Tonight's date was going to be a mess because I was so confused, and I couldn't do anything about it except sit back and try to keep an open mind.

"My date last night with Lyanna was a lot of fun. We had a delicious dinner and a great conversation." Denise motioned for me to continue, but I wasn't in the mood to embellish. I wanted to cross my arms and scowl for the rest of the day. "She's very ambitious and nice. We talked about family and food."

"Savannah, you're going to have to try harder. This is coming across as flat," Denise said.

"I'm sorry, but the magic wasn't there. I know you want me to say we felt a spark last night, but we didn't." At least not during that date. I definitely had one when Lauren visited. "I had high expectations because I felt I had something special with Lyanna this whole time, but the one-on-one date disappointed me."

"All right, everyone. Let's take a quick break," Denise said. She was frustrated, and with good reason. I needed to be professional. I had signed up for this. I walked from the interview room and found a quiet place away from people on the patio. I needed to clear my head and redirect my energies into my upcoming date. I smiled when I thought of Alix. They were wonderful, and I knew the date would be perfect. When we had been poolside this afternoon, the contestants were asking me what I liked to do, what the perfect date was, except Alix. They just sat back and smiled. Something amazing was going to happen, and I hated that I wasn't one hundred percent in. I needed time.

Mandee found me on the patio. "Denise is looking for you."

"I'll be there in a minute." This had been an emotionally draining day, and I still had to be spot-on for at least another eight hours. I wanted to crawl upstairs and hide under my blankets until I felt stronger.

Instead of leaving, she sat next to me. "I can tell you're having an off day. I'm sorry you can't postpone it."

"Is it that obvious?"

"Your makeup has never been harder to apply, and I haven't seen you smile at all. Did you have a bad date? You don't have to tell me if you don't want to."

Given that this was probably the most Mandee had spoken to me, I decided to keep the conversation going. I needed to talk, just not about what had happened last night. "The date was fine. Not spectacular, but not bad. I just didn't sleep well, and I woke up crabby. The demands of the show must be starting to get to me."

"You're doing better than most."

"Oh?"

"Usually someone has a breakdown before it starts." She looked at me wide-eyed. "Not that you're having a breakdown. I just meant that usually the flame needs a few days to herself because everything becomes overwhelming. Trust me. You've held it together longer than most."

"I don't know if that makes me feel better or not." I sat up and gave a deep sigh. "Okay. Let's do this."

Mandee pulled me up and walked me back to the makeup chair. It took only a few minutes to touch up my face and hair. I squared my shoulders and marched into the interview room, prepared with canned answers and a smile.

"Are you ready to jump back in?" Denise's words weren't bitter. I think she understood that this was wearing on me.

"I am, and I apologize about losing it. It's just been pretty stressful as we get deeper into the season." That was partially true. The rest of the interview went smoothly. I smiled and nodded and said all the right things, and when it was over, Mandee marched me into the other room to find Alix to start our date.

"I'm so excited. Are you ready?" Alix looked amazing. They were wearing black trousers, a white button-down shirt with the first two buttons undone, and loafers. It was a classic look that could be taken as formal or casual, depending on the activity. When Buzzy had showed up with short evening dresses, I wasn't pleased. I felt cranky, bloated, and emotionally unwell, with no desire to go out. Standing in front of Alix and feeding off their excitement, I had a change of heart. They deserved my attention, even though my heart was swirling in a different direction.

"I'm looking forward to whatever you have planned."

They raised their eyebrows and grabbed my hand. "I promise you that it's a lot better than just dinner. I can't believe Lyanna blew her first one-on-one with a boring meal. The whole house gave her a hard time."

I bit my tongue to keep from laughing. "Maybe she was stressed. It can't be easy trying to find the perfect thing to do." They had to plan a romantic date with the help of the show's event planner because they weren't allowed access to the internet. It had to be tough not being able to do it themselves.

"When you have perfection on your arm, anything and everything is perfect," they said.

A part of me wanted to tease them for sucking up to me, but I believed them. Alix was here for me, and I wasn't here for them. Guilt pricked my heart. "Thank you. That was sweet. Can you give me a hint of what we're doing?" They opened the limo door for me and slid in beside me. I didn't mind their closeness. They smelled like wood sage and sea salt, my favorite Jo Malone cologne. I'd mentioned it was my favorite during a group date, and somehow Alix got their hands on it. I smiled.

"I know you have a journal and that you like to read when you have downtime. I decided to go with something a little different to start our date. How do you feel about Ernest Hemingway?"

"Oh, he's one of my favorite American authors. He used to live down here, right?" I knew the answer. There was only so many things you could do in the Florida Keys that weren't water-related, and visiting his home was one of them.

"Yes, he did. I wanted to inspire you to write in your journal by taking you to his house," they said.

"That sounds perfect."

"I told you. If you are with perfection, then life is perfect."

They leaned over and gently kissed me. Their touch was organic and soft, and I hated every slow second of it. A vision of Lauren flashed in my mind, and as much as I tried to be present for the kiss, I just wasn't. "Is this okay?" Alix asked after pulling back.

"It is. I'm sorry. I'm having a rough day, and it's not about you or this wonderful date." I told myself to stop talking. "I need to get out of my head and have a good time."

"Whatever you want, you let me know. We can just go to the beach and grab some chairs and watch the sunset in total silence."

I touched their arm. "No. Let's see Hemingway's house. It sounds like fun. We can do the beach later." Alix held my hand and rubbed the side of my fingers with their thumb. It was a nice, calming feeling, and I decided to throw everything I had into the date to be fair to both of us. Lauren was a crush, unavailable. We had little in common, and she was out of my league. Alix was down-to-earth and fun and flirty. They always made me feel like I was somebody special. By the time we reached our first stop, I was relaxed and had convinced myself that I had nothing with Lauren and should focus on why I was on *Sparks* in the first place. I wanted to find love and prove to the world that dating shows could be real.

"Hello there, buddy." Alix reached down to pet a cat that greeted us at the door. "Are you going to give us the tour?" The cat meowed and flopped over on its back for belly rubs.

A woman stood in the doorway. "I see Bernard has greeted you. He loves attention. Hello. I'm Marion Smith, and I'll be your tour guide this evening."

Alix and I introduced ourselves, even though she knew who we were and why we were there, because the show had rented the house for the afternoon.

"How many cats are here?" I asked. Once I looked around, I saw several of them in the garden and in the windows.

"Fifty-four at the moment. Are you both Hemingway fans or cat fans?"

"I'm both," I said. I loved *The Old Man and the Sea* but didn't want to say that for fear Marion would quiz me on a book I'd read over ten years ago. The moral of the story had stayed with me, but the details were fuzzy.

"Me, too," Alix said.

"Hemingway loved cats, as you can tell. He loved the absolute emotional honesty of them." Marion air-quoted his words. Hand in hand, Alix and I followed her around the house, asking questions and petting the cats who wanted attention.

"They are so beautiful and friendly," I said. Being around them made me want to have at least two. They could entertain each other while I worked.

"Most of them are, but some run and hide," she said.

By the end of the tour, I was relaxed and ready to start my date with Alix, even though we had technically already been on it for an hour and a half. We said our good-byes to Marion and the cats and crawled back into the limo.

"Are you ready for dinner? Or would you like to hang out at the beach?" The attention Alix gave me was sincere.

"Can we do both?"

They kissed my hand. "Of course, we can. We can even get dinner to go if you'd like."

"I think dinner inside would be nice and free of sand. Let's keep the date like you planned it." They looked down at my mouth and back up to my eyes. I could tell Alix wanted to kiss me again.

"Well, how about off the sand and in a controlled environment?" Alix shrugged. The restaurant, Latitudes, was part of a gorgeous resort that I would never be able to afford in any other circumstance. Alix had a large, private outdoor tent pitched on the beach near the restaurant, filled with candles and flowers and as romantic as it could be. Three solid walls were up for privacy, but the front that faced the ocean was wide open. I walked in, delighted the air was cool. "This is amazing, Alix." I touched their face and kissed them softly. "Thank you. It's exactly what I need today."

"I hope you're having a good time."

I nodded. "I am."

They pulled out the chair and waited for me to get situated before sitting across from me. A waiter appeared with a wine list that Alix and I reviewed and decided on Rudd Sauvignon Blanc 2019.

"The food here is great, according to all the reviews. I hope you like seafood, but even if you don't, we have a ton of options. I've only ever seen you eat fruit and cheese and crackers," they said.

I wanted to laugh about the food restrictions I was on because of my predetermined wardrobe. "I'll eat anything. I don't have a lot of seafood because I live in Arizona, but I do enjoy it."

"Oh, I can't wait for you to visit Portland with me. Tons of fresh seafood, and just so you know, I'm an awesome cook."

"Do you fish?"

They nodded. "My brother and I have a boat."

"You two are very close, aren't you?"

"He's my best friend."

"That's beautiful. Be still my heart," I said and even threw in a flirtatious wink. "Are you close with your parents?"

Our conversation was smooth and easy, and for a few minutes of my night, I didn't think about Lauren or the cameras or saying the right thing. After dinner, Mandee did a touch-up, and I brushed my teeth. Alix was waiting on the beach, near a small bonfire and a double chaise with cushions. It looked like a stretched-out hammock for two.

"This is cozy," I said.

"We even have blankets if the evening gets chilly."

Alix handed me a thin blanket, and I covered my legs. Since my dress was short, I needed it more for discretion than warmth. I didn't need my crotch on national television. They carefully crawled onto the chaise and put their head next to mine. It was sweet. The light from the fire was too bright to see the stars directly above, but we looked anyway. "How are you with astrology?"

"I could write a book on it," they said.

I laughed. "Let's pretend we just saw a shooting star. What would your wish be?"

"My wish is right here next to me," they said.

I rolled onto my side to look at Alix. They gently played with my hair, and when their dark blue eyes met mine, I knew we were going to kiss. It was soft, and when it heated up, I didn't stop it.

## CHAPTER TWENTY

I don't know why I'm here," Lauren said. When I heard her voice, I accidentally swallowed a mouthful of water and choked. "Don't drown. We need to talk."

I kept swimming. I couldn't get out of the pool, afraid for this moment now that it was here. She looked too vulnerable sitting on the edge of the lounge chair, and I knew tonight was going to break me. After four long laps, I decided I couldn't hold off the inevitable and climbed out. Lauren handed me my towel.

"How are you feeling?" I asked.

She gave me a weak smile. "I'm okay. Thanks for asking."

I wiped off the excess water and slipped on my robe. I still felt naked physically and emotionally. I sat on the lounge chair next to her and waited for her to speak first, even though millions of words were perched on my tongue, threatening to tumble out.

"You had a good date tonight." Her voice was low, as though she was defeated.

I stopped her after noticing the cameras were uncovered. "Not here. Do you want to go inside?" I nodded in the direction of one of the cameras, so she got the hint. She stood and motioned for me go ahead of her. We were quiet on what felt like the longest walk of my life. By the time we reached the master suite, my stomach was twisted in a knot so tight I had to sit down. Lauren paced in front of me. "Would you please sit down and talk to me?" I asked. "I've been wrecked since last night."

"I want to apologize for yesterday. I should have never said anything to you. It was unprofessional, and I'm embarrassed by my outburst," she said. Her eyes flashed with remorse and sadness. Her apology could have waited until morning. She wanted more. That gave me the boost of confidence I needed to speak my truth.

I took a deep breath. "I think you're here because you want to be." She stood and moved away. I walked closer. She held up her hands for me to stop. "I get that you don't want to ruin the show or career that you've worked so hard for."

"That's not fair."

I held my hand up. "Please let me finish. I don't mean anything bad. I just mean I respect what you've built. You've worked hard and have sacrificed so much to get where you are. It's hard for your career to be on the line. I understand you have more to lose than I do, but I just want to talk about options." I hated how clinical that remark sounded, but I needed her to know I had a level head about our situation. "I just want to know if you think we have anything between us because I—" I took a deep breath to clear the waver in my voice. "Lauren, I can't stop thinking about you."

"Please don't."

Cautiously, I took another step toward her. "I remember when you breezed into the conference room after I flew out to talk to everybody before agreeing to be on the show. I hadn't watched the show since you took over, but I knew that you had and that it was thriving. You were so warm and made me feel comfortable enough to put myself in the exact situation I was in ten years ago. It was the worst time of my life, but your confidence in me made me throw all caution to the wind and sign on the dotted line. Honestly, I had a crush on you then. I had no idea you were a lesbian." I couldn't stop talking, and she wasn't interrupting. "I've been tamping down my feelings because I'm not being fair to anybody involved."

"That's what I've been saying. This isn't right. Nothing can happen between us. It wouldn't be right," she said.

My heart stopped, but not because she said no. In her message, I heard the confirmation that she felt something, too. "Isn't the goal to find someone? Isn't that the whole premise of the show?"

"Yes. One of the contestants."

Silence hung in the space between us. I didn't want to give up. I was so close. "But you're here, in front of me. That means everything." I touched her hand. When I felt her respond, I pulled her closer. I was damp, my hair was finger-combed and slicked back with pool water, and I smelled like chlorine. I wasn't sexy, but she made me feel sexy. I touched her face and gave her a small smile when she didn't pull away. She wanted to be here. I could see the struggle in her eyes. I ran my thumb over her bottom lip and moved even closer. She didn't move away. When my lips brushed hers, she stepped back. "Please don't," I said. "Can't you tell how much I want you? Out of everyone here, I choose you." I knew it was bold to go all in, but I had only one shot here before her walls went up again. I closed the gap and waited. She had enough room to get by if she wanted to, but what I wanted and was offering was clear.

"Fuck," she said and pulled me into her arms.

Her lips were on mine fast and furious at first. I couldn't get close enough. The lapels of my robe pressed between us, and I reached down to untie the sash. She moaned when my partially naked body pressed against her clothed one, but her hands never left my neck. It was perfect.

I felt a stirring deep inside. Every important part of me throbbed when her tongue dipped into my mouth. I felt her resolve weaken as she moved her hands down to my waist, and a moan bubbled up from her throat. Her lips were hot and her mouth wet, and I never wanted this to end. I wanted to forget the last few months and not think about anybody I might be hurting by kissing Lauren. When her hands slipped inside my robe and rested on my hips, I almost whimpered with delight. Her fingers burned into my skin, and I wanted them all over me, but she pulled away.

"Savannah, wait, stop," she said.

I instantly dropped my hands and opened my eyes. The passion in hers made me weak with need and strong with desire. I had never wanted to touch and be touched this badly before. The weeks of lusting after her, dreaming about her, wishing for her was finally a reality, but she stopped me. "What's wrong? Don't say *this* is, because it's not. I'm not going to let a television show define me or tell me who I'm supposed to be with."

"We're halfway through the season, Savannah. Let's just wait it out. I know there are people you care for, and it's only fair you let it play out."

"I don't feel for them what I feel for you. It's not organic. Even if I was dating Alix and met you after, I would still want to be with you. And that's the truth," I said.

"Look, I think you're wonderful, and I know we have something, but it's not a good idea right now. We're both under contract, and it would be a legal nightmare to try to get out of this. We don't have a choice."

She held my face in her hands and looked deep into my eyes. She didn't appear happy or sad, only hungry. I knew if I pressed, she would crumble, and we would be in bed in a matter of seconds, but I had to respect her. I took a deep breath and closed my robe. "You're right. We need to finish the process. I promise not to do anything that would compromise you or the show. This thing between us affects too many people."

She tucked my hair behind my ear and rubbed her thumb across my cheek. "I'm going now. We need to stop our late-night swimming dates, too."

I pressed her hand against my face just to feel her touch one last time. "I know."

"Try to get some sleep. I'll see you tomorrow."

And just like that, she was gone.

Lyanna and Charlotte stood in front of me with their candles. My one-on-one date with Lyanna was boring, but I almost died on my date with Charlotte.

Okay, that might have been a slight exaggeration, but we had a mishap with the parasailing equipment. The cord started to unravel when they tried to pull it in, so I had to "hang tight" until they were able to get another person in a different parasail to slowly work their way over to me and hook me to another tether. It was the longest hour of my life.

Once I was safely on the beach, I threw up. Lauren was beside me in a flash, ensuring I was okay. I told her I just wanted to go back to my place. Charlotte rubbed my back and handed me a water bottle. It would have been sweet had I not seen her laugh at me stuck up in the air. I hated myself for agreeing to the date, knowing heights weren't my thing.

"Ladies, Savannah can choose only one of you." Lauren stood with the sparkettes who had already gotten my flame. She was wearing a simple black dress that fell to her knees and hugged her hips and waist. It was sleeveless and allowed me to secretly drool over her sexy, toned, tanned arms. I was happy my peripheral vision could soak her in.

"Actually, Lauren, tonight I'm going to say good-bye to both lovely ladies. I don't want to keep them here if I haven't made a connection with them." Every single person froze, including Lauren. Somebody must have nodded at her or said something in her invisible earpiece. "Thank you both so much for being here with me. I know it was a big sacrifice, and I wish you nothing but happiness."

Lyanna took the news the best. "Hey, it's been fun, and I hope you find the perfect person for you." She high-fived me and then pulled me into a quick hug before walking out of the room.

Charlotte seemed dumbfounded. I grabbed her hands and squeezed them. "You're wonderful, and I'm sure you'll find the one who fills your heart. Good luck." I gave her a hug, and she left.

Somebody waved me into the interview room, and Mandee pounced the moment I entered. "Sit down. We have a lot to do."

She pulled at my hair and stabbed bobby pins in it to keep it on top of my head. My makeup took longer because the humidity and my nerves sweated it off. She said something only when I was done. "Good luck."

Lauren entered the room, and we did a quick comm check. Her expression was unreadable. Was she angry that I didn't tell her? I thought for sure Denise would've filled her in on the plan, but she must have wanted to get her reaction.

I'd pleaded with Denise to allow me to excuse two contestants this week and used the parasailing mishap as my reason. After Denise reviewed the tapes and saw Charlotte's reaction, she reluctantly agreed.

"Are you ready?" Lauren asked. Still no emotions.

I gave her a weak smile. "Yes."

"That was quite a surprise, even for me, when you eliminated both Lyanna and Charlotte. Can you tell us why?"

"I think they're lovely women, but my connection fizzled with both of them. Lyanna is fun, beautiful, and will surely find somebody soon. And Charlotte is amazing and intelligent, but the chemistry wasn't there."

"Your one-on-one dates didn't go as planned."

"No, Lauren, they didn't. I can't even talk about the parasailing incident."

"You're afraid of heights, but you still agreed to Charlotte's date. Why?"

I wasn't prepared to answer that question and felt somewhat attacked. We always reviewed questions, but these were new to me. I decided to be honest. "It was her date to present to me, and honestly, I wasn't sure I could get away with saying no. Rules and all."

Lauren clearly felt the punch of my words and leaned back. "I understand. I'm sure Charlotte was convincing, and it's hard to say no sometimes." That was a horrible message, and I thought it was directed at me, but before I could respond, she continued. "The good news is that we can push up the Mexico trip. Are you excited about that?"

More sun, more sunscreen that made me feel greasy and heat I wasn't prepared for. "I am. I have a feeling that good things will happen there."

"More alone time but also eliminations. Can you give us a hint on where you stand with the contestants?"

"I think the sparkettes are on an even playing field." That wasn't remotely true, but I knew the rules and some of the canned answers expected from me. Lauren didn't respond. She wanted more. "I mean, I feel a deep connection with two people here, and I'm excited to see how this experience plays out."

"We're excited for you, too. Now how about going back inside and celebrating with the final four?"

"Sounds perfect." I stood, completely done with this interview. She didn't attack me, but she gave me no warning about the questions, which wasn't like her.

"So, we're going to Mexico, huh?" Alix handed me an old-fashioned when I entered the giant living space. The other contestants rushed me so we could do the stupid toast for the cameras.

"Here's to good times in Mexico and no dates that take me high in the sky."

"That was horrible. I would never do that to you," Ophelia said.

"Well, Charlotte didn't do anything wrong. I agreed, but I don't want any future dates involving heights."

Kaisley put her lower hand on my back for my attention. "We've already discussed it and agreed to not put you through anything like that again."

"Then, cheers," I said. I stayed for a few obligatory minutes and made a quick exit. I wanted to curl up on the bed in a little ball and maybe cry myself to sleep. I wasn't even going to swim laps, knowing that Lauren wouldn't be there. I said good night to the two security guards up front and walked straight up the stairs to my bedroom to get out of my clothes. When I saw the pink box of doughnuts and a stack of newly released lesfic books, I stopped short, and my sour mood instantly changed. I smiled at the note Lauren had tucked inside the warm box.

*Don't forget to do laps if you eat these. Two laps for every doughnut.—L*

Inside were four warm, freshly baked ones. I looked at the time. It was midnight. How did she get me fresh doughnuts at midnight?

## CHAPTER TWENTY-ONE

How good is your Spanish?" I asked Emma. We were in Cancun on a little bus that was taking the five of us to Chichen Itza to see the Mayan ruins and swim in the waters of Saamal. It was so beautiful in Mexico, and I knew the cameras wouldn't be able to do it justice.

"I took three years in high school, so I can get you to the library, the bathroom, order you a beer, and sing a few lyrics from several Shakira songs," she said.

Her Kentucky accent was so strong I doubted anyone here would be able to understand her if she spoke Spanish. Most of her words were drawn out, but she didn't care. Emma was a go-with-the-flow kind of woman. She was going to have a good time here regardless of any upcoming candle ceremonies. We had two ceremonies in Mexico, and then the two sparkettes left standing would go home to visit my family.

My shoulders sagged when I thought about my mother being put on the spot. I'd offered up Jane as my family until I had a chance to discuss it with my mother. I was sure by now she and Jane had chatted about my impromptu decision. Everything had happened so quickly that I knew I would have to beg for her forgiveness. I couldn't imagine she'd want to talk on television and be on the show. She loathed attention.

"Hello? Savannah?" Emma tapped my arm to get my attention.

"Oh, sorry. I have a lot on my mind."

"It's too beautiful here for you to have anything heavy on your mind," she said and laid her head on my shoulder.

I tried not to panic. It was a move that she could've made in private, but we were getting angry stares from Ophelia and Kaisley. I sat up straight, prompting Emma to move. "Oh, look at that." I pointed to a road sign as we whizzed by.

"What'd I miss?" Emma looked around, moving her head from side to side.

"Five kilometers to our destination. We need to gather our things." I heard Alix laugh and cough to cover it up. They saw the whole thing. I gave them a wide-eyed look and grimaced. At least they knew that it had been uncomfortable for me. Hopefully the cameras on the bus didn't pick it up.

Our tour guide, Luis, met the bus when we pulled up in a parking lot near the pyramid. The fact that we were here was incredible. I wasn't likely to visit another one in my lifetime, so I was going to be damn sure I appreciated today. We had the private tour, which gave us the place to ourselves for an hour so no one could leak who the final four contestants were. I was surprised when Lauren joined us.

"Hi," I said with a little too much enthusiasm. I toned it down. "Will you be on the tour with us?"

"I'll be here only because this is amazing, but I'll be behind the crew."

"Take lots of pictures," I said and pointed at her phone.

She nodded. "After the tour, you're going to have a break, so we'll have an opportunity for one-on-one time." She waved good-bye before disappearing behind the five or six camera people, who fanned out to get all kinds of footage from different angles.

"Luis, what can you tell us about Chichen Itza?" I wanted to bring the group together so the tour would go fast and maybe I'd get a chance to see Lauren again.

"Thank you." He nodded his appreciation at me being able to quiet our little group and started spouting off historical facts. His theatrics made for a better tour, and at the end of it, we all shook his hand and thanked him for being wonderful at his job. I wished I could've tipped him but was sure the show compensated him well.

"Would you like to take a walk?" Kaisley said before we'd even reached the rest area that *Sparks* had set up with a local hotel.

"Can we eat first? I missed breakfast."

"Oh, sure. When you're done."

I liked Kaisley. She was second out of the contestants, but I was afraid I'd break her heart. If my own heart was in it, it was a tough matchup between her and Alix. Kaisley had showed me her passionate side, which was a massive turn-on. She was sweet, kind, gentle, attractive, and one of her luxury items was a photo of her son, Kaden. She was perfect, just not for me. She was going to get hurt. I hated leading people on, but I'd gotten myself into this mess and was going to have to ride it out.

"Can you believe all of this food?" Emma asked.

"I'm hungry. How about you?" I picked a plateful before I even got halfway down the table. We were given half an hour to eat, with minimal cameras. Privacy was a no-no, thanks to my impromptu visit to the contestants' house weeks ago. I had a camera trained on me all the time.

"Has anyone been here before?" Alix asked the group.

"I've never been out of Kentucky, except for a trip to Disneyworld and a road trip to Nashville," Emma said.

I had been on many road trips with my mother, and we'd even traveled up to Canada, but once my business started, I stayed in Arizona. I went to New Mexico with Jane to pick up supplies, but that didn't count. What the fuck had I actually done the last ten years of my life?

"I've been so many places, including Mexico City and Guadalajara," Ophelia said. "This is my first time to Cancun, though." She turned to Emma. "I can't believe you haven't traveled more."

I rushed to Emma's defense. "I've done nothing but build my business, so I haven't been to many places either. I'm sure Emma's had her reasons."

Ophelia smiled but backed down. I refused to let anybody make anyone else feel bad for their life decisions. Traveling wasn't for everyone, and it required money. As a preschool teacher, Emma probably wasn't rolling in the dough. Even though I had my own business, I still lived paycheck to paycheck.

"The important thing is that we're here now, and we get to swim in the most amazing caves in the world. Eat up. I'm ready to see more," Alix said. They approached everything with gusto. Their attitude was refreshing and contagious.

"Yes. I'm almost ready." I shoved the last of my sandwich into my mouth and looked for Mandee. A small tent was set up for privacy behind us, and she waved me over when our eyes met. I excused myself and followed her into the cool tent. "Why can't we pick somewhere like Iceland or Finland, where it's not so damn hot and my makeup doesn't need touched up every few minutes?"

She shrugged and pointed to the back of the chair. "Then we wouldn't see you all frolic in your bathing suits."

I looked at her, offended at first, but she was right. "Maybe if we had a full season, there would be some sled-dog races somewhere very north, where my hair wouldn't fall limp and my makeup wouldn't sweat off."

"Then we'd have to worry about static electricity and dry hair and pale skin. There's no perfect place. Now sit back, and let's get your makeup ready for swimming."

"That sounds ridiculous."

"That's because it is."

Tomorrow was a blackout day, and we were instructed to stay in our rooms. The weather was going to be crappy anyway. The contestants bunked together in swanky suites on the other side of the resort, but I had one all to myself. It looked like the honeymoon suite, with beautiful roses everywhere and a giant Jacuzzi tub. I immediately knew what I was going to do with my downtime. I was surprised to have a television in the room, but only local channels were aired, and they were in Spanish. My journaling was going nowhere. I was bored. And when I was bored, bad things happened. The knock at my door scared me. I opened it and found a guy I'd met before on the set of the contestants' house.

"Hello, Miss Savannah. My name is Jason. I'm security for the show and will be here in the hall if you need anything."

"Thank you, Jason. I should be good for the evening." I locked the door and flopped onto the bed. We had four days in Mexico, and then the remaining two contestants and I would head to Scottsdale. In less than three weeks, it would all be over.

I was dreading the "Secrets Revealed" show before the final candle ceremony. Madison and Thea were for sure going to come guns blazing and say awful things, but most of the audience wouldn't take them seriously. I was more worried about the people who I'd either already hurt or was going to be hurt. It was unfortunate but a must.

I turned on the shower and found a casual skirt and an off-the-shoulder shirt. I knew I was going to sneak out before I even made plans. The balcony was a foot off the ground, so getting out would be easy enough. There were bars down the street, and since it was a weekend, the town would probably be packed. I had all Mandee's makeup at my disposal and had watched her enough to know how to put it on. I grabbed a large, obnoxious, floppy straw hat and sunglasses, even though it was dark out. I had a minimal amount of cash at my disposal, but enough for at least a drink or two.

I turned off my lights and sneaked out the sliding door. Climbing over a railing in a skirt was a zero out of ten for me. I fell the short distance to the mulch below and basically flashed everyone in slow motion. I popped up and pretended I was fine and did this all the time. I slipped into foot traffic and walked to the next street over, where I heard music and laughter. I felt free and smiled for the first time in forever. I walked into the first bar and ordered a shot of tequila. I deserved to let loose on my terms, not whenever the show expected me to.

"What are you doing here?"

Somebody twirled me in my bar stool, and I yelped in surprise. "Lauren. How did you know I was here?"

"I saw you fall off your balcony and followed you."

I downed the second shot and hissed as the sharpness of the alcohol slowly coated my throat with liquid fire. "I needed a moment. I needed to be around people and not cameras."

"I get it, but you can't be out here. It's not safe, and it's against the show's policy."

I leaned into her personal space, starting to feel relaxed. "You're so pretty when you're angry."

She stepped back and brushed her hair back with her hand. "Finish up so we can get back."

I pulled her hand. "Come on. Let's loosen up for a night. Nobody knows who I am. I'm in disguise. Look at this hideous hat and glasses. People are going to recognize you before me."

"The hat and sunglasses draw more attention. And I don't think you realize your popularity. It's exploding," she said.

I shrugged, even though the thought made me smile for a moment. This season was going down in flames, too, and once again, I would become an internet joke. "I just wish it would be for the right reasons."

"Well, right now the world is pulling for you. And when I say world, I mean everywhere, including Cancun, so we need to get out of here now."

"Fine." I slid off the stool and threw my only twenty-dollar bill on the bar. "Let's go, boss." She didn't say anything but followed me out and onto the street. We were only two blocks from the hotel, and I could feel the impending loneliness squeeze inside of me. Even though Lauren had a longer stride, I stayed ahead of her like an angry, pouting child.

"We're not going to climb your balcony. We're going in through the door," Lauren said and directed me away from the bushes.

"Won't we get into trouble?"

"As long as I'm with you, we won't. Do you need anything tonight?"

"You mean before I'm locked up?"

We turned down my hallway, and Jason looked surprised. Lauren pulled him aside, and he nodded at whatever she told him. He walked away. I turned to her when I reached my door.

"I don't have my key." She pulled out one from her back pocket and swiped it in the lock. The button changed from red to green, and she pushed the door open. "You have a key to my room? Have you been inside?" I should have been shocked that she had, but at the same time, I knew she would never do anything sinister with it.

"I just got it from Jason. It's for safety reasons."

"Do you really think it's safe to be in my room?" Ah, the tequila was kicking in right on time.

"I want to make sure it's safe. You left your patio door unlocked, and anybody could've crawled in."

She moved past me and checked the closets, under the bed, and in the adjoining room. I stood there as she zipped around me on her safety mission. I was pretty sure Jason could have done this. "What do you think about the place?" I swooped my hand around like I was Vanna White on *Wheel of Fortune.*

"It's lovely."

"Why are you so grumpy?" That question made her stop checking for hidden cameras.

"Because you're doing reckless things, and it's stupid when we're this close to the end. You're going to ruin our chance." She put her hand over her mouth and shook her head.

I pointed at her. "Aha! I knew it. You want this, too. You don't want me to find a connection with Alix or Kaisley. You want to explore this thing between us." I realized how immature I sounded, so I put my hand down and casually sat on the couch as though this bombshell hadn't just exploded in the space between us.

"I'm leaving."

And just like that, I was up again and in front of her. "Don't go. Nobody knows you're here. Hell, everybody is probably asleep." I put my hand on her arm. "I miss you. I hate that I'm in this beautiful place and can't even share it with you."

"You know this isn't a good idea. I can't be seen with you."

"Would you quit fighting this? We have this beautiful private suite in Mexico, and nobody can get in." For effect, I slid the locks in place. I knew she had bolted the patio door. "It's just us. No cameras, no contestants, just us." She stood in front of me with her arms crossed and that unbreakable, unemotional expression. "Just stay. Even if it's just to keep one another company. I could turn on the television, and we could try to—"

She put her hand on the back of my neck and pressed her gorgeous, full lips against mine. I whimpered with delight. She tasted like mint and heat. I regretted the two shots of tequila, as my mouth felt dry and hot, but I didn't care. I wrapped my arms around her and walked her back to the bed, my mouth still eager against hers. I slid beside her onto the plush comforter with my hands on her, afraid that if I stopped touching her, she would vanish. It was the first time I'd seen her in jeans and a T-shirt. No wonder she wasn't worried about being recognized out in public. She didn't look like herself. She still was sexy and beautiful, but more relaxed and natural. Her makeup was minimal, her hair pulled back with a clip at the nape of her neck.

"I need to tell you something." She broke our heated kiss and leaned up on her elbows. I'd never seen her look more serious, so instead of pushing her to relax and go with the moment, I rolled onto my side and waited for her to continue. "I need to tell you about why I quit reporting."

"Okay." I touched the soft skin that was exposed above her belt line where her T-shirt had risen when we fell on the bed. She stopped my hand from slipping underneath. I pulled back. "I'm sorry. Please go ahead." Whatever she had to say was important to her, so I reined in my lust and waited for her to talk on her terms. She grabbed a pillow and tucked it under her head, then reached for my hand and linked our fingers.

"I was in Afghanistan on assignment, and a bomb went off when we were reporting on a school nearby. Somebody got mad that they were teaching English there and planted a bomb that detonated while we were filming the story."

"Oh, my God. Are you okay? I mean, physically, yes, but are you okay?" I sat up and stared at her. I sounded ridiculous, but I couldn't find my words. "That must've been horrible. No wonder you got out."

"We lost one of our cameramen, Tommy Umbre. And Nathan Dover, our sound tech, had his leg blown off. I got hit in the chest and needed surgery. I'm fine now, but I have a pretty horrific scar on my sternum where they cracked my chest open."

I looked at her. "Can you show me?"

Her fingers hesitated on the hem of her T-shirt. I gave her a soft smile and a nod of encouragement. She pulled the shirt over her head and laid her head back on the pillow. I noticed her pale-blue bra first because it was almost the color of her eyes. Running along the smooth valley between her breasts was a puckered scar that started about two inches below her collarbone and ended almost at her navel. I touched the scar where it had marred her smooth stomach and moved my fingertips up until I had touched every millimeter of it.

"Does it hurt?"

"Not really. It just feels weird, like it's not supposed to be there," she said.

"I can't even imagine the pain you went through when this happened." My voice was a whisper as I carefully placed my hand on her stomach.

"I thought I was dead. I don't remember when it happened, but I remember waking up with everybody screaming. I was wearing Kevlar at the time, and it saved me."

"This is why you always dress so conservatively when we swim." I leaned forward and placed a small kiss on it.

"It's ugly and crooked, and it embarrasses me."

"Are you kidding me? There is nothing ugly about you. You're beautiful. This scar is just a part of you now." I leaned over her and slid a leg between hers. "I'm so thankful you survived that horrible ordeal and are here with me now."

She touched my cheek and pulled me down for a kiss. The fast passion I felt when we had kissed earlier was replaced with a tenderness I didn't know I had. The scar didn't take away from her beauty. I deepened the kiss to let her know it didn't scare me or make me think less of her.

"You're lovely. Every part of you." I wasn't surprised when she flipped me and settled between my legs. Lauren was a take-charge kind of person, and I welcomed her control. I held her close and gasped when she rolled her hips against mine. I lifted my knees so she was in direct contact with every part of me that throbbed. My skirt was a twisted mess around my waist, and my shirt was bunched up right under my breasts. Feeling Lauren's warm, bare stomach against mine made me want to rip everything off so that nothing prevented us from touching.

"Are you sure about this?"

I heard the words, but it took me a few seconds for the meaning to settle in. "Hell, yes." I pushed her up so I could yank off my top. Sensing my frenzy to be naked, she tugged down my skirt and tossed it somewhere behind us. "Take off your jeans," I said. She twisted on the bed and lifted her hips to slide her jeans off. She was wearing light blue silk panties that matched her bra. I paused to look at her and swallowed hard at her perfection. A lump settled in my throat as I thought about how long it had taken to get here and how my journey just took a turn. "Is this what you want? I don't want you to have any regrets."

"I'm done fighting my feelings. I want to be here. I know it's only going to complicate things for the next few weeks, but I want tonight to be about us. No tomorrow, just right here and now."

That wasn't exactly what I wanted to hear, but it was close enough. I pushed the covers down and pulled her onto me. She pulled the clip out of her hair, and I smiled as her long tresses cascaded around my head. My heart thudded when she smiled at me. Her sexy, unguarded expression made me feel like we were meant to be. I kissed her because I was afraid of letting her see how this moment affected me. She knew I was into her. I had made that perfectly clear time and time again. But having Lauren Lucas in my bed, in my arms, was always a dream, never a reality.

I slipped my hand between our hips and massaged her over her panties. I wanted them off but was too impatient to wait the three seconds it would take to remove them. She moaned against my mouth and pushed herself up to her knees so I had access. A mixture of a growl and a whimper came out of my mouth when I pulled the soft, silky fabric to the side and slipped a finger inside her wet pussy. She was tighter and warmer than I expected. She scraped her teeth along my neck and down my shoulder. When I slipped a second finger inside, she threw her head back.

"That feels…" She stopped talking when I sped up. I slowed so she could finish what she was saying. "Incredible."

Empowered, I flipped her and pulled her panties down. I needed to taste her. I kissed both thighs as I crawled up her body to the junction of her thighs. I smiled when she dropped her bra off the side of the bed. She wrapped her fingers in my hair as I licked up and down the soft, bare skin of her pussy. I was going to do everything in my power to show her how much she meant to me. I slid two fingers inside. She gasped in pleasure and groaned in disappointment when I immediately pulled them out. I did that several times in a row until she writhed and begged me to fuck her. Her request was honest and raw and empowering. I kept my fingers inside but moved them as fast as I could. Her fingers clenched in my hair, and I smiled, knowing I was giving her pleasure and she was allowing me control. I flicked her clit with my tongue, and she jerked in response. She was ready to climax just from my fingers, so I crawled up her until we were face to face and slipped my fingers back inside. "Do you like this, Lauren?" The guttural moan followed by a fast, hard kiss gave me my answer. "Do you want to come like this?"

"Yes," she said against my mouth.

I sped up my motion and watched as she climbed. One of her hands was pressing the headboard behind us, and the other was wrapped around my neck. She quivered in anticipation. I'd never been with a woman so sure and confident before. My hand was drenched, but I didn't stop until she exploded and collapsed. Every part of me soared. I kissed her neck and snuggled into her warmth and held her while she shook. I felt her smile against me. I didn't have words for this moment, so I pulled the sheet over us and relaxed against her in silence.

"Why do you still have clothes on?"

"I was too excited to get to you," I said. My voice was hoarse, and my throat was dry, but I was in heaven.

"It's not fair," she said. For a moment, I thought she was talking about the show, and panic squeezed my chest. "I'm almost completely naked, and you're fully dressed."

I smiled in relief and at her playfulness. "I mean, to be fair, you've seen me naked and what I look like when I come."

She laughed and pulled me closer. "Trust me when I say I remember everything—how beautiful you are, how your cheeks turn bright red right before you orgasm. But I want to be the one to do that to you, not the Jacuzzi." She paused as though in deep thought. "Although the idea has merit."

"Desperate times call for desperate measures. Besides, I was thinking of you," I confessed.

She stared at me. "You're lying."

I tried to come up with a joke and a smile to laugh it off, but my smile disappeared, so I shrugged instead. "It's true. I've been thinking about you this whole time." She crawled on top of me and kissed me softly.

"I shouldn't believe you, but I do."

"I've wanted you here for so long," I said. Why was I being so emotional? The impact of her here, in my bed, in my arms was hitting me hard. I kissed her because I was afraid of revealing too much. She ran her fingers over the swell of my breasts and smiled when chill bumps popped up under her touch.

"Are you cold?"

"No. It's just been a long time since I've been touched, and it's perfect that it's you." Fuck. I needed to quit being so open and honest.

She nodded as though she understood but didn't say anything. Instead, she slid down me and slowly pulled off my horribly plain white panties while I unclasped my mismatched bra. Of all the fucking days to not look my best or wear a sexy matching set. She hooked my knees over her shoulders and pressed into me. We both moaned at the intimate contact. I was swollen and ready for release. She leaned forward to kiss me and slipped her hand between us. The pressure of her body against her hand gave me the friction I needed to move and find my orgasm. When she shifted her hips and slipped two fingers inside, I gritted my teeth and told myself to hold off. This felt a million times better, and I wanted it to last. With her fingers inside me, she thrust herself into me hard and fast. I didn't have time to think or figure out why every part of me was on fire, why my heart and soul fluttered. I allowed the feeling to build until I couldn't contain it. I exploded and didn't drift away because Lauren was on top of me, kissing my face and whispering words I couldn't comprehend. The only thing I could hear was the roaring beat of my heart. I thought we were done. When she pulled away, I closed my eyes and gave in to the shakes. I wasn't expecting to feel her mouth and tongue on my slit.

"Oh, fuck," I whispered and spread my legs apart. I wanted everything she would give me. She spread her tongue and licked me up and down until her tongue settled on my swollen clit. I was sensitive, but the spark turned into a flame the harder and faster her tongue moved against me. I grabbed a pillow and put it over my head to muffle my ecstatic cries. I didn't want any staff member guarding the halls to hear me. I was throbbing and dripping with sweat.

"That was even better than I imagined," Lauren said.

Her voice was gravelly and sexy, and I could barely move or breathe. "Yes." It was the only word I could form between gasps. I was spent. I laughed only because I didn't want to read too much into the moment and cry.

"What's so funny?" She smiled, and I brushed my finger across the dimple high up on her check.

"Nothing. I just feel good. Thank you for staying." When I leaned up and kissed her, she tasted like me. I wasn't sure what this meant, but I knew that after tonight, we were back on the show. I was expected to find love, and she was expected to guide me. The thought made me sick.

"I have a few hours before I have to get back to my room. Any ideas on what we should do?" She looked at me innocently, as though the last hour and a half hadn't just happened.

I kissed her hard. "I know exactly what we should do."

## CHAPTER TWENTY-TWO

S avannah, I have to go."
I leaned up and rubbed my eyes. Lauren was fully dressed and sitting on the bed beside me. "No. Don't go." I reached for her, but she stood and stepped out of my grasp.

"I'm sorry, but it's getting light out, and I can't be seen here. I didn't want to leave without saying good-bye."

I held my finger up and took a drink from the bottle on the nightstand. At some point during the early morning hours after another incredible round of sex, I'd crept over to the mini-refrigerator and downed two bottles of water. I was dehydrated and exhausted but felt alive for the first time in forever. I knelt on the bed and, completely naked, crooked my finger at her. Watching her gaze roam my body made me feel sexy. "At least a kiss good-bye?"

"Like I could say no to you." She kissed me deep and hard. I whimpered as I instantly blossomed with need. "Fuck. I have to go, Savannah."

"I like it when you say my name." I watched as she quietly unlocked the door and cracked it open. She closed it softly and came back to me.

"We have a problem."

"What?" I clutched the sheet close to me as though her bad news had eyes.

"A security guard's in the hall right outside the door."

I jumped up and slipped into my clothes from last night. "Maybe I could ask him to get me something."

She shook her head. "He'll just radio it in."

"How did you get rid of Jason last night?"

"I asked him to do a security check in the lobby in case we were followed."

"I have an idea. Here. Put these on." I handed her my floppy hat and ridiculously oversized sunglasses from last night, then stepped out onto the balcony and waved her over. "The coast is clear. I'm sure you'll do a better job of climbing over the railing than I did. It's private, and nobody is awake yet."

She slipped past me and climbed over it. "Thank you for last night."

I grabbed her shirt and pulled her close enough to brush my lips over hers. "My pleasure. Now go." I watched as she carefully made her way through the shrubs and onto the footpath. She didn't look back. It was too risky now that she was in full public view. I locked the sliding door and crawled back into bed. I couldn't believe she had just been in my room, the last seven hours punctuated by rounds of incredible sex and cat naps. I wanted to take a long, hot bath, but sleep was too important. Mandee would hate me tomorrow if I showed up with dark circles under my eyes. Since it was a blackout day, my options were limited anyway. I shut all the blinds and pulled the covers over me. The bed smelled like sex and Lauren's perfume. I fell asleep exhausted, thrilled, and sated.

"Huh. You look relaxed and refreshed," Mandee said.

"I took the blackout day and did everything I was supposed to. Absolutely nothing." Not true, but the world didn't need to know that. "Isn't your boyfriend down here with you?"

"He's back at the resort. One good thing about working on the show is that, as long as he pays for his airfare, we get to travel together," she said.

"That's a nice perk."

I couldn't wait to see Lauren today. I had an afternoon date with Alix and an evening date with Emma. I couldn't help but frown when I knew I was hurting at least two contestants. Kaisley and Alix were the most invested, and I had to get rid of them first. I wanted to walk away from this job, but legally I couldn't. The best I could do was cut the people who I'd gotten the closest to and not lead anyone else on during the next two weeks. I dreaded any future awkward kisses with the contestants, knowing full well that Lauren was watching.

"Since you'll be at the market with Alix today, I'm going to pull your hair back in a fishtail braid, so even if it's windy, your hairdo will hold up," Mandee said.

The whole process took over an hour as she straightened and then braided my hair. I was highly flammable after she was done spritzing and spraying it into place. The makeup took an additional thirty-five minutes, so by the time I was ready for my interview before my date, I was exhausted.

Lauren looked beautiful wearing a white, sleeveless blouse and a light blue tulip skirt. She was showing more leg than she had in the past, and in my head, she wore the outfit for me. I'd told her how it turned me on to see her cross her calves during our interviews.

"Hi, Savannah. How are you?" She touched my arm, and nobody cared.

I smiled when she gave me a soft squeeze and dropped her hand. "I'm great. How are you?"

"Mexico has been a wonderful experience so far. Have a seat. Today I'm going to ask you about Alix and how the relationship is progressing. We'll also talk about Emma, since your date tonight is with her. Just go with the flow and be as truthful as you can," she said.

I almost snorted. *Oh, like grab your hand and run away with you right now?* "Okay. I'm ready." I cleared my throat and smiled at Lauren, whose expression was soft and encouraging. It was harder to do this than I thought. Scott quickly finished comm checks, and Denise gave Lauren a nod to start the interview.

"What's been your favorite part about Mexico?"

"The scenery, for sure. This is such a beautiful country. We've seen and done amazing things so far. I can't wait to see what my dates have planned here." Did the word I loathe most in the world tumble from my lips? I stopped myself from rambling and waited for the next question.

"We're down to the final four. Do you think you had enough time to find the perfect person for you, or does this process seem rushed? The whole world wants nothing more than for you to find somebody, and we're all hoping for good things."

Lauren folded her hands in her lap and waited patiently for my answer. She didn't seem affected by my nearness or that I was going on dates with other people. She warned me that she would have to be professional on set, and I didn't—no—couldn't blame her. "Some really wonderful people are here looking for the same thing. I hope that by the end of this season, I will be carrying the proverbial torch for someone."

"I think I can speak for everyone and say we hope you find that spark."

I could see Denise getting excited about our cheesy exchange. It was exactly what she was looking for and made for good reality television. "I hope that as well."

"Shall we go find Alix so you can start your afternoon date?" Lauren asked.

We both stood, and she followed me into the room where the four remaining contestants sat. Alix stood when we entered. They were wearing shorts, a button-down, short-sleeve shirt, and boat shoes. Thankfully, I knew ahead of time that it was casual. Buzzy had hooked me up with a short summer dress that rested at my knees and was tapered enough that it wouldn't fly up if the wind caught it. I didn't want all of Mexico to see my panties since half probably saw them the other night when I sneaked out.

"Alix, have you planned an amazing date with Savannah?"

"I certainly hope she enjoys it. It's fun and adventurous, but don't worry. It's mostly on the ground," they said and gave me a wink.

"Mostly?" I smiled at them until guilt pricked my heart. I felt rotten for the deception. I was attracted to Alix, but with Lauren in my world, Alix didn't stand a chance.

"I promise you won't do anything that makes you feel uncomfortable. We're going to have a good time. Shall we?"

I held their hand when we slipped into the car. It didn't feel right to do it in front of the other contestants, and even though everyone told us to have a good time, I knew they didn't mean it. I had kissed three of the four remaining contestants. I know I would be jealous and had been when I was in their place. "So, can you give me a hint of where we're going?"

"I like to shop. There's an enormous marketplace I thought would be fun to hit while we're inland. Maybe get a few things for our families."

"That sounds like a lot of fun. I love to shop, too." I could tell they wanted to kiss me. Pre-Lauren, I would've gladly accepted it, but now, I felt like a cheater. They kissed my cheek softly and ran their fingertip on my neck. Shit. I knew the cameras were on us, and I kept my expression simple. My eyes briefly fluttered shut out of habit, and I left my lips pressed against theirs but didn't deepen the kiss. I was sure it looked fake, like most reality-television kisses, but Lauren was too fresh in my mind and on my body. Alix must have sensed my mood because they pulled away and pressed their lips together.

"Let's go have fun, shall we?"

I smiled at them and inwardly groaned. Poor Alix. They were nothing but kind to me. They deserved better. I grabbed their hand and nudged them with my shoulder. "Let's do this."

"Great. Because I have a surprise. Let's hit the market first."

We walked through a very crowded market. How was the camera crew handling the throngs of people and keeping the cameras steady? "I'm surprised they haven't swept the area." Most people gave us a wide berth when they saw me and Alix and four cameramen, a sound operator, and two lighting technicians headed down the street. But once the street vendors realized we were on a television show, they were very engaging.

"What looks good? I don't even recognize some of these fruits." Alix picked up what might be a type of melon. "Want to try this? It smells like cotton candy."

"Maybe some kind of sweet melon? I'm sure it's delicious. Everything we've had here has been so good." Alix picked one that the vendor insisted was the best. "We can eat it on the beach."

"Yeah. It would be perfect for lunch. Maybe throw some vegetable kabobs on the grill, with a side of this melon."

"Why can't we do that?"

Alix stopped walking and looked at me. "We can. I'm serious about just keeping it simple. Who can't make the beach work for any mood? Happy? Let's go to the beach. Sad? Let's go to the beach. Indifferent? Hey, let's go to the beach. I'm there every weekend."

"It sounds wonderful. Since you own your own business, it's probably easy to get away. Maybe if I had the ocean to go to every day, I would adjust my schedule."

"Maybe Portland would be a good place for a store. Or do you have more of an online presence? Because you can make your candles anywhere, right?"

They weren't wrong. "I can."

"I'll just say that Portland is booming." Alix pulled me closer and brushed their lips over mine. "Keep that in mind."

Alix bought me a colorful scarf and a small watercolor of Cancun to remember our date. "So, I know we have to go back, but are you up for one more thing?"

Their devilish look was heartbreaking. "I can't say no to you. What did you have in mind?"

They hugged me fast and hard. "I promise that even though it's kind of up in the air, it's nothing like parasailing."

I stopped. "Wait a minute. Tell me."

"A tandem zip line. I thought it sounded like fun." They leaned down to whisper, "I'd like to see the cameramen keep up with us on it."

I knew the show would make us wear GoPro cameras, so even though they thought they were being sneaky, we weren't going to get away with anything. I looked down at my sundress. "Why do I think this will be a problem?"

"They'll give us jumpsuits."

"Have you been here before? How do you know so much?"

"Google is my friend."

I slowly nodded. "And if we fall?"

They threw their head back and laughed. "I promise not to let anything happen to you," they said. "We'll be only a few feet off the ground. No more than ten. And if we do fall, you can land on me."

"How romantic," I said, still a little traumatized by my date with Charlotte.

"I zip-line all the time, so you'll be with a professional," they said.

"As long as you'll be right beside me, it should be fine," I said and linked my arms with theirs. At the end of our walk was the zip-line excursion. "Well, that was fast."

Alix shrugged. "I get you for only a short time before I have to hand you over to Emma." They looked sad when they mentioned my next date.

I touched their face. "But we still have an hour, so let's have some fun until then." I pulled on the ugliest orange, button-down jumpsuit that was a size too large for me and let a stranger strap me in. I checked all lines for any fraying, and after adjusting a new *When Sparks Fly* decorated helmet, we got into position and began our descent. Alix reached for my hand.

"See? This is easy and fun."

We weren't high off the ground so my anxiety wasn't too bad, but things got worse as we went. We crossed two small rivers, part of a town, and ended at the beach. I closed my eyes through most of it. My anxiety was off the charts, and once my feet touched solid ground again, I was angry.

Alix helped take my helmet off. "Wasn't that amazing? That was incredible. I had such a rush."

I peeled off my jumpsuit and sat on a bench to catch my breath. I wasn't happy. As wonderful as Alix was, they had pushed me into something I wasn't prepared for, something I explicitly said I didn't want to do. Their ten feet was more like forty or fifty.

A cameraman came out of nowhere with a bottle of water and an apple juice.

"Wait. Are you okay?" Alix finally realized I wasn't doing so well.

My voice was shaky. "That was higher than ten feet."

"But only in a few places. Besides, I saw you had your eyes closed through a lot of it," they said. "Which, by the way, only makes it worse."

"What makes it worse is you telling me that it wasn't bad. Who are you to judge me? I told everyone after the parasailing incident that I didn't want to go up in the air."

"You could have said no," they said.

"I already said no. You lied to get me to agree. That's not okay."

They looked horrified as it dawned on them how upset I was and how badly they had screwed up. And just like that, we were in our first fight, and I had a viable out with Alix.

"A spa date followed by an amazing dinner sounds lovely, Emma," I said. And it did. We were having a couples' massage at six, followed by dinner. The elimination cocktail party was after that, but we didn't talk about it.

"I thought so, too. I'm sorry other people here didn't listen to you," she said. She held the door to the expensive spa open for me. "I could spend half a day in here easily. I've scheduled us facials, too."

Go big or go home, I thought. According to the drive over here, neither one of us could afford such pampering at home, so we intended to enjoy every minute of it. "I definitely need this after today."

"It still blows my mind." She handed me a nonalcoholic juice with umbrellas and fruit pieces jabbed on a very long skewer that somebody off-screen gave her. "Let's hydrate, relax, and then indulge."

We wrapped up in fluffy robes and sat in facial chairs. I fell asleep in the middle of Emma telling me a story about one of her students at preschool and then again during the hot-stone massage. I had warned her that I might sleep during the massage but didn't expect it to happen immediately and for the entire time. She woke me up gently when she said we would miss dinner if we didn't get ready now. I felt relaxed, so I knew the massage worked, but I wished I'd been present for it.

"Since we're in Mexico, I've asked for some authentic food. They're taking us to a restaurant called Mextreme. According to all reviews, the vegetarian street tacos are to die for," she said.

"I really enjoy your accent."

She smiled and playfully smacked my arm. "I don't know what you're talking about. I don't have an accent." She crinkled her nose.

"You heard it, didn't you?" I asked.

She nodded and covered her face with her hands. "Ack. I'm so embarrassed."

I pulled her hands away from her face. "It's adorable, and you shouldn't be embarrassed." She took the opportunity to link her hands with mine, and we drove the entire way to the restaurant holding hands. I was hyper-aware of the contact, which made me jumpy more than anything else.

"Mexico is so beautiful."

"I wish we had more time here," I said. I didn't. I wanted this to be over, but I had a camera hanging three feet from my face recording my every word, my every expression, and it was daunting. I had to play along. I smiled and listened to Emma talk about the small toys and candy she'd bought for her students. When we reached the restaurant, I was surprised at the small crowd gathered near the entrance. The limo driver lowered the glass.

"I guess the world found out you planned to be here," he said.

Emma and I stared at each other. "What should we do?"

"I'll phone Denise," the cameraman directly in front of me said. He made a quick call. "Yes, about thirty people. Okay. We'll leave."

"Oh, no," Emma said. She turned to me and pouted. "I was really looking forward to the food."

"There are so many street vendors. Let's hit one closer to the hotel. I can't imagine things getting out of control there," I said. The people trying to peek inside the limo were starting to scare me. "Or we can just eat at the resort." Security was tight there. The limo driver honked until people moved, and he zipped us away, making sure nobody followed us.

"Let's just go back to the resort. It's gated, and we can find privacy there. Plus, we need to be there anyway for the candle ceremony later tonight." Emma's pale face told me this incident had shaken her up more than she was willing to admit. It wasn't a threat to us physically but an attack on our privacy.

I took Emma's hand again. "It's okay. The evening isn't ruined. Maybe we can place a to-go order since you were really looking forward to that restaurant. And then we can fake-eat whatever they put in front of us later for the camera."

"What do you want to order?" the cameraman asked. He was looking at the menu.

"I really wanted some vegetarian street tacos," Emma said.

"I can order them, and they do deliver," he said.

Emma looked at me for approval. I shrugged. "Whatever you want. This is your date."

"Yes, please. Can you order us two dinners and then whatever else you think we might like?"

"Let me make a quick call. Their delivery service is very fast. They might beat us back to the resort." He laughed at his own joke.

"Thank you. That would be wonderful." I looked at Emma. "See? Problem solved."

She impulsively kissed me, then tried to deepen the kiss, but I kept my lips together. It probably looked as awkward as it felt. "Thank you. It's the one thing I've been looking forward to the most." The weird kiss didn't seem to faze her. I couldn't seem to get away from people who planned their dates around what they wanted without any thought to my feelings.

## CHAPTER TWENTY-THREE

This is the final candle of the evening. Savannah, please take your time. This is a big decision, and there's no rush." Lauren looked amazing standing beside me. Her hair was down and styled the way I liked it. Her tight, red dress hit right at her knees. It was conservative but still sexy. I barely saw her before the happy hour, but every time I did, my heart exploded with memories of being in her arms two days ago.

I returned my attention to Alix and Emma, who were standing in front of me. Ophelia and Kaisley were on my right, holding lit candles. Every single person there thought they knew what was going to happen, including Emma, who was near tears.

"Thank you both for making Mexico memorable. I know we're all on this journey to find somebody we can spend time and maybe find love with. I have so much appreciation for both of you and hope that if I don't pick you tonight, you will continue searching and find the perfect person for you." I took a deep breath. "Emma." Every single person in the room was in shock. Alix's mouth fell open. Emma looked at Alix, then back to me, then back to Alix. I heard a camera person say "no way," and both Kaisley and Ophelia gasped. I repeated myself. "Emma." That got her attention. She walked up to me. "Emma, I feel a spark with you. Do you feel it, too?" She nodded. I lit her candle, and she moved to where the other two sparkettes stood.

Lauren swooped in and took over immediately. "Alix, I'm sorry. Please take all the time you need."

I waited patiently as Alix hugged the remaining contestants. I was getting emotional over the moment, and when Alix reached me, they took my hands in theirs. "Can I walk you out?" Alix looked numb. They were still in shock. I sat next to them on a bench outside, where the limo to take them away from me forever idled twenty feet away. Two cameramen were already set up.

"What happened? I thought. I mean…" Alix hung their head.

I knew they were fighting tears. I blinked back my own and squeezed their hand. "You are a wonderful person, and I've had the best time with you."

"Is it because of the zip-lining? I knew I should've changed our date. Why did I do something so stupid?" They smacked their forehead in disappointment.

I cupped their face and brushed the tears that fell on their cheeks. "It's not that. Well, not really. You're adventurous, and I really like that about you. It's just too easy for me to get swept up in what you want and ignore what I want. The zip line wasn't good for my health, but I ignored that feeling to make you happy. That's not a good relationship dynamic. I know you will find that perfect person. We had a wonderful time, and I really felt a connection with you, but we're just at different places right now. In time, you will find that I'm right." The tears were flowing down my face, too. Fuck, this was hard, and we were both ugly criers.

"Are you sure?"

"No. I'm not sure about anything. I just know you're wonderful, and I want you to stay this gorgeous and fun, and you will find the perfect person," I said. I pulled Alix close, and we cried for a few minutes in each other's arms. I refused to rush back in so I could stage a toast. I planned to stay here as long as it took to make them feel better and understand that they did nothing wrong. The world would think I got rid of them because of the zip-lining excursion. That was the price I had to pay for wanting a relationship with Lauren.

"I want us to stay in touch. I want to hear about your life and see you shine. You're a wonderful person, and I'm so honored to have met you."

Alix nodded and wiped their tears away. "I want that, too. Even if we didn't have the right connection, I think we can be the best of friends."

"I agree. As soon as I get my phone back, I want you to DM me."

They kissed me softly, and I let them. Alix would have been the one had my journey not taken a turn. I watched as they climbed into the limo and drove away. I looked up to the sky and tried hard to stop crying but couldn't. I sobbed for the shitty timing of all of it and how bad Alix felt.

After a few minutes, the cameras went back inside, and after Lauren peeked out to see if I was okay, I cried in her embrace. I didn't care if I was getting makeup on her dress. We had a whole crew of people who would be able to make us both look unaffected by what just happened.

"Come on. Let's go somewhere more private," she whispered.

I let her guide me to the large bathroom on the main floor, away from the three remaining contestants, whose low whispers irked me. She held her finger up, untethered my microphone from my dress, and slipped it underneath a pile of towels. I walked into her outstretched arms and cried. She stroked my hair and didn't say anything. We both knew what was at stake and how it was going to hurt. We had never talked about how, but I'd known I had to get rid of Alix first because I felt the strongest for them. When I had cried all the tears I could, I pulled back and looked at her. "That wrecked me."

She wiped a few of my tears. "I know. That was the hardest thing to do."

She held my hands and took deep breaths with me until I was ready to talk. I looked at my reflection. "I'm the world's ugliest crier. Mandee's going to have her hands full trying to get me to look good again."

"Don't even worry about it. We don't have to do the obligatory toast tonight. It was hard on all of us. Denise said we can wrap it up."

"Really?"

"That's translation for it was good television. Honestly, I think we all need to break and just regroup in the morning."

I nodded. "Thank you for understanding and being here for me."

She kissed me softly. "I know this has been incredibly emotional for you, and I completely understand. I just wish I could comfort you more. Let's get you back to your room." She opened the door to two camera people and Denise waiting on the other side of the door.

"Are you okay, Savannah?" Denise asked. She gave me a weak, somewhat supportive smile, and I nodded.

"I'm numb and really tired."

"That was quite the surprise." Denise walked with me and Lauren back to my suite. "I know this is hard, but we got some really good, authentic footage."

"Alix is great. They all are, but Alix is young and still fresh to relationships. They aren't ready for what I need and want." That wasn't the truth, but it was what I was willing to believe to make it easy.

Denise touched my forearm. "Take the night off. Lauren, stay with Savannah for a bit if you have time."

"I'll make sure she's taken care of," Lauren said.

"Thank you," I said.

"See you in the morning. Get some sleep. We have another big day tomorrow." Denise excused herself while Lauren opened the door to my suite.

"Let's get you comfortable for the night," she said.

I was still upset about saying good-bye to Alix but happy that Lauren was with me. It couldn't have been easy for her to watch the night unfold. She was a professional, though, and the only emotion that visibly seeped through was shock.

"Go change into something comfortable. I'll be right here," Lauren said.

I was overly emotional and needed a moment to collect myself. I knew what I'd done was for the best, but it still hurt. I turned on the shower and picked a pair of boxers and a T-shirt. I wanted to wash away the day and curl up on the bed with Lauren. The hot water felt wonderful.

"I guess I was in there a long time," I said. Lauren was wearing yoga pants and a T-shirt that I assumed she'd grabbed from her room while I was in the shower. She stood when I entered the bedroom.

"I figured you needed some alone time to deal with such an emotional night," she said. She pulled me into her arms and held me. She wasn't jealous or mean. She was being Lauren, and it was perfect.

"Thank you for understanding."

"It's such a hard journey."

I looked at her. "But it's worth it. Can we sit down? I'm exhausted."

She pulled back the covers and fluffed the pillows on the bed. "Come here."

I crawled onto the bed and patted the space next to me. "My turn. Come here." The knock on the door made us separate. "Who's that? It's so late."

She held up her finger. "Hang on."

My heart sped up when she answered the door. I couldn't hear who it was, but the moment she closed and locked the door, I asked, "Who was it? What did they want?"

"It was Denise's assistant checking to see if you needed anything. Also, security is guarding your suite like a hawk, so I'll have to leave at some point."

"But we have time, right?" I asked. I reached for her when she crawled back onto the bed.

"We do. There's no rush. Do you want to talk about tonight?"

"Not really." I wanted to be held. I needed her comfort. I wasn't sure when it turned from compassion to passion, but I forgot everything when her lips found mine. I sank against her, weak with desire.

She spread my legs apart with hers and ran her forefinger across my bottom lip. "Are you sure about this? You've had such a hard night."

I nodded. "This is perfect. You're perfect and exactly what I need." I knew time was precious. She leaned up and stripped off her T-shirt. I ran my fingers over her tight stomach as she tossed the shirt over onto the chair. I touched her scar, which was partially covered by a white sports bra. "You're beautiful."

She stopped my hand. "It's ugly."

I leaned up and kissed her. "Nothing about you is ugly." She moaned when I kissed her and pushed her back onto the bed. I wasn't usually the aggressor, but I couldn't keep my hands off her. "How did I get so lucky?" Her skin was warm under my lips as I made a trail from her sensitive neck, over the swell of her breasts, down her quivering stomach, until I hit the waistband of her pants. She lifted her hips, and I pulled both her pants and panties off. We didn't have a lot of time, and I needed to show her how I felt because words were too much. What if I said the wrong thing? What if I pushed too far? I could say things with my hands and body that I couldn't any other way. I sat on my heels and pulled off my shirt. Lauren automatically reached up to rub my breasts and slide her fingertips over my hard nipples.

"I'm the lucky one," she said. She ran her fingers over the smooth skin between my cleavage.

As much as I enjoyed her touch, I knew that something bigger was happening here. "Take off your bra," I said. Her eyes met mine, and I gave a small nod. I wanted us both to be naked, so I slid off my boxers while she wrestled with her tight bra. I helped her when it got tangled in her hair. She squeezed my breasts and sucked one of my nipples into her mouth. I moaned my appreciation.

"Shh. We can't have anybody hear us," she said.

"They can't hear us from here, can they? I mean, the bed is far away from the door." I bit my lip to keep from making noises as Lauren continued to lick and suck every part of me she could reach with her mouth while I straddled her.

"The walls are surprisingly thin," she said. When my shoulders slumped, she quickly added, "But don't worry. We have fluffy pillows to moan into, and I'll make sure things don't spiral out of control."

I touched the dimple high up on her cheek. "But I want things to get out of control with you." I meant my emotions, because they were already teetering, but she took it a different way.

"Let's wait for that until we can be somewhere entirely more private."

I kissed her because I was done talking. I just wanted to find bliss in her arms and not worry about other people, a schedule that was entirely too demanding, and the shitshow that was going to be my life for the next two weeks.

She wrapped her arms around my back and quickly flipped me so she was on top. "It's so hard to see you and not be able to touch you every day."

"I can't ever see that on your face," I said.

She kissed me hard. "Never think that. I'm just trying to get through the day as much as you are."

That was the last thing she said before leaving my mouth to run a trail of hard kisses and soft bites down me until she reached my hips. Just as I was about to spread my legs, she grabbed my hips and turned me over. My excitement level jumped from a ten to a thousand at the delicious thoughts that flooded my brain. Facedown in the pillow, I waited with anticipation. She ran her tongue over the back of my knees, and I jumped at the sensation. When she reached the back of my thighs, I wiggled for friction. She was so close to my pussy that I could feel her body heat. I knew what her mouth and hands were capable of. She spread my lips apart and darted her tongue over my opening. I lifted my hips higher so she had better access, but she pushed them back down into the mattress and climbed over me until I could feel her hot breath on my ear. Her voice was a gravelly purr. "Here's the part where you're going to need the pillow." She spread my legs with her knees, slid her fingers expertly over my slick pussy, and pushed two inside. I threw my head back and gasped at the raw pleasure that rippled through me. "Shh, Savannah. You have to be quiet."

How was I supposed to be quiet when she was fucking me this way, at this angle, getting so deep inside that my legs were shaking and I wasn't even close to coming? "Yes, okay." I dropped my face to the pillow. The moans that were coming from me were out of my control as I felt her slip a third finger inside. I was tight but so wet it didn't take me long to adjust. I had to lift my hips to accommodate, and she slid deeper inside. She moaned and bit my ass while I buried my face and let out a cry. "Oh, my God. Yes, Lauren. Fuck. Yes." My words failed, and I moaned with every thrust of her hand. I was going to orgasm, and it was going to be magnificent.

My knees were barely able to support me, and when I finally reached the peak and my orgasm crashed into me, I slowly slid to the mattress and cried. Not because I was sad, but because I had never experienced something that powerful before. The fact that Lauren had given me such pleasure only intensified my experience. She carefully slipped her hand away and curled up behind me. She ran her fingertips over my neck and down my back as I waited for my shakes to subside. "Sorry about not being quiet," I mumbled. I wasn't, and she knew it.

"I think we got away with it."

I tried to laugh, but my body and mind weren't working the way they should, and my laugh came out more like a whimper. My body was sore, but I'd never felt so alive. "If this is how it's going to be every single time, I feel a very combustible spark with you. Do you feel it, too?" I spoke in jest, but when I turned to look at her, her expression was very serious. I thought maybe I'd crossed the line, but she smoothed out the lines on my forehead with her thumb and smiled.

"I feel it, too."

## CHAPTER TWENTY-FOUR

It was our last night in Mexico, and I was in the same awful position of sending another person home. The shitty part was that Kaisley and I had had a wonderful time horseback riding on the beach. It was romantic and beautiful, but I was there with the wrong person. Emma and Kaisley stood in front of me. Ophelia, off to my right, held a lit candle and seemed to be trying hard not to smirk. I wondered if she thought she was my final pick since she was the first.

"This experience has taught me a lot about people and relationship expectations. I came onto the show looking for love, or at least the possibility of love. We all did. I truly believe everyone left is here for me and what I want. That's why this is so hard." I imagined all the tabloids and entertainment shows were going to roast me, again, only this time for getting rid of fan favorites. "Please understand that I care for each of you so much and respect you for sacrificing so much to be here." I looked at Emma and Kaisley and knew Kaisley was going to be crushed. Deep breath. "Emma." Tears instantly welled in Kaisley's eyes. Fuck, it killed me to do this. "Emma, I feel a spark with you. Do you feel it, too?" She hugged me first and then held her candle to my flame. Kaisley started swaying back and forth, and I knew I had to get to her and explain.

Lauren reached her first. "Kaisley, I'm very sorry. Please say your good-byes."

She turned and embraced Ophelia, who smiled at me over Kaisley's shoulder. I looked away. I didn't want the hint of any scandal on this season that involved me. I waited patiently while Emma handed Kaisley a tissue, and she desperately tried to remain calm and in control, but the minute she walked toward me, she started sobbing. I held her tightly until her sobs were somewhat under control.

"Let me walk you to the limo," I said.

"Do you mind if I just go alone?"

I was shocked that she didn't want me to explain myself and completely embarrassed that she said so in front of the cameras. "I'm completely fine with that. I understand your need to be alone." I really did. I hugged her one last time and watched her walk out the door and climb into a limo waiting to take her far away from here.

Since I didn't have the emotional breakdown like I did with Alix, I stayed behind and toasted with Emma and Ophelia. They were the ones who would meet Jane and hopefully my mother next week. The thing I liked about *When Sparks Fly* was that I got to meet their families as well. Final candle was in a week. Episode four out of ten was dropping tomorrow. The pace astounded me, but I was warned upfront that it was a whirlwind of a season.

"Ladies, how is everyone feeling this evening?" Completely unscripted and unplanned, Lauren sat in a chair opposite the couch. My heart soared, and it was difficult to keep from dreamily smiling at her. "It's been a very hard week, and I'm excited to go home and meet families and see mine again." I wondered how the business was doing. I knew Jane could handle it, but it wasn't easy being so cut off.

"At least Kaisley can go home to her son," Ophelia said.

She wasn't wrong. but I found her comment in poor taste. "Hopefully, she finds somebody soon. She's really a wonderful person." I was worried about her mental state. She wouldn't have closure, and that would make the "Secrets Revealed" episode even juicier for fans of the show. Too bad I'd already had my appendix removed.

"Okay, ladies. Have a good evening. I have a surprise for you when we get back to Florida," Lauren said.

I couldn't read her expression and was going to have to wait to find out with the rest of them. It didn't seem like bad news though. Surprises were usually good, right? "Sleep well." We watched Lauren walk away.

"She's so pretty. Is she single?" Ophelia asked.

I wanted to say keep your hands to yourself and leave her alone, but that would blow my cover, and she *was* pretty. "I don't think so. I mean, she never said she was."

"Is she even gay?" Emma asked.

"She's probably dating somebody ultra-rich and famous. Like royalty in a foreign country. She literally could pick from anyone she wanted," Ophelia said.

"There's not a lot of personal information online. I did a social-media dive when I was chosen to be on the show, but it was never confirmed or denied that she's a lesbian or bi."

I stood because we'd reached the gossiping stage of the conversation, and I wasn't going to partake any longer. "Okay. I'm leaving. I'll see you both in the morning."

"Oh, you can't stay for just a bit longer?" Emma asked.

I shook my head. "Thank you, but I'm drained. Have fun." I walked back to my room, sad because I knew I wouldn't see Lauren privately until the show was done. I locked my door, and even though I didn't have the energy, I packed my clothes and crawled into bed early. I was beyond exhausted, and life wasn't about to get easier.

When I opened the door to my mansion, Jane was standing in the foyer. "Jane! You're here!" I grabbed her and hugged her. "I can't believe it. Wait. Is everything okay?"

"Everything is fine. The business is fine, your mother is fine," she said.

That's when I started crying. The stress of the entire show and me being so alone was too much.

"Come here. Has it been that bad?" she asked.

She stroked the back of my head while I cried out my frustrations. "Let's go upstairs." I needed my best friend, and our conversation didn't need to be filmed. I grabbed her hand and walked quickly up the stairs. I had so much to say and wasn't sure where to begin.

Jane sat on the couch and leaned forward, obviously eager to hear about my journey. "Mexico, huh?"

"I have so much to say, but I need to shower."

A knock at the door startled me. It was Evelyn, one of Denise's assistants. "Denise wants to see you."

"Right now? We literally just got back, and I've had two minutes with Jane."

"She was pretty adamant."

I sighed and wiped my eyes. "Jane, I have to go, but hopefully I'll be back in just a few minutes. If you want something to eat, ask Josef with an 'ef.' He's the chef of the manor, mansion, whatever this place is. I won't be long." She gave me a playful salute and waved me off.

I followed Evelyn down the stairs. Instead of entering the information room or the office, she walked out of the house. "Wait. We aren't meeting here?"

"No. We're going to the office."

I hadn't been there since the initial meeting. "Okay." I climbed into the back of the car and tried to clean my smeared makeup the best I could with a tissue and a compact. The drive took about twenty minutes in minimal traffic. I wanted to get back to Jane. She said everything was fine, but I needed more information.

"Right this way, Savannah." The driver opened the door and ushered me inside.

The same receptionist greeted me. "Ms. Edwards. It's nice to see you again. I'll buzz you through the door." She hit a button and pointed me to the side door. Cole was walking toward me.

"There you are. I'm sorry I wasn't downstairs to greet you," he said.

"What's going on, Cole?"

"I'm not one hundred percent sure. Follow me, please."

I followed him down the hall until we reached the same conference room where I had signed my life away months ago. Denise, Peter Meyers with his great hair, and two men I didn't know were sitting on one side of the table.

Denise waved me in. "Savannah, please sit down." Her lips were pressed so tightly that they disappeared into a straight line. This wasn't good.

I sat opposite them and folded my arms. "What's this about?"

She pulled out an eight-by-ten photo, slapped it onto the conference room table, and pushed it in front of me. "We're being blackmailed because of this photo. What in the fuck were you thinking?"

I looked down at a photo of me kissing Lauren. It was when she sneaked out of my room in Mexico. I went from extreme cold to extreme heat and was starting to sweat.

"Who is she, Savannah?"

They didn't know. I looked closer. The hat and sunglasses disguised her features, and the world hadn't seen Lauren in jeans and a casual T-shirt. They weren't looking for Lauren in the photo, so they didn't see her. It didn't look like any of the contestants either. It was obviously me. I couldn't deny that, but I could pretend it was just a hookup. "She's somebody I met when I sneaked out. Not a contestant. Somebody who I found at a bar like two blocks from the hotel."

"This has royally fucked everything up. What in the hell were you thinking?" she asked again. "I don't even know how to do damage control," Denise shouted.

I was two seconds from freaking out when Lauren burst in.

"I'm so sorry I'm late. What's going on?" she asked.

I wanted to protect her, so I started talking immediately. "I hooked up with somebody in Mexico, and some rando took a photo and is blackmailing the show. Here." I thrust the photo at Lauren.

"Wait, what?" Lauren grabbed the photo from me and looked at it closely.

"Nobody even knows who it is," I said.

"Who the fuck is it?" Denise asked.

"None of your damn business," I said, my anger boiling over at my own embarrassment.

"Everything about this show is my business," Denise yelled.

Peter stood. "Okay. Let's settle down and focus on damage control. Obviously we're not going to pay anybody anything. Let's figure out how to get out of this."

"The show is ruined," Denise said.

I dropped my head iton my hands. This wasn't happening. "I can quit. I can walk away."

"Will any of the contestants say it's them? Maybe we can throw money at one of them," Cole said.

Now I was offended. "They aren't like that."

"They're on television, aren't they?" Peter said.

I wanted to argue with him, but he wasn't wrong. "Can't we just say I was kissing somebody?"

"She is literally hanging off your balcony. This isn't just a kiss. This is a fuck session," Denise said.

"Don't be rude, Denise. We've had scandals in the past. What are our legitimate avenues?" Lauren asked the two men sitting next to Peter, whom I assumed were the show's lawyers.

"We can let the scandal blow up, and Savannah can take the blows. She's a favorite, and fans will probably forgive her. Maybe tonight she can tell Emma and Ophelia that she kissed somebody else and let it play out," Denise said.

"Nobody's throwing Savannah under the bus," Lauren said.

I put my hand on Lauren's arm. When she looked at me, I shook my head. I didn't want her to sacrifice everything. Her job was too important to her. "Don't worry about me. Let's just figure out the best way to get out of this with the least amount of damage for the show." Including you, I added silently, hoping that she knew what I was doing.

"Lauren, you're the level-headed one of this group with the best ideas. You have your pulse on the audience. Do you have any ideas?" Denise asked.

Lauren pushed her chair out and stood, putting both her palms on the table. I shook my head at her, but she ignored me. "I don't know how we're going to fix this, but I want everyone to know that the person in the photo with Savannah is me."

## CHAPTER TWENTY-FIVE

O kay, slow down. What do you mean it's over?"
In the living room, Jane pulled me over to the plush couch I'd never sat on before and put her hands on my shoulders. I was overwhelmed and didn't know how to get my head above water.

"I hate that we haven't talked yet. We need to go upstairs," I said.

"This is a gorgeous place. Why can't we talk here?"

I leaned forward. "Trust me." She followed me up the stairs, and I dropped onto the bed.

Jane dropped beside me. "So, what's going on? Why'd we have to come up here?"

I rolled over and looked at her. "Cameras are everywhere but here and in the bathrooms. Brace yourself. I slept with Lauren."

She sat up. "Shut up. Lauren Lucas? The beautiful hostess of your show? How did that happen?"

"She was just super sweet and really nice to me, and we bonded over swimming and doughnuts, and then I slipped and crossed the line," I said.

"That's amazing. She seems so genuine and classy. On the show you look like you're really into Alix and Ophelia," Jane said.

"I really liked Alix and Kaisley, but then spending time with Lauren and really getting to know her changed my feelings for the people I was supposed to be falling in love with." I flopped onto the bed. "This is the worst thing ever. I'll be lucky if I leave here without a lawsuit."

"What could they sue you over?"

"Violation of my contract, I guess. I came here to at least make money and restore my reputation, but there's no way that's happening."

"You mean they won't pay you? Aren't they contractually obligated to give that to you?"

"Nope. Only if I finish the season without a scandal, and this feels like a monumental one," I said.

Jane moved so she was right next to me. "To be fair, you did find someone, and it was because of the show."

"I hope nothing bad happens to Lauren. We need to play along so she can keep her job. I can't believe I'm going to be the laughingstock of *When Sparks Fly* and the internet again," I said.

"Let me tell you how things appeared on television. First of all, you looked beautiful and happy every time the camera was on you. I was so proud of you, and I still am."

"Ugh. I don't know if I want to hear this right now." I was still too worried about Lauren and repercussions for her.

"It's something to talk about. But I guess we can discuss the massive upswing in business instead," she said.

I sat up. "Really?"

Jane nodded. "Yep. Almost everything is gone, and we have orders for the fall candles when we start production on them again." That was code for when I made a huge batch of candles. While Jane was fully capable of making candles, she knew I was a perfectionist and would rather do everything myself.

"Oh, and our Instagram followers have multiplied."

"Do you have your phone here?"

"No. They took it. But I have my iPad that has cellular."

"I'm going to need you to get the tablet without anyone seeing it and bring it up here right away. I want to do some investigating." I paced while Jane went downstairs to get her messenger bag. First, had the photo been leaked yet? Probably not, since the blackmailer was looking for cash. Then I wanted to find out everything on Lauren, which I should've done in the first place. I stopped my back-and-forth trek when I heard her footsteps.

"I brought a friend," Jane said and stepped aside. Lauren walked into the bedroom, and I immediately hugged her.

"Why did you do that?" I pulled away to look into Lauren's eyes. "I didn't want you to risk everything for me. I'm more than willing to take the hit. I have nothing to lose. I mean, I survived this show before, and I'll do it again." She squeezed my hands and asked me to sit with her.

"I'm going to the kitchen and find something to drink," Jane said.

She bolted before I could tell her to stay. I wanted her close because she was my best friend and I needed her strength, but Lauren looked like she had a lot to say. I would fill Jane in later.

"So, I'd like to say there's good news and bad news, but there really isn't anything but bad news."

I leaned back and sighed. "Fuck."

"You for sure have to finish the show. You're under contract. If you don't, they will sue the hell out of you. So, I have a plan," Lauren said.

"I'm going to hate it, aren't I?" I threaded my fingers with hers and braced myself for news I knew I was going to dread.

"It's a solid plan. It's the only thing that'll work for the network, you, and me. You have to continue the hometown dates. Jane will meet Ophelia and Emma, and then you'll have to meet with their families and do the 'Secrets Revealed' episode." She held up her hand when I tried to interject something. "Hang on. Please let me finish. At the end, ideally, it would be great if you picked one and then did a few publicity stunts and broke up."

"Well, I hate that idea. I don't want to hurt anyone. What's the bare minimum I can do without losing everything?"

"Still do the visits and the 'Secrets Revealed' episode. You're not getting out of that one no matter how hard you try, but at the end you can say it didn't work out for you. It was too rushed. You didn't find the connection you wanted."

"But that's a lie," I said.

It was the first time she smiled. "That's probably not what they're expecting."

"But it's the truth, and I'm not ashamed of it. I found what I wanted, what I needed on this show, even if it wasn't the way everyone expected." I looked away. Confessions were tough, and my emotions were already scraped raw. "You're perfect. Completely out of my league, but here we are, and I'm going to do whatever it takes to keep you in my life." I braced myself for words that would shred me but, instead, made my heart soar.

"We're going to make this work. You just have to put on a show and give them what they want, and once it's done, we can focus on us," she said.

The next two weeks sounded emotionally exhausting, but I could do it. "That sounds wonderful." I rested my forehead against hers. "What do we do now?"

She kissed my lips softly. "We get through this. You smile for the camera and give them the show the world expects. I pretend it's wonderful to watch you date other women."

"You know I don't want to."

"I know. I'm not insecure, but that doesn't make it any easier."

"I need to prep Jane for everything. Can I tell her what's happening?"

"As long as you do it here in the bedroom. The producers don't want the crew to get wind of all this."

"Good to know. And I trust Jane. She would never say anything to anyone." I stood. "I'll bring her up here so you can really meet her."

We both looked at her phone when it rang. "It's *Sparks*' lawyers calling. I'd better take this." She answered it as I was closing the door.

"Jane, where are you?" The mansion was huge, and for the first time ever, I didn't run into a single person. I found her sitting on the couch eating a sandwich and immediately wondered where she got bread. I plopped down next to her. "Would you like to eat upstairs?"

"Are you done talking?"

"For now. We had to discuss the upcoming family dates both here and at their hometowns." I was totally dreading them. I was expected to sit in front of parents and tell them how much I cared for their daughters, when I knew it was a bold-faced lie. I liked Emma and Ophelia, but not in the way everyone thought.

Jane eyed me carefully, understanding that we were under scrutiny. "Okay. I want to see this gorgeous home. Give me the tour."

She played along perfectly. *Sparks* had several cameras staged on both floors, so I knew to keep the conversation on the show. Jane didn't ask a lot of questions but followed me and nodded at the appropriate times.

"It's a gorgeous house. A bit larger than yours." Jane laughed.

As soon as we reached the bedroom, I opened the door slowly, hoping we weren't disturbing Lauren's phone call. She was sitting on the chaise, scrolling through her phone as though everything hadn't just blown up. "Hi. Is everything okay?"

Lauren nodded. "They decided to buy some time and throw money at the blackmailers. I told them you were going to finish the show. As long as we get through the next two weeks without another incident, you should be in the clear."

"Okay. Let's talk. What's going on?" Jane asked. She sat at the desk and waited for one of us to start.

"I don't even know where to begin. I fucked things up. And we're trying to salvage the show and our lives," I said.

"It wasn't only you. I was right there with you on that balcony," Lauren said.

I smiled at the memory and launched into the story of the past six weeks and how Lauren and I were photographed in Mexico. "I was going to walk away from the show, but the lawyers got all lawyerly with me, and now I have to finish. We have to do the family visits, and then I have to record the 'Secrets Revealed' and the last episode, where I will pick nobody."

"How will that go over?" Jane asked.

"Contractually, I'm in the clear. Ideally, they want me to pick somebody, then dump them down the road, but I can't do that. Stringing people along isn't my thing."

"I hate to do this, but I have to go," Lauren said. She waved her phone at us. "I have some damage control to take care of on my end. Tomorrow is a big day. Jane, I'm sorry to have met you under these circumstances, but I'm glad you're here. Savannah has really missed you over the last few months."

"I'm happy to be here. And it's a pleasure meeting you, too."

I walked Lauren to the bedroom door. "Let me know if things change and I need to do something different."

She pressed her lips softly against mine. "I will. Get some sleep. Mandee will be upset if you show up with puffy, sleepy eyes."

"I'll be lucky if I get any sleep at all," I said.

"Good night," Lauren said, flashing us a brilliant smile before leaving us alone.

"Oh, my God. I need all the details. Tell me everything, especially the part about hooking up with Lauren. She's gorgeous."

I took a moment to appreciate the positive in my downward-spiraling life. "She really is. She's smart, worldly, beautiful, funny, empathetic. Jane, I love her. I know it sounds bonkers that I came here agreeing to date ten people but found love with somebody not on the roster."

"She makes you happy, and that's all I care about. Who made the first move? I'm here for the romance. Spill."

"Honestly, everything's been a blur, but one night she let it slip that there was something between us, and I pushed."

Jane gave a little squeal. "Yes. I love this so hard."

"Well, it's hard, trust me. I will be distancing myself from her, and that's going to be difficult now that we've crossed the line."

"Okay. Let's get through the next two weeks, and then you can celebrate together. In the meantime, let's talk about tomorrow. Can you think of anything I should do or say or ask the contestants? I can play bad cop if you need me to."

"That's sweet. I don't really know right now." Too much had happened today, and I was starting to shut down. Jane saw it, too.

"What time are we supposed to be on set tomorrow? Or downstairs or wherever?"

"We'll probably start recording at noon. I think we're filming here," I said.

She gave me a tight hug. "Get some sleep, and we can talk in the morning. I love you, and I'll see you bright and early."

Sleep was difficult because my brain wouldn't shut off. It had been one of the worst days of my life yet somehow the best thing that had ever happened to me. When everything came crashing down, I wanted Lauren to save herself. I even gave her the out, but she didn't take it. Instead, she came up with a way to keep us going without getting hit with career-crushing lawsuits. But that wasn't even the best part. The best part was while the dumpster fire raged behind us, she was still all in.

❖

"Ophelia, this is Jane. She's my best friend."

"It's so nice to meet you. Savannah has told us all so much about you," Ophelia said.

That wasn't exactly true. I'd brought up Jane only a handful of times.

"It's nice to meet you too," Jane said.

We were sitting in the living room facing the ocean. Ophelia had showed up wearing a green, sleeveless summer dress that hugged her curves and landed mid-thigh. Jane kept her eyes focused on Ophelia's face, but I knew she already had an opinion of the way Ophelia was dressed. She looked sexy and confident. Jane knew my feelings for Lauren, but she was a good sport and still charming with her.

"What do you like most about Savannah?" Jane asked. *Sparks* had given Jane a list of possible questions to ask, and this one was high on the list.

"I'm going to grab some wine and let you two get to know one another better." I didn't want to hear the answer. Hearing compliments always made me uncomfortable, especially if they weren't true. As nice and beautiful as Ophelia was, it was becoming obvious with each passing day that she was in it for herself. Maybe she was on the show to find more clients as a life coach. I didn't blame her, nor did I really care. Now that I'd found what I was looking for, I only wanted the best for her. I opened the glass door and stood on the oversized patio overlooking the water. It was so beautiful here. Hot, but the ocean breeze made it bearable. For a split second, I forgot I was on the show until a cameraman slid into my peripheral vision. Oh yeah. I was here to break hearts. I went back inside. "How are things?"

"Great. It's so nice chatting with your best friend," Ophelia said.

She patted the empty cushion beside her. I sat and gritted my teeth but smiled when she held my hand.

"Jane's been telling me about your life back home and how good you are with her kids."

"I'm an amazing aunt." Weird that Ophelia had picked that subject to start the conversation with. She didn't even like children. Maybe she was worried that I wanted a slew of them, because she made it perfectly clear that she didn't.

We had an awkward lunch together, and once it was over, I walked her out. The good-bye kiss was terrible, but she pretended it was the best kiss she'd ever had.

"I can't wait for you to meet my family," Ophelia said.

I waved until the limo was down the drive. *One down, one to go.* Emma wasn't supposed to arrive until dinner. That meant I had time to chill with Jane.

Lauren swooped in. "Ladies, can we have a quick chat?" Mandee was a half-step behind her with her makeup brushes and palette in hand.

"Definitely. Where would you like to have it?"

"Right here is fine."

Lauren looked beautiful in her pastel-blue sleeveless dress. Two bracelets dangled from her wrist, and a simple diamond necklace rested against her neck. Her hair was down and pulled over one shoulder. It was hard not to touch her. My chest swelled with pride. This beautiful woman was mine. I watched as she charmed Jane while Mandee powdered my shiny face and fixed my eyeshadow.

"Almost done," Mandee said. She smacked her lips together, wanting me to mimic her, and slipped a soft cotton pad between my lips to pat down the lipstick and remove any excess from my mouth. I didn't like lipstick, but judging from the smoldering look Lauren shot me, that might change. Lauren took a seat in the chair next to the couch, so we were all on the same side, with four cameras ready to capture every reaction.

"Jane, thank you for being here."

Jane squeezed my hand. "Anything to help my best friend find true love."

I squeezed hers in return. "Thank you."

"You've known Savannah for a long time. What has her dating life been like since you've known her?"

"Not great. But not because she isn't lovable, because she is. Savannah has the biggest heart in the world. I'm lucky to have her as my best friend. But it's hard to find somebody when you work seventy to eighty hours a week. Her business is everything, and I get why she works so hard."

"It's difficult to find time to date when you put all of yourself into your work," I said. At Lauren's encouraging nod, I continued. "I want somebody in my life. I just wanted to have a foundation first. Suddenly, it's ten years later, and I'm on a reality dating show to find true love."

"You're down to the final two contestants. And we know it's a fast season, but do you believe you're going to find that special someone?" Lauren asked.

"Yes. I believe I'll find love on this show."

## CHAPTER TWENTY-SIX

The bugs were the worst. Kentucky in July was unbearable. Emma's family was fun and over-the-top nice, but they did everything outside. Mandee aged two years the two days we were there just trying to keep my makeup from sliding down my face and making me camera ready.

"Come dance with me." Emma pulled me to the makeshift dance floor on her parents' front yard. The lights set up by the show attracted every single winged insect within a five-mile radius, and her family didn't seem to care.

"Why are you so tense?" she asked.

"Because I don't want a bug to get stuck in my hair or crawl down my shirt." My fear was obvious.

"Come on. The bugs are more afraid of you."

"That's a solid no," I said. I'd begged Buzzy to let me wear tight clothes and had Mandee put my hair up to avoid any possible altercation with a flying insect.

I had to give it to Emma. She was playful and charming around her family. Whenever I started having a good time with the family, pangs of guilt jabbed my heart. Last night I'd had dinner with her parents, and tonight was a grill-out with the whole family. Her five-year-old niece clung to me most of the night. Whenever Emma tried to get me alone, I pointed to her and shrugged. I felt terrible for using her as a buffer. I knew alone time was coming, but I intended to prolong the wait.

My sit-down with her parents was a lot less stressful than the conversation I'd had with Ophelia's family. Emma's parents were so relaxed and didn't press me on my intentions. Ophelia's parents, her siblings, and her aunt had grilled me relentlessly. I was handed from family member to family member until it became obvious they were talking to me only to get on television. *Sparks* would edit the shit out of that hometown date.

"Let's get out of here," she said.

"As long as it's inside." Camera people scrambled to get in front of us and cue the one guy in the house.

"Fine. Let's go hang out in my old room." She wagged her eyes at me and grabbed my hand.

"Let's not get too carried away. Your parents are here." I was starting to sweat.

She brushed her lips over mine. "My parents won't mind. They like you. A lot. And so do I."

She applied more pressure to the second kiss. I had to remind myself that this was what I needed in order to give the show what they wanted. I responded, but not passionately. There was a rule about open-mouth kisses on the show, and I was going to be a stickler for the rules. I broke the kiss first. "Okay, show me your room." It came out sexier than I intended.

"Oh, that sounds like fun."

Emma jogged up the stairs, then back down so a camera person could go ahead of her to film both of us jogging up the stairs like giggling teenagers. I felt stupid doing it because I was thirty-two.

Her room was full of show ribbons and crafting supplies. "What are the ribbons for?"

"Horseback riding. I've been riding since I was five."

I put the large blue ribbon back on the shelf. "That's amazing." Fuck, that word again. "I don't think I've ever been on the back of a horse."

Emma sat on the bed and patted the mattress. "Come here." Her sexy smile left nothing to the imagination.

A cameraman was in the small room with us. Denise barked for him to leave and asked Emma to shut the door. The situation was suggestive, and I hated it, but Lauren knew this was part of it all. I had to give it to Denise. After the blowup in the conference room, she was nothing but professional toward me.

"They're gone." Emma sprawled on the bed. "So, why did you pick me out of everyone else? I'm happy you did, but honestly, I didn't think I was top two."

Though the camera people had been kicked out, they'd probably still placed cameras and microphones everywhere. I proceeded with caution. "You're a very special person with the kindest heart. You're gentle, great with people, great with kids. You always look for the good, and that's hard to find in people anymore." I spoke from the heart. Emma was all that and more. She would make somebody very happy one day. All the sparkettes would. Even Madison.

"That's the sweetest thing anyone has ever said about me."

She kissed me again. It was sweet, but I felt no sparks. It only reminded me what I'd been missing the last week. Lauren was not allowed in my private quarters. They were keeping us apart so we could honor our contractual obligations and not get caught by paparazzi. Again. The photo had not been leaked, and we were trying hard to reach the end of the show without our relationship ruining everything.

I slowly pulled away. "It's time for me to go." She pouted. "I know, but they're trying to keep everything equal, although I think I've spent more time with you than allowed."

"Thank you for visiting and getting to know my family. I hope they've made a lasting impression on you," she said. Her niece cried as Emma walked me to the limo. Emma gave me a warm hug and another soft kiss. "I'll see you in a week."

I climbed into the limo and slouched into the seat. I didn't care that a guy with a camera was three feet from me. I knew I had to say something clever and convince the world that my heart was torn, that it was going to be so hard to decide. I took a sip of water and sat up. "The two of them are very different. Ophelia is driven and sexy, whereas Emma is fun, cute, and perky. It will be a difficult decision because I admire them both for different things. I'm not even sure

I can make a decision. I have a lot to think about over the next few days." That was an understatement.

❖

"Let's welcome this season's flame, Savannah Edwards."

Lauren's applause was my cue to join her on stage for the dreaded "Secrets Revealed" episode. The stage was beautifully decorated. I was invited to sit on the small neutral-color love seat with round, muted-orange pillows. It was hard not to stare at Lauren. She looked so beautiful in her dark gray, short-sleeved dress with black heels. Her hair flowed in waves down her back. Her beauty took me aback, and I stumbled on my way to the stage. She reached out to steady me.

"Are you okay?"

I tried to recover. "That's a tricky step." I sat down after giving Lauren a quick hug. It was so good to see her and feel her in my arms again, even briefly. I had to mask my feelings because I was an easy read. "Glad to be seated." The audience laughed nervously for me. I took a moment to look around the room. Eight unhappy contestants were sitting among approximately eighty audience members. The next two hours were going to be hell. The show would whittle it down to forty-two minutes, but I was obligated to be there for two hours. The producers had given me a list of questions Lauren would ask me and a stack of ways I could answer possible questions from the contestants.

"Savannah, welcome to the show." Lauren's eyes shone when they met mine. Our secret was giving me strength.

"Thank you."

"We have a lot to talk about so let's get down to it. I'm sure people want answers," Lauren said. She was rewarded with applause from both audience and contestants. "Have you found your person here?"

I knew to keep the answers vague and dangle hints. "It's been a difficult road, but I think I've found someone special on this show."

Lauren couldn't mask her surprise. Everyone in the audience gasped, too. Apparently that was too much of a hint, especially after only a few minutes.

"I think that admission has shocked all of us." She smoothed back her hair, even though it was perfect. She was nervous. Maybe she thought I was about to reveal something I shouldn't.

"To be fair, I've met a lot of special people on this show, and I wish nothing but the best for them."

"Let's talk about the contestants. The show started off a little rocky," Lauren said. She looked directly at Madison, who sat in the audience on one side of the room, and then at Thea, on the opposite side.

"Yes. I mean, the whole Madison and Thea hookup was a surprise at first, but then I realized they did me a favor." The crowd shifted uncomfortably in their chairs.

"Why do you say that?" Lauren asked. She paused. "Wait a minute. Before you answer that, why don't we have Madison come up?"

She started the applause, but the crowd's participation was minimal. They were pissed at her. "Hello, Madison." My emotion had switched from anger to pity. Her mouth pinched into a small smile.

"Hello, Savannah," she said. She clasped her hands together and entwined her fingers. She was either nervous or angry about having to be here. I couldn't blame her. "I want to start off by apologizing for my bad behavior. I came here with every intention of being a sparkette, and I got swept away with the decadence of the situation. You remember what it was like, right?"

I bit my cheeks to keep from smiling when several audience members booed her. I held up my hand. "Don't. Just let the apology be that. An apology."

"Madison, I think we're all curious to find out if you and Thea are still together. Are you?" Lauren asked.

Madison waved her hand as though it was a mere dalliance. "Oh, no. Nothing happened there. We went our separate ways."

I watched Thea's eyes narrow angrily for a moment right before she shrugged like it was no big deal.

"We'll have Thea come up in a minute," Lauren said and refocused on Madison. "How has the show changed your life?"

Madison nodded, obviously expecting the question. "I think people need to know that I wasn't portrayed in the best light. The viewers didn't get to see the good. The show only displayed the bad."

I tuned her out. She was here to clear her name and attempt to salvage how she came across on television. I didn't blame her for trying, but it was futile. She wasn't likable. When Thea was invited up, she assured the world that she was happily in a relationship and regretted the hookup with Madison. After the second commercial break, Lyanna had the stage.

"We decided on our one-on-one date that we would be better friends than anything else," Lyanna said.

"That's true. Lyanna is great, and I think we'll be really good friends," I said. Lyanna smiled at me, and we had a sweet moment. A friendship moment.

"I love this so much," Lauren said. She turned to the camera. "When we come back, we're going to ask Alix to join us. Stay tuned."

She gave me a sweet look and a small nod. I saw concern in her eyes, but also encouragement. The next twenty minutes were going to be the toughest for me. For us. Lauren knew that I once had feelings for Alix, and it would be hard to talk to them in front of the world. During the scheduled break, Lyanna gave me a hug and joined the audience. Alix made their way over to the stage.

"Hi."

They were as lovely and charming as ever, wearing dark gray trousers, a light gray shirt with the sleeves rolled up to reveal new ink, and black boots. My heart raced, and I started tearing up. "Hi, Alix. You look as dapper as always." I welcomed their hug and sat next to them on the couch. Lauren pretended not to have noticed our exchange, but I knew it affected her. She pressed her hand to her ear, getting instructions from Denise.

"Okay, we're back in thirty seconds," Lauren said.

Alix quickly gave Lauren a hug before reclaiming the spot next to me on the loveseat.

"It's good to see you again, Alix," Lauren said.

"Just like old times." Alix's smile didn't quite meet their eyes. They were still hurting, and I couldn't blame them. I reached over and squeezed their hand.

"Welcome back, everyone. Alix is up on the stage. Thank you for joining us," Lauren said. The room erupted in applause and even a few whistles. Alix blushed. "You probably have a lot of questions for Savannah, and we'll get to them soon, but first tell us about you. How are you doing?"

Alix crossed their ankle over their knee and tried to look as casual as possible, but I could feel their nervous energy. It rivaled my own.

"I'm doing well. Business is booming. The show really helped our little shop."

"I see you have a few more tattoos," Lauren said.

More whistles made their blush spread down their neck and blossom across the span of skin showing at the opening of their shirt. "It's hard to stop once you get started."

"Let's talk about the show. Why did you decide to become a contestant on *When Sparks Fly?*" Lauren asked.

"I've never had a serious relationship, and I was ready for one. I figured this was no different than dating apps. My brother talked me into applying for the show, and I didn't know Savannah was the flame. The show was very secretive and gave us only information sheets about the flame, no name, but it listed all the qualities I was looking for in a partner," they said.

"Let's talk about what happened in Mexico." Lauren paused for everyone to switch gears from playful banter to a more serious matter. "The world was shocked when Savannah didn't pick you."

Alix looked at me. They were still hurting. It wasn't the same shock and sadness that I remember seeing that night, but it was still there under the smile. "It didn't go as planned. I screwed up." They turned to me and took my hand. "I'll always regret planning the worst date in history. It was insensitive and I'm sorry."

It hurt watching them suffer. I squeezed their hand. "You're a wonderful person, Alix, and I wish you nothing but the best. I have no ill will toward you."

They placed a small kiss on the back of my hand. "And I hope you find what you're looking for. You seem to be happy, and that's all I want for you."

"Alix, don't you dare make us all cry," Lauren said. The audience laughed, and a few of them dabbed tears from the corner of their eyes. "We wish you the best and hope you find that special person soon."

Kaisley hugged me but didn't sit close to me when it was her turn on the couch. She had no hard feelings about the experience, but she wasn't as warm as she used to be. She was happy to be home with her son and wished me nothing but the best.

When Lauren and I finished the segment, I relaxed and smiled. One really hard show down, and one to go. I looked at Lauren as Mandee circled her to ensure every part of her was perfect. It was hard not to swoon as my heart expanded. I was a few feet and a few days away from having the woman of my dreams.

## CHAPTER TWENTY-SEVEN

W hat are you doing here?" I quickly pulled Lauren into my bedroom in shock. I stood in front of her with my hand on my chest, my heart beating furiously. We were supposed to keep our distance. That was the agreement.

"I wanted to check on you. I know it's been hard, and we're so close to being done with all of this." She ran her fingers through my hair and smiled.

I melted under her gaze, which was filled with hope and longing. "I miss you. I miss our late-night swims and our early morning talks." I leaned against her for strength and comfort. She smelled like soothing vanilla and jasmine. I wrapped my arms around her waist. I tamped down the panic that was rising. I needed to be strong.

"I miss us, too. I can't wait for all of this to be over."

I locked the door out of fear that somebody would burst in, even though I knew only a few people were downstairs and wouldn't bother me this late. I didn't trust Denise. If she realized Lauren was here, she'd probably send security up.

I forgot about the dangers of Lauren being here the moment her mouth pressed against mine. I moaned when her warm fingers slipped under my T-shirt. Her tongue slid into my mouth, and I threw my arms around her neck to get closer. I broke the kiss after twenty seconds and touched her face. Was she really here?

"How's it going behind the scenes?" I kissed her before she had a chance to answer. I wasn't gentle, and neither was she. Her mouth was demanding as she pressed into me.

"I don't want to talk about that. I want to talk about you. You're so beautiful," she said.

My cheeks heated. "I can't believe you're here."

"I shouldn't be, but I wanted to see how you were doing," she said again. "I know it was hard to see everybody tonight."

She kissed me again, and even though we had limited time and anyone could have knocked on my door at any moment, we tumbled around the bedroom until we ended up on my bed. I wanted to know how she was, but more than that, I needed her. I wanted to show her that I still wanted her after all of this. I shifted so she was between my legs. I couldn't stop touching her. She kissed my neck and the sensitive skin around my collarbone. I'd been tired twenty minutes ago, but the adrenaline rush of her presence gave me energy. "I still can't believe you're here. Am I dreaming?" That sounded cheesy, but I meant it. I was never going to tease people for saying sappy things again.

"I'm here, and I'm yours."

"Come here." Tears stung my eyes, and my throat constricted. I was close to crying. I needed to be held. I needed Lauren to tell me we were good over and over again until I believed her.

"It's all going to be okay," she said as her mouth found mine again. I loved the way we kissed. Her mouth fit mine perfectly. She pulled at my bottom lip with her teeth and soothed the sharpness with her soft tongue. The move was sexy and made me want more. I moaned when she slid her hand between us, under my pajama bottoms, and ran her fingers up and down my slit.

"I've missed this. How wet you are for me, how tight you are," she said.

We were new lovers, but Lauren knew exactly how to touch me, how to build me up, and how to hold me when I crashed. I was never into dirty talk, but the sweet heat she whispered in my ear made my clit swell and my heart dance to an exciting, fresh rhythm. These were stolen moments.

"Please," I said. It was a simple word, but she understood what I meant. She slipped two fingers inside, and I groaned. The faster her fingers moved, the harder she kissed me. I wanted to come, but I didn't want her to stop. I gave myself thirty selfish seconds of intense arousal before my orgasm crashed over me and I crumpled in her arms. "I can't move."

She pulled me close and held me for a few minutes. "I have to go. I'm sorry, but I needed to hold you again."

"I'm glad you did. What a wonderful surprise." I propped up on my elbow to look at her. "Are you really okay?"

She ran her fingertips over my face and gave me one of her brilliant smiles. "I am now." She kissed me and slid off the bed.

I looked at the clock. She had been here for only fifteen minutes. I hated that we were rushed but thankful we got the alone time. "Be careful. I'll see you tomorrow." One last press of her lips against mine and she was gone. I crawled into bed knowing that soon we'd be together and wouldn't have to sneak around.

While Mandee and Buzzy worked on my wardrobe and makeup, I tried hard not to throw up. Today I was going to give the world my answer. I practiced my speech over and over in my head, knowing I might forget everything once I was in front of the cameras. Emma was up first, and she would be the hardest to let down.

"Quit frowning. You're going to make me smear your lipstick," Mandee said.

Buzzy came at me with the alterations on the black, strapless dress that narrowed at my knee. The black heels were sexy and tall. I spent the morning walking all over the mansion in my pajama bottoms, a spaghetti-strap tank, and these shoes that screamed sexy. I'd never looked at a pair of shoes before and thought, "Damn, these are going to make the outfit," but I did today. I fought Mandee when she wanted to pull my hair into a updo, but she promised that if I didn't like it, we would do it my way. One look in the mirror reminded me that I needed to trust the staff. I was afraid to move. "Wow. I look stunning."

Buzzy clucked at me. "Now stand and let me adjust. We don't have all day."

They were right. We were pressed for time, but the show wouldn't start without me. The cameras recorded me pretending to finish putting on my makeup in the mirror while I did a voice-over about my thoughts on the process. I read from a script that I edited because some of the things they wanted me to say weren't true. I wanted to leave the show with some integrity. I sat on the bed and slipped on my heels. I was supposed to grab a clutch and glide gracefully down the stairs, but that shot took twice, because even though I wore the heels all morning, I didn't wear a restrictive dress while I practiced my walk. I had to take smaller steps and pull my shoulders back for perfect posture. "I'm not a Neanderthal," I repeated.

We were going off-location to a bluff that overlooked the ocean. Trapped in a limo with two camera people and Mandee, I had to repeat questions and answer them during the twenty-minute drive. "What did I enjoy most about the journey?" They gave me the questions ahead of time, so I was prepared. "I enjoyed finding out more about myself. More about what I want out of this life." I was directed to stare out the window for a few seconds. "Finding a forever person is very difficult. I was presented with ten incredible people, and making a decision after ten weeks is almost impossible." There was a pause. I knew they didn't want me to give too much away, but they could always edit it out. "But I think I have my answer."

My stomach lurched when the limo rolled to a stop in front of the garden that overlooked the ocean. My moment was here. Everyone vacated the limo, and I had to wait for my cue.

Lauren was waiting for me. Stunning, she was wearing a charcoal jacket with matching cropped pants and a stark, crisp white shirt with the first button undone. Her hair was in an updo, like mine, instead of her signature tight bun. She was breathtaking. I teared up as a burst of a foreign emotion crashed over me. I was in love with her, but what I was feeling was so much more than just love. I felt complete, like the jigsaw pieces of my life were finally fitting together. This was the one piece that had somehow fallen under the table or stuck to the inside of the box, and I hadn't known I was missing it until I saw it. Until I saw her.

I blinked back the tears because I knew Mandee would kick my ass if she had to do my makeup all over again. Now was not the time to cry.

"You look so beautiful, Savannah. How are you feeling about tonight?" she asked.

I walked to her, smiling as though I had a massive secret, which I did, but nobody knew it except me. I was about ready to give *Sparks* everything they'd asked of me and then some. "I'm pretty excited."

Lauren cocked her eyebrow at me. "That's great to hear. This is a big day for you. Your last night with the show. Hopefully, you've found what you are looking for."

I knew she had to be vague, too. "I feel very comfortable with my decision. A little nervous, but I hope everything works out."

"I hope so, too. Just follow the stone path to the back. I'll be here if you need me," she said.

I hugged her because I needed her strength. "Thank you." I felt the tight squeeze of her hand as I slid away from her and followed the path to where Emma stood. She looked lovely. Like all the other contestants, Emma would find her perfect person. I hugged her, too, and reached for both of her hands. "You look so beautiful."

She looked hopeful, and it killed me that I was going to have to turn her down on national television, but I planned to be damn sure to do it nicely.

"You look amazing." She didn't know my aversion to that word, but I kept the smile on my face.

"Thank you." I knew she needed to know, and so did five million viewers, but I was obligated to drag it out. "Emma, you are a wonderful and fun person. I love how open and friendly you are with your family. You're so nice and sweet, and you are pretty damn close to perfection." To look into such hopeful eyes shredded my insides, but I pressed on. "I know that someday, you will find the perfect person, but unfortunately, it's not me. Thank you so much for giving so much of yourself and pausing your life to be here. I wish nothing but the best for you. I really mean that." She was clearly shocked, but she recovered quickly.

"I understand. You need to do what's best for you and your heart." She wiped away an errant tear and sniffed. "I hope you find her."

It started off as a hug, but I ended up holding her while a few more tears spilled. "You really are a special person, and you will be so happy one day soon. I just know it." She let me go and brushed her lips over mine. "Good luck, Savannah."

I watched her walk away and stood there as instructed. Mandee rushed over with her powders and brushes, and somebody on the set put up a shade so I wouldn't roast in the heat. Thankfully, we were slipping into evening. On the other side of the garden, Ophelia was pulling up in a different limo. I took a deep breath. Delivering the news to Emma had been hard, but that little burst of self-awareness before I stepped out of the limo really helped me stay grounded.

"Places, everyone," somebody shouted. The crew scattered. I felt the energy and excitement of the people around me. They thought I was choosing Ophelia. I stood under a garden arch full of red roses and looked out at the ocean. The coast was beautiful. I could get used to this view. I turned when I heard footsteps and watched Ophelia walk the path toward me. She was all smiles and looked incredible, but the reality of the last two months had dulled her shine. We were in completely different worlds, and no way would it ever work between us. I visualized fans of *Sparks* yelling at their televisions, thinking Ophelia was the one I chose, knowing we weren't suited at all.

"Hey, you," she said and gave me a quick hug.

I wasn't going to tell her how beautiful she was because she knew it. Most of our conversations had been about how gorgeous we looked or how people didn't understand our passion for our jobs. "Hi. How are you?"

She held one of my hands and swayed slightly. She was nervous. "I'm excited but worried about tonight. Am I the only one left?"

I reached for both her hands. This was going to go quickly. "Ophelia, thank you so much for spending your summer here and taking the time to get to know me. We've had some good times, haven't we?"

She smiled. "We have."

She purred the words. She still had the expression of a victorious person. My words weren't exactly encouraging, so I didn't know where her confidence was coming from. "I know that you will find a person someday who can keep up with your energy and your passions, but I just don't think I'm that person."

Ophelia looked stunned. An angry wince pinched her features, but she quickly recovered. "Oh, I see."

I don't think she did, but it didn't matter. "I'm so grateful to have met you and have had fun with you, but our journey ends here. I hope you understand. You're such an energetic and vivacious person, and I wish you the best."

She stared at me for what seemed like minutes but was probably five seconds. "Okay. Well, I guess, good luck. I hope you find what you're looking for."

She walked by me without a hug. I stood there awkwardly until I saw the limo drive off. "Can somebody get Lauren?" I asked. The world changed in that moment. I shook my hands as though relieving stress and waited for her. Where was she? I was surprised she didn't jump right out as soon as Ophelia left. Reality shows were extremely edited.

"Savannah, are you okay?" Lauren quickened her step on the path up to the archway.

I reached for her. "Keep rolling," I heard from behind me. I was about to give the show exactly what they wanted—a fucking rock-star ending that people would talk about for years, even if I crashed and burned.

"Lauren."

"What's wrong?" She was holding my elbows as if she expected me to faint. I reached out and touched her face, and she didn't shy away. I saw nothing but concern in her ocean-blue eyes. She didn't care about the cameras.

I blew out a deep breath and said a little prayer that I, as the flame, wouldn't get burned. "It's you. You're the one I want."

Lauren kept her eyes on me, even though there was a flurry activity as camera people scrambled to position themselves in the best possible way to capture this moment. I even heard Denise say, "What's going on here?" Lauren's fingers pressed gently into my skin, but she remained quiet.

"I love you, Lauren. I know that sounds bananas after everything I just went through with these wonderful contestants, but somewhere along this journey, I found somebody perfect for me. It's you." My heart stopped when she looked away and down at the ground. The heaviness of the fear of rejection made me almost drop to my knees, but I refused to give up now. "I know this wasn't supposed to happen. I was supposed to fall in love with one of the ten sparkettes, but my heart found you. Please say something before I faint or run to the closest car and drive off. Well, run as fast as I can in this dress." I gave her a pleading half smile. She looked at me with zero expression. I swallowed hard as my heart lodged at the base of my throat. This situation felt bad. I braced myself when I saw she was going to speak.

"I don't know what to say first," she said. She dropped my elbows and slid her hands down my arms until our fingers interlocked. "I love you, Savannah," she said.

I thought I'd misheard her. I turned my head and looked into her brilliant eyes. She gave me a soft, vulnerable smile and repeated her words.

"I love you, Savannah. I have for a long time."

She kissed away the tears that slid down my cheeks and held me when the words finally seeped in. "I don't deserve somebody as wonderful as you," I said. The weight of the show and my emotions started to crack me. I tried hard not to cry but was overwhelmed.

"I think you're perfect. We're perfect, and hopefully the world can see that we belong together," she said.

"Hopefully, we're forgiven."

"You came here for love and found it. I came here to host a show and wasn't expecting to fall for anyone," she said.

"Lauren Lucas, I feel a spark with you. Do you feel it, too?"

She laughed and pulled me close. We kissed under the arch of roses with twilight draped around us. I didn't care that people were staring or that we had ten cameras focused on us. I didn't care that I'd had to wait so long to find true love. I only cared that at the end of such a public process, I was finally holding my forever person.

## EPILOGUE

F irst of all, I want to say thank you both for being on *Reality Bits*. The world has been dying to hear your story."

Ellie Stevens invited us to do a special live edition of her show the night after the season finale. She got wind of what had happened before it aired and booked us immediately. So the very next night, we were back on television, only this time as an out and happy couple. The fandom was still processing what had happened, but the reactions were mostly positive so far.

"Thank you for having us," I said.

"Where do we begin?" Ellie asked. The audience laughed and applauded. "Let's start at the beginning. Savannah, when did you start having feelings for Lauren?"

I looked at Lauren, who appeared calm and beautiful. One month later and it was still hard to believe she'd taken the chance with me. "Every night, Lauren would check in on me to make sure I was okay. You have to understand that everyone is extremely sequestered on set. We don't have access to the internet or television, so not only was I bored, but I had nobody to talk to."

"It's important to remember that reality shows take a toll on the mental health of contestants. They are cut off from their lives and the comforts of home, including loved ones. How many times do you call your best friend or your sister or parent because you need advice? That isn't allowed to happen on a show like *When Sparks Fly*," Lauren said.

She held my hand. The audience cooed at the gesture. Ellie noticed it too, and her smile for us seemed genuine.

"I'm so happy for both of you. Last night's jaw-dropping episode blew up social media," Ellie said. She made a mind-blowing motion with her hands by her head. "I'm still trying to process it."

"It feels like yesterday," I said and looked into Lauren's eyes. We'd been sequestered, not only because we wanted the show to be a surprise, but so we could get to know one another.

"It was yesterday for the rest of the world. What have you been doing in the meantime?" Ellie asked.

Lauren tilted her head and raised an eyebrow. I blushed because I couldn't get away with saying it was the best month of my life and the sex was incredible. I could have, but that was private, and I needed a break from my private life being out in the open.

"Getting to know one another really well," I said. The audience roared. "I'm with my forever person." Lauren looked at me so lovingly that Ellie cleared her throat to get our attention.

"How do you both feel about Alix as the new host of *When Sparks Fly*? Do you think they will do a good job?" Ellie asked.

I clasped my hands together. "I love the idea. Alix is so flirty and fun, and I wish them the best of luck. They'll do great." I was so happy when I heard the news. Lauren told me yesterday, and the first thing I felt was pride. I was so proud of them.

"I have no doubt that Alix will blow everyone away. They're young and fresh, and that's exactly what the show needs now. Charisma, and better representation, and more diversity," Lauren said.

"And Kaisley is going to be the next flame. I couldn't be happier for her," I said. That news had dropped this morning. Unlike with my season, where they had created several teaser videos where I was blurred in the background, they wanted fans to know right away. The transition from my short season to hers was a quick turnaround, with production starting next month. Scandals were expensive.

"Since you seem to be freed up at the moment, Lauren, what's next for you?"

Lauren shrugged. "Right now I'm just spending as much time with Savannah as I can. She's moving to California to be with me once she sells her house."

Ellie touched my arm. "I can't tell you how happy I am that you wanted this fairy tale, and you got it. I can't think of a more deserving person. So, you're selling the house and moving to California. What's next for you?"

I wanted to roll my eyes because my plans sounded typical of fallen reality stars. "I'm writing a book about being on both sides of the show. First as a sparkette and then as the flame. Kind of a tell-all journey." I wasn't allowed to discuss certain things, but I had enough of a story that I could easily fill the pages of a book.

"I want a signed copy. In advance," Ellie said.

"I promise you'll get one of the first copies of *My Forever Flame*."

"I love the title," she said. The person behind the camera made the wrap-it-up motion. "Unfortunately, that's all the time we have. Thank you so much for telling us your story. Is there anything you want to say to your fans?" Ellie asked.

"I want to say thank you for your support over the years, from the first season to this one. I appreciate your kind words and encouragement." I took a moment and a deep breath to keep myself from crying. Ellie squeezed my hand and smiled, knowing full well I was close to tears. "We both found love, even though it was in an unconventional way. We hope the show remains successful, and we wish Alix and Kaisley the best," Lauren said.

"I'm sorry to see you go as host of *When Sparks Fly*, but if you're interested in a co-host job at *Reality Bits*, let me know." Ellie turned to the audience. "Wouldn't that be wonderful? Lauren Lucas on this show?"

The audience clapped and cheered. Lauren smiled at their reaction. Ellie knew Lauren's worth and that she would be a great addition to the show. Lauren was a hot commodity, but she wasn't in a hurry to start elsewhere.

"Thanks, Ellie. I will seriously consider your offer."

"Savannah and Lauren, the hottest couple in Hollywood now, I wish you the best."

We signed autographs and took photos with fans before we were whisked away in a limo to take us back to the hotel. Ellie had invited us to a private dinner at her place later, and while we just wanted to be alone, now was the time for Lauren to network.

"What do you think about being on *Reality Bits*? Is that something you'd like to do?" I asked Lauren on our way up to the suite.

"It would be fun, but do I want fun, or do I want to get back into something serious again?"

My heart stopped when I thought about what had happened to her overseas. "I don't want you to put yourself in danger."

Her warm fingers held mine. "I wouldn't do that. There's plenty to do without going into a war zone. I want to see what my options are before I commit."

"*Reality Bits* would be local, and you and Ellie respect each other. But I get it. Options. You could always learn how to make candles and work for me." I had used my money from the show to lease a small building in Goodyear, Arizona. It wasn't too far for Jane, part-owner, to drive. I planned to hire a shipping manager and three employees to make candles. I was sure after the information bomb that Lauren and I had just dropped, the business would grow. She put her arm around my shoulders. I felt loved and treasured.

"Right now, I just want to think about us and finally getting out in public. I want to show you off," she said.

"And all I want is to get you behind closed doors so we can finally be alone. This was a long day." I placed my head on her shoulder and watched as she dug in her purse for the room key.

Lauren checked her emails and phone messages before joining me on the couch.

"Everything okay?"

"Everything is perfect. *World News Tonight* wants to talk about reporting for them, but that means overseas work, so I politely declined. *Celebrity Buzz* offered me a co-hosting job. The money is great, but I don't know that I want to do what I already did. I mean, if that's the direction I want to go, I might as well take Ellie's job offer."

I put my head on her shoulder and held her hand. "I'm sorry this is so difficult for you. Hopefully something will come along that you'll love."

"Something did come along, but I wanted to talk to you about it first," she said.

I looked at her. "Tell me now."

She kissed the tip of my nose. "You're so impatient."

I pulled her to me and kissed her. "But you love me anyway." Her blue eyes sparkled, and my heart swelled. I loved this woman so much and couldn't imagine my life without her.

"*Hollywood Hills* offered me a spot on their morning show that would start this fall. I would interview celebrities and notable figures. They would air the segments weekly. We'd start off with one a week and see how it goes. The money is great, and I would be here. If I had to travel, they would allow me and a guest to go wherever we needed to."

I was trying not to squeal and cling to her with excitement. "What do you think about *Hollywood Hills*? Are they reputable? Do you feel good working for them?"

"They're an ABC company, so I know the money's there, and they're in the top three morning shows in California. I'll set up a meeting next week and see what they have to say."

I loved that she was so laid back about her career path. I would be beyond stressed trying to figure out where my next paycheck was coming from, but Lauren had money and time. "That sounds great."

"We'd be closer to your mom, and maybe you can work on that relationship. I'd like to meet her sometime," Lauren said.

My mother was pissed when she found out I did the show. Again. But I had no doubt that she would love Lauren. Who didn't? "I think we should probably do that sooner than later."

"Let's plan on it this weekend. Meantime, we need to get ready for dinner with Ellie. Do you want to take a shower with me?" Lauren lifted her eyebrow at me and wiggled it.

She was so sexy and all mine. I stood and led her by the hand to the incredibly large bathroom, where I unbuttoned my shirt and kicked off my shoes. "You know, as much as a shower with you sounds delightful…" I turned on the faucet of the massive tub and adjusted it to the right temperature. "I want to introduce you to my other best friend during my stint on *When Sparks Fly*, the beloved Jacuzzi."

# About the Author

Multi-award-winning author Kris Bryant was born in Tacoma, WA, but has lived all over the world and now considers Kansas City her home. She received her BA in English from the University of Missouri and spends a lot of her time buried in books. She recently discovered a passion for kayaking and spends her weekends at the lake when she's not racing toward a deadline.

Her debut novel, *Jolt*, was a Lambda Literary Finalist. *Forget Me Not* was selected by the American Library Association's 2018 Over the Rainbow book list and was a Golden Crown Finalist for Contemporary Romance. *Breakthrough* won a 2019 Goldie for Contemporary Romance. *Listen* won a 2020 Goldie for Contemporary Romance. *Temptation* won a 2021 Goldie for Contemporary Romance. Kris can be reached at krisbryantbooks@gmail.com, www.krisbryant.net, Twitter @krisbryant14, Instagram @kris_bryant14, and Tik Tok @lesfic_author.

# Books Available from Bold Strokes Books

**A Long Way to Fall** by Elle Spencer. A ski lodge, two strong-willed women, and a family feud that brings them together, but will it also tear them apart? (978-1-63679-005-3)

**Barnabas Bopwright Saves the City** by J. Marshall Freeman. When he uncovers a terror plot to destroy the city he loves, 15-year-old Barnabas Bopwright realizes it's up to him to save his home and bring deadly secrets into the light before it's too late. (978-1-63679-152-4)

**Forever** by Kris Bryant. When Savannah Edwards is invited to be the next bachelorette on the dating show When Sparks Fly, she'll show the world that finding true love on television can happen. (978-1-63679-029-9)

**Ice on Wheels** by Aurora Rey. All's fair in love and roller derby. That's Riley Fauchet's motto, until a new job lands her at the same company—and on the same team—as her rival Brooke Landry, the frosty jammer for the Big Easy Bruisers. (978-1-63679-179-1)

**Inherit the Lightning** by Bud Gundy. Darcy O'Brien and his sisters learn they are about to inherit an immense fortune, but a family mystery about to unravel after seventy years threatens to destroy everything. (978-1-63679-199-9)

**Perfect Rivalry** by Radclyffe. Two women set out to win the same career-making goal, but it's love that may turn out to be the final prize. (978-1-63679-216-3)

**Something to Talk About** by Ronica Black. Can quiet ranch owner Corey Durand give up her peaceful life and allow her feisty new neighbor into her heart? Or will past loss, present suitors, and town gossip ruin a long-awaited chance at love? (978-1-63679-114-2)

**With a Minor in Murder** by Karis Walsh. In the world of academia, police officer Clare Sawyer and professor Libby Hart team up to solve a murder. (978-1-63679-186-9)

**Writer's Block** by Ali Vali. Wyatt and Hayley might be made for each other if only they can get through noisy neighbors, the historic society, at-odds future plans, and all the secrets hidden in Wyatt's walls. (978-1-63679-021-3)

**Cold Blood** by Genevieve McCluer. Maybe together, Kalila and Dorenia have a chance of taking down the vampires who have eluded them all these years. And maybe, in each other, they can find a love worth living for. (978-1-63679-195-1)

**Greener Pastures** by Aurora Rey. When city girl and CPA Audrey Adams finds herself tending her aunt's farm, will Rowan Marshall—the charming cider maker next door—turn out to be her saving grace or the bane of her existence? (978-1-63679-116-6)

**Grounded** by Amanda Radley. For a second chance, Olivia and Emily will need to accept their mistakes, learn to communicate properly, and with a little help from five-year-old Henry, fall madly in love all over again. Sequel to Flight SQA016. (978-1-63679-241-5)

**Journey's End** by Amanda Radley. In this heartwarming conclusion to the Flight series, Olivia and Emily must finally decide what they want, what they need, and how to follow the dreams of their hearts. (978-1-63679-233-0)

**Pursued: Lillian's Story** by Felice Picano. Fleeing a disastrous marriage to the Lord Exchequer of England, Lillian of Ravenglass reveals an incident-filled, often bizarre, tale of great wealth and power, perfidy, and betrayal. (978-1-63679-197-5)

**Secret Agent** by Michelle Larkin. CIA agent Peyton North embarks on a global chase to apprehend rogue agent Zoey Blackwood, but her commitment to the mission is tested as the sparks between them ignite and their sizzling attraction approaches a point of no return. (978-1-63555-753-4)

**Something Between Us** by Krystina Rivers. A decade after her heart was broken under Don't Ask, Don't Tell, Kirby runs into her first love and has to decide if what's still between them is enough to heal her broken heart. (978-1-63679-135-7)

**Sugar Girl** by Emma L McGeown. Having traded in traditional romance for the perks of Sugar Dating, Ciara Reilly not only enjoys the no-strings-attached arrangement, she's also a hit with her clients. That is until she meets the beautiful entrepreneur Charlie Keller who makes her want to go sugar-free. (978-1-63679-156-2)

**The Business of Pleasure** by Ronica Black. Editor in chief Valerie Raffield is quickly becoming smitten by Lennox, the graphic artist she's hired to work remotely. But when Lennox doesn't show for their first face-to-face meeting, Valerie's heart and her business may be in jeopardy. (978-1-63679-134-0)

**The Hummingbird Sanctuary** by Erin Zak. The Hummingbird Sanctuary, Colorado's hottest resort destination: Come for the mountains, stay for the charm, and enjoy the drama as Olive, Eleanor, and Harriet figure out the meaning of true friendship. (978-1-63679-163-0)

**The Witch Queen's Mate** by Jennifer Karter. Barra and Silvi must overcome their ingrained hatred and prejudice to use Barra's magic and save both their peoples, not just from slavery, but destruction. (978-1-63679-202-6)

**With a Twist** by Georgia Beers. Starting over isn't easy for Amelia Martini. When the irritatingly cheerful Kirby Dupress comes into her life will Amelia be brave enough to go after the love she really wants? (978-1-63555-987-3)

**Business of the Heart** by Claire Forsythe. When a hopeless romantic meets a tough-as-nails cynic, they'll need to overcome the wounds of the past to discover that their hearts are the most important business of all. (978-1-63679-167-8)

**Dying for You** by Jenny Frame. Can Victorija Dred keep an age-old vow and fight the need to take blood from Daisy Macdougall? (978-1-63679-073-2)

**Exclusive** by Melissa Brayden. Skylar Ruiz lands the TV reporting job of a lifetime, but is she willing to sacrifice it all for the love of her longtime crush, anchorwoman Carolyn McNamara? (978-1-63679-112-8)

**Her Duchess to Desire** by Jane Walsh. An up-and-coming interior designer seeks to create a happily ever after with an intriguing duchess, proving that love never goes out of fashion. (978-1-63679-065-7)

**Murder on Monte Vista** by David S. Pederson. Private Detective Mason Adler's angst at turning fifty is forgotten when his "birthday present," the handsome, young Henry Bowtrickle, turns up dead, and it's up to Mason to figure out who did it, and why. (978-1-63679-124-1)

**Take Her Down** by Lauren Emily Whalen. Stakes are cutthroat, scheming is creative, and loyalty is ever-changing in this queer, female-driven YA retelling of Shakespeare's Julius Caesar. (978-1-63679-089-3)

**The Game** by Jan Gayle. Ryan Gibbs is a talented golfer, but her guilt means she may never leave her small town, even if Katherine Reese tempts her with competition and passion. (978-1-63679-126-5)

**Whereabouts Unknown** by Meredith Doench. While homicide detective Theodora Madsen recovers from a potentially career-ending injury, she scrambles to solve the cases of two missing sixteen-year-old girls from Ohio. (978-1-63555-647-6)

**Boy at the Window** by Lauren Melissa Ellzey. Daniel Kim struggles to hold onto reality while haunted by both his very-present past and his never-present parents. Jiwon Yoon may be the only one who can break Daniel free. (978-1-63679-092-3)

**Deadly Secrets** by VK Powell. Corporate criminals want whistleblower Jana Elliott permanently silenced, but Rafe Silva will risk everything to keep the woman she loves safe. (978-1-63679-087-9)

**Enchanted Autumn** by Ursula Klein. When Elizabeth comes to Salem, Massachusetts, to study the witch trials, she never expects to find love—or an actual witch…and Hazel might just turn out to be both. (978-1-63679-104-3)

**Escorted** by Renee Roman. When fantasy meets reality, will escort Ryan Lewis be able to walk away from a chance at forever with her new client Dani? (978-1-63679-039-8)

**Her Heart's Desire** by Anne Shade. Two women. One choice. Will Eve and Lynette be able to overcome their doubts and fears to embrace their deepest desire? (978-1-63679-102-9)

**My Secret Valentine** by Julie Cannon, Erin Dutton, & Anne Shade. Winning the heart of your secret Valentine? These award-winning authors agree, there is no better way to fall in love. (978-1-63679-071-8)

**Perilous Obsession** by Carsen Taite. When reporter Macy Moran becomes consumed with solving a cold case, will her quest for the truth bring her closer to Detective Beck Ramsey or will her obsession with finding a murderer rob her of a chance at true love? (978-1-63679-009-1)

**Reading Her** by Amanda Radley. Lauren and Allegra learn love and happiness are right where they least expect it. There's just one problem: Lauren has a secret she cannot tell anyone, and Allegra knows she's hiding something. (978-1-63679-075-6)

**The Willing** by Lyn Hemphill. Kitty Wilson doesn't know how, but she can bring people back from the dead as long as someone is willing to take their place and keep the universe in balance. (978-1-63679-083-1)

**Three Left Turns to Nowhere** by Nathan Burgoine, J. Marshall Freeman, & Jeffrey Ricker. Three strangers heading to a convention in Toronto are stranded in rural Ontario, where a small town with a subtle kind of magic leads each to discover what he's been searching for. (978-1-63679-050-3)

**Watching Over Her** by Ronica Black. As they face the snowstorm of the century, and the looming threat of a stalker, Riley and Zoey just might find love in the most unexpected of places. (978-1-63679-100-5)

**#shedeservedit** by Greg Herren. When his gay best friend, and high school football star, is murdered, Alex Wheeler is a suspect and must find the truth to clear himself. (978-1-63555-996-5)

**Always** by Kris Bryant. When a pushy American private investigator shows up demanding to meet the woman in Camila's artwork, instead of introducing her to her great-grandmother, Camila decides to lead her on a wild goose chase all over Italy. (978-1-63679-027-5)

**Exes and O's** by Joy Argento. Ali and Madison really only have one thing in common. The girl who broke their heart may be the only one who can put it back together. (978-1-63679-017-6)

**One Verse Multi** by Sander Santiago. Life was good: promotion, friends, falling in love, discovering that the multi-verse is on a fast track to collision—wait, what? Good thing Martin King works for a company that can fix the problem, right…um…right? (978-1-63679-069-5)

**Paris Rules** by Jaime Maddox. Carly Becker has been searching for the perfect woman all her life, but no one ever seems to be just right until Paige Waterford checks all her boxes, except the most important one—she's married. (978-1-63679-077-0)

**Shadow Dancers** by Suzie Clarke. In this third and final book in the Moon Shadow series, Rachel must find a way to become the hunter and not the hunted, and this time she will meet Ehsee Yumiko head-on. (978-1-63555-829-6)

**The Kiss** by C.A. Popovich. When her wife refuses their divorce and begins to stalk her, threatening her life, Kate realizes to protect her new love, Leslie, she has to let her go, even if it breaks her heart. (978-1-63679-079-4)

**The Wedding Setup** by Charlotte Greene. When Ryann, a big-time New York executive, goes to Colorado to help out with her best friend's wedding, she never expects to fall for the maid of honor. (978-1-63679-033-6)

**Velocity** by Gun Brooke. Holly and Claire work toward an uncertain future preparing for an alien space mission, and only one thing is for certain, they will have to risk their lives, and their hearts, to discover the truth. (978-1-63555-983-5)

**Wildflower Words** by Sam Ledel. Lida Jones treks West with her father in search of a better life on the rapidly developing American frontier, but finds home when she meets Hazel Thompson. (978-1-63679-055-8)